To Cooty, with all my love

Extract from *Rogue* by Anonymous

Bears, clowns, cats, butterflies, demons and angels cavort along the banks of the canal, dancing, laughing and twirling their capes in ceaseless balletic arcs. Music drifts through the night air from the square up ahead, growing louder and more frenetic as I approach. My feet stamp along with the beat.

A black and white chequered mask looms out of the crowd. Man or woman? I have no way of telling. It points directly at me and beckons. A strange force compels me forward. As if under a spell, I have no choice but to follow. The light-footed creature tiptoes onto a tiny bridge, stands in the middle, claps silently in time to the music then runs backwards, drawing its arms together, suggesting an embrace.

Aroused and afraid of losing sight of this hypnotic stranger, I cleave from the crowd and speed up, breaking into a run over the ancient stone edifice after the disappearing figure. A flash of white down an alleyway catches my eye and I give chase, my breath ephemeral clouds in the February chill. Moonlight barely penetrates these tiny backstreets, and when it does, merely illuminates skeins of gauzy mist rising from the Venetian waters, creating a theatrical dry ice effect. A whistle from above makes me look up.

The china-faced harlequin, high above me on a crumbling balcony, lit by an arcane street lamp, genuflects in an elaborate bow. I tilt my head back as far as it will go and stare up at the apparition. How did it get up there so fast? Impossible, unless whoever it is has wings. And how am I supposed to follow? I pace backwards across the deserted street until my back grazes the stone wall and fix my attention on the balcony – a stage no bigger than a dining-table – as the performance begins.

The harlequin spreads its arms wide, revealing the dramatic scarlet lining of its black and white cape. Each arm makes a sweeping gesture, once left, once right, acknowledging a vast imaginary audience. The head rolls in figures of eight, apparently seeking someone in the crowd. Then with catlike precision, the mask looks directly at me. One hand floats to its mouth and it blows me a kiss. I press my fingers to my mouth, offer them upwards and blow one in return.

The harlequin clutches at its heart with one hand; the other reaches out to snatch the kiss from the ether. The clenched fist remains in the air while the head is bowed in gratitude. Long hair, black as midnight, spills around the frozen features. This is a woman, I am now sure. With a slow, ritualistic gesture, the figure brings her fist to her mouth and raises her chin in ecstasy.

Once more the arms widen, as if receiving rapturous applause, and then the figure bows to the left, right and centre. She brings both hands to her painted mouth and blows an expansive kiss to her public. Her arms mime a giant heart shape as she embraces her watchers and holds them close. She repeats the gesture, her beautifully chiselled mask somehow evoking modesty, pride, love and passion without a single movement. The third time her hands return to her heart, they are no longer empty.

In the left, a single red rose, striking against the white diamond on the front of her cape. In the right, a handgun, aimed upwards beneath her chin. She kisses the rose and lets it fall from the balcony to the street below. I watch it tumble to the ground, its petals scattering on the cobbles. The shocking report of a gunshot whips my head upwards.

Against a blood-spattered backdrop, her body crumples over the stone balustrade. Long black hair dangles from the remnants of her blasted skull and the white diamonds of her cape turn dark. Something breaks at my feet. Her mask, cracked into shards. I lift one to the light. Her mouth, painted in a silent, frozen smile.

He jerked upwards with a gasp, his torso covered in sweat. The sheet fell to his waist and his breathing rasped in the silence of the bedroom. He stared at the mirror on the opposite wall, replaying the flamboyant brutality of his dream. The monochrome cape, the crimson rose, the decaying balcony and those scarlet china lips. In the mirror, his own face reflected back at him through the roseate light of dawn.

Beside him, the girl shifted, curled up like a dormouse. He laid a hand on her shoulder to ease her back to sleep. When her breathing had deepened, he slid out of bed and used the torch on his phone to locate his clothes. He backtracked, recalling the feral passion of the night before. His jeans lay in the bedroom doorway, his shirt was on the living-room couch and he found his jacket in the entrance hall. His wallet was still in the inside pocket, its contents intact.

Two problems presented themselves. His boxer shorts and shoes were missing. Underwear he could manage without but no way was he going to tramp the streets of Venice barefoot. He closed the bedroom door silently and risked switching on a lamp.

He found one sock dangling from the lampshade. The other could have been anywhere. His brogues, dusty from the previous night's dancing, lay half under the sofa. In the absence of his boxers, he was forced to go commando. Time to leave. On the glass coffee table, he spotted her handbag, all quilted leather, gold chain and to his amusement, his own initials. He opened it, took out a lipstick and wrote on the table. *Grazie. CC xx.* The front door creaked as he crept away into the early morning light.

As he wended his way back to his hotel through the detritus of last night's *Carnevale*, mist wreathing over midnight-blue canals brought back his dream. His subconscious had ways of making itself heard, so he did not simply dismiss his nocturnal visions as after-effects of a night on the town. Turning his collar up against the frosty air, he concentrated on revisiting each lurid element to articulate what he'd seen.

A caped reveller in black and white with the classic mask, at once beautiful and unnerving. The performance, just for him. The rose, the gun, blood dripping from the long black hair onto the petals.

He crossed a little bridge over Rio de San Andrea and came to a sudden halt as he saw the sign. *Albergo Arlecchino*. Harlequin Hotel. The morning chill was forgotten as he stared at the multi-coloured joker.

Harlequin. In the dream, he had thought of her as a harlequin. But now, awake and lucid, he knew Harlequins were male, colourful characters, figures of fun. Not a black and white image of bloody suicide.

That was when it clicked. He broke into a run, sprinting through grey littered streets, past empty café tables and overflowing bins. It took him fourteen minutes to reach his apartment, during which time he'd worked the whole thing out.

Out of breath after leaping up two flights of stairs, he opened the safe and fired up his laptop. He logged into PIN and entered his high-level access code. Ten seconds later, he received a second code via his mobile and punched that into the security portal. After speaking his name into the microphone and allowing the camera to compare his right eye to his left, the Police Intelligence Network granted him permission to enter. Sweaty and uncomfortable after racing across the city wearing one sock and no underwear, he adjusted himself and began his search.

It took him three minutes to review the entire Code Red report on potential terror attacks during a major European national festival. Intelligence services had earmarked suspected agitators with allegiances to three right-wing groups and intercepted a certain amount of traffic which pointed to Venice as a potential target. As a high-level undercover agent fluent in Italian, he'd been the natural choice for the task of locating this gang and preventing a terrorist action. Venice at party time. Perhaps he'd thrown himself into the celebrations with too much gusto.

But he'd done his homework and now it began to pay off. One of the names under surveillance was Zanni2, whose avatar on the chat site was a coat hanger bearing a black shirt. This faceless commentator had made occasional references to *My Darling Columbine*, leading the police to suspect a planned mass shooting.

He printed out all the comments from Zanni2 and sat in the kitchen with an espresso, underlining what he could see as an emerging pattern. It was not yet seven in the morning, but he was so close that the excitement buzzing through his whole body rendered the caffeine surplus.

Harlequin. A character from the theatrical *Commedia dell'arte* tradition involving two characters named Zanni. The first Zanni always took the lead, driving the plot, backed up by his comic sidekick. The second Zanni was a trickster clown in a colourful diamond-patterned costume, half masked, known as *Arlecchino*, or Harlequin. His love was for Colombina, although he slaked his lust wherever he could.

Decoding the simple disguises became child's play. He identified Zanni2's collaborators from their use of similar terminology or characteristics and put them through a simple program to search for lexical overlap. What words were these guys using and what did they mean?

The first, *Littorio*, an Italian emblem from the days of Mussolini. Intelligence had correctly labelled the term as the terrorists' utopian ideal of a return to Fascism. The second, *Colombina*, was the name of Harlequin's true love. This was harder to pin down as all four collaborators used it differently. He decided to identify it as Venice itself. Thirdly, *la spiacevole sorpresa*. The unpleasant surprise.

He recoiled in horror, his cup clattering into its saucer. It wasn't a shooting Zanni2 was planning. It was a bomb.

He reached for his phone but hesitated. Yes, he now knew what and where and why. But a crucial element was missing. When. He scrutinised the exchanges again and picked out key words: Glory. Right. Joy. Fight. People. Flight. Angel. Dove.

He stopped and reread. *Il Volo dell'Angelo*. The Flight of the Angel. He checked the date on his watch, smacked his palm on the table and snatched up the phone. He hit number 7 on his speed-dial list, typing his notes into PIN as he waited for a reply.

"Good morning sir, how can I help?"

"Wake him up. I've got bad news."

Twenty minutes later, this time wearing cotton briefs beneath his black jeans, he ran back downstairs. While intelligence agencies were comparing notes and alerting *carabinieri* across the city, he had a job to do. Few taxis patrolled the streets this early, so he swung a leg over his rented Vespa and sped towards Piazza San Marco.

Street cleaners, security officers, city officials and pigeons still had the freedom to roam the enormous square. In a matter of hours, every inch of space would be packed with costumed revellers, hawkers, food stands and media, awaiting the annual Flight of the Angel. From the bell-tower of San Marco, a wire ran to the Doge's Palace, where the angel would 'fly' across the crowds, a tradition stretching back centuries.

Originally known as the Flight of the Turk, a real acrobat used to cross the square on a high-wire, to the thrill and delight of the crowds below. In 1759 they renamed the event *Il Volo della Colombina* – The Flight of the Dove. That was the year the acrobat performing the stunt fell to his death.

Human beings were replaced by a large wooden dove for some time after that tragedy until the performer's safety could be guaranteed. Nowadays, he or she would be winched across the square in a harness, scattering glitter and confetti onto the celebrating crowds below.

He put himself in the mind of a terrorist. How could one

cause maximum damage during such an event? If the high-wire artist scattered something else, such as hydrofluoric acid, he could inflict horrific carnage on those upturned faces. A homemade bomb made less sense. Detonated at that height, the device would wreak limited damage, even if it was filled with nails or ball bearings. Most would fly harmlessly into the air. No, he was sure the attack was a ground-based explosive. He was equally sure this was not a suicide bomber. These individuals had bigger plans. The perpetrators had no intention of dying or getting caught. This was merely their opening scene.

Angel. Dove. *Dove?* He snorted in not-quite amusement. Good question. *Where are you, you bastards?* His stomach clenched as he considered the possibility that these people had long since planted their little box of tricks and were now watching from a comfortable distance.

He had just parked the Vespa up a side street when his earpiece buzzed. He listened in silence. Latest intelligence on the suspects' communication included repeated mentions of The Triumph of Venice. Could he shed any light? For the first time that day, he allowed himself a smile.

Yes, he could. Although the café was no longer called *Alla Venezia Trionfante*, it had a long history of hosting revolutionary ideas and described itself as the oldest café in Europe. With its famous artworks and live concerts, it had attracted the powerful and beautiful for nearly four centuries. Most crucial of all, it nestled under the arches of the Procuratie Nuove in Piazza San Marco. Which, in a few hours from now, would be crammed with people.

He set off with a purposeful stride while giving his intelligence agents all they needed to know. They'd found him.

Get ready, Zanni Two, I'm on my way.

The café was almost empty this early in the day. The waiters had little interest in a solitary coffee drinker, and after serving his espresso they retreated to the counter to argue about the distribution of tips. Most patrons, sitting in his spot, would be looking outwards, absorbing the architecture of the most famous piazza in the world.

Not him.

He took in the café's interior, its distinctive decor and proud heritage, trying to comprehend the layout of such an historic building. With a yawn, he got up and went in search of the bathrooms. The waiters ignored him as he passed and descended a stairwell bearing the universal male/female toilet signs. At the bottom, he stopped and checked the other doors.

The clanging of utensils and scent of baking bread came from the kitchen, a smell of detergent and air freshener seeped from the toilets and the only other room released no clues other than the sign on the door. PRIVATO.

He pressed himself back into the doorway of the Gents and listened. Clattering cutlery, voices raised in banter, the thin sound of a radio from the kitchen. Not a sound from either toilet and the private room stayed silent. An unoccupied cellar office, probably. It looked like he was in the wrong place. But his job was to chase each lead till it ran out. He had to be sure Zanni2 was not on the premises, and flush the terrorising little bastard out if he was.

Like every field agent, he had an ASK – an Access Skeleton Key – which could open pretty much anything. In this situation, it was unnecessary. The lock was old enough to be defeated by sliding in his credit card. He withdrew his gun and pressed himself up against the PRIVATO door for one final check before he attempted to prise it open. At that moment, he heard a whispered curse.

"*Merda! Mi manca la quarta sorpresa.*"

'Shit. I'm missing the fourth surprise'.

Two things sent a chill through his veins.

One: He had found Zanni2, preparing to detonate no fewer

than four bombs in the heart of Venice during the most popular event of the year.

Two: Zanni2 was a woman.

He messaged PIN, calling a ground team for back-up, and slid his platinum AMEX into the gap. Silent as he was, he still couldn't prevent the door mechanism from clicking. In the dim basement light, she turned from the laptop, her long black hair swept over one shoulder, eyes dark hollows in her pale face. An oil-fuelled heater sat in the centre of the room, its paint peeling and one wheel missing.

"Put your hands up. It's all over. We have everyone now," he lied. "You were the last, Zanni Two. Hands in the air, please, and back away from the computer."

Seconds ticked away. He took a step forward and repeated his instructions in Italian.

Her hands floated upwards and she swivelled slowly in her chair, obscuring her left arm for a second. With a twist she lifted a handgun and aimed it at him.

On instinct, he dived right and shot at her wrist as a bullet smashed into the door jamb behind him. He rolled backwards out of the doorway, scrambled to his feet and listened. He could hear liquid dripping onto tiles.

He crept back into the room, his weapon readied, but it proved unnecessary. His shot had done double duty, passing through her wrist and into her face. Zanni2 flopped across the radiator, a broken puppet. Her long black hair hung down like a stage curtain. Blood pooled from her shattered skull and dripped from the remains of her left hand. A small square of sunlight streaming through the stained glass rhomboids of the basement window threw colourful diamond patterns across her white shirt.

With one eye on the doorway, he picked up her undamaged right wrist to feel for a pulse. Tattooed on her forearm was a crimson rose. He let her hand fall and stepped past her dead body.

He had a bomb to defuse.

Chapter 1

"Ah-kah."

The muffled cough was barely audible in the quiet of the third floor bedroom, but Doctor Elisabete Silva heard it. She held her breath and tilted her head so both ears were free of the pillow. Another cough and an accompanying snuffle. She reached to throw the duvet off her legs, but a hand pressed on her chest, fingers splayed.

"Stay there," he said.

"No."

"Yes."

"Samuel, you have to get up in an hour. I'll go. You need your rest."

"I'll see to her," he replied. "My last chance before I leave." He rose from the bed like a wraith and pulled on a T-shirt, graceful and grey in the chiaroscuro of the shadowed room.

Elisabete relaxed and smiled up at her husband even though she couldn't quite make out his face in the dark of their bedroom. "Thank you, *o meu amor*. Call me if you need any help."

She closed her eyes and her head sank back into the pillows, listening to the rasp of the door, the slap of bare feet on tiles and the soft murmurs and groans as Samuel lifted their daughter out of the cot. Sleep dragged at her consciousness and the creak of the rocking chair next door lulled her body into a doze.

But her mind refused to go back to sleep. Part of her brain

was awake and ready for duty, running through a checklist. His suitcase, his documents, itinerary and police issue weapon all floated across her vision. His presentations and handouts all prepared, almost as familiar as the first photographs of Marcia. Once more she calculated his journey time from leaving home on Rua dos Anjos. Crossing Lisbon by car to Santa Apolónia station, taking the train to Porto, another to Viana do Castelo and a taxi to the venue. Samuel would be travelling almost the length of the country.

She stretched and faced the fact the night was over. Instead of getting into the shower, she wrapped a robe around her nakedness and padded into the adjoining room, her need for them both a palpable thing. The nightlight on the landing shed a soft pink glow, illuminating her husband rocking gently back and forth, his hand supporting the child's dark head against his shoulder. She watched him, returning the contented, weary ghost of a smile when he looked up.

"I'll miss her," he breathed.

"She'll miss you," Elisabete said, resting her head against the door. "Maybe I will too, just a bit."

"I already regret doing this conference. It's too soon and not worth..."

"Sssh. It is worth it. This is your career. It's only a week and it's a high-profile, well-paid appearance. Anyway, you can't cancel now..."

He pressed his lips to their daughter's forehead, his long lashes brushing the thick hair on top of her head.

"But the timing..."

"Samuel, she's still only two. She's absorbing everything and finding her place. Yes, the absence of Papa will confuse her to begin with, but as long as I'm here to take care of her and shower her with love, she'll continue to adapt. Then when you come back she'll be delighted to see you all over again. Seven days, that's all."

He eased out of the rocking chair and with great tenderness, placed their daughter back in her bed, where she clutched her pillow with her small fist.

"I think I meant the timing for me." He reached out and Elisabete slid into his arms. They gazed at the sleeping figure, as if unconvinced she was real.

"After everything we did to bring her here," he whispered, "it feels as if every minute without her is a waste of time. I wonder if natural parents think the same."

"Some, maybe. Those who tried and tried and then conceived a child after they'd given up all hope. But many others regard children as a nuisance. So when Marcia grows up and we tell her the story, she'll know she was no accident or afterthought. We wanted her so badly we went through two years of bullshit to rescue her. Now we are her parents and her daddy loves her so much he doesn't even want to go to work."

Samuel laughed softly through his nose. "I do want to go to work. I just don't want to think about a week without you two."

"When she's older, we'll come with you. I want her to see the whole of Portugal and then travel all over the world. I just don't want to drag her away when she's only just getting used to this place as her home. This time, we stay here. You go to the conference. Speak, socialise, network and tell everyone about your plans for publication. Build a fan base and make sure the name on every police bigwig's lips is Samuel Silva. Then come home to your family."

Morning light spilling through the window began to add shades of clarity to the pink glow. She studied his complexion as he faced her. His usual frown of concentration was absent but the lines on his skin remained. The grey in his hair stood out against the black and even his stubble was now stippled with white. He kissed her and pulled away to direct his intense stare into her eyes.

She knew that look. "We don't have time! You should get into the shower while I finish your packing. Nelson will be here at seven to take you to the station and it's already half past five. Samuel, listen to me!"

His arms slipped around her waist and he nuzzled her ear. Her body responded as inevitably as an egg on a hot pan.

Samuel murmured in her ear. "I'll be ready by the time Nelson arrives. Of all people, he would never let me miss the train. But as my daughter is now asleep and I won't see my wife for seven days, not to mention nights, I think I should say *até logo*, in my own way."

He took her hand and led her back to their bedroom. She paused for a second, then ran ahead of him and flung off her gown as she leapt onto the bed.

"The doctor will see you now."

Chapter 2

Acting Detective Chief Inspector Beatrice Stubbs. 'Acting' was about right. She was making it up as she went along and the sense of being an utter fraud was omnipresent. Even her new desk made her uneasy. This was the headmaster's office; the place one was summoned to be carpeted or given bad news. The usual chatter, banter, laughter and inexplicable smells of the open-plan area were all shut out of here. She craved the hum of a busy office, grease stains from a half-eaten pizza, stale whiffs of lunchtime booze and damp of tobacco from those who forced outside to smoke in the rain. This was Hamilton's place, not hers. This room smelled of polish and whisky and punishment. It smelled like politics.

Her discomfort was exacerbated by the knowledge that every time she'd stood here fuming with dislike of the man behind the desk, his feelings had been quite the opposite. Six months had passed since she received Hamilton's final missive before he chose to end his life. Time had not healed and she still found the realisation too much to bear. It was odd to discover your nemesis had actually loved you.

And as the gods love to play with our fates, so they had in this instance. The powers-that-be at Scotland Yard met and came to a decision. The Superintendent's position was to be awarded to Rangarajan Jalan, a choice universally approved, especially by Beatrice. The man was a diplomat, an admirable detective and made of the sort of moral fibre immune to erosion.

Which left the position of his junior – Detective Chief Inspector. Despite her insistence that she intended to take early retirement, that she hated managerial responsibilities, that she would be far better employed as a detective than a boss, Beatrice Stubbs was appointed to 'caretake' the role of DCI until a suitable replacement could be found.

Beatrice scowled at the brilliant London summer sunshine streaming in past the plants Melanie had added to the windowsill.

"Hamilton wouldn't even of had a cactus in here, even though I told him about Feng Shui. Bit of green, few flowers, instant karma, innit?"

She decided to avail herself of one of the few privileges the position afforded and picked up the phone. The administrator answered immediately.

"Hello, Beatrice! What can I do you for?" That particular joke had never worn thin. At least for Melanie.

"Hi, Melanie. Could you bring me a coffee, please? Latte macchiato, no sugar."

"You want that much caffeine before the meeting with the Super? If you're thirsty, Beatrice, I'll bring you some water or a camomile tea. Thing is, you don't wanna go over there wired even if it is only Ranga. You know what you're like. Gotta keep a clear head, know what I mean?"

"Never mind, I'll get it myself."

So much for privileges. She considered visiting the coffee machine and ignoring Melanie's advice, except the interfering little cow was right.

She sent a text message to DI Dawn Whittaker.

Feel like I'm in solitary confinement. What did I do wrong and when can I get visitors?

Dawn pinged back in seconds.

It's what you did right that counts. Word is, time off for good behaviour. Large glass at The Speaker tonight?

Beatrice smiled and sent a thumbs-up icon, entering into the whole txt-spk shorthand for civilised communication with barely a regret. She checked her hair, picked up her brand-new briefcase and walked the length of the building for her meeting with Superintendent Jalan.

"Beatrice, punctual to the minute. Come in, sit down and let's have some coffee. This machine can make the concoction of your choice and I ordered a pastry selection from Paul's. This whole position of power deal has its perks, don't you think?"

The elegant glass table sat in a corner window with a view across St James's Park, where swans glided across the water and the perfectly maintained lawns were as yet free of tourists.

"If you can get the staff," replied Beatrice, dumping her bag on a leather chair and reaching for a plate.

Ranga laughed and sat down opposite, the skin around his warm brown eyes crinkling. Apparently he was pleased to see her. "Melanie has our best interests at heart. By the way, are you going to her wedding?"

Beatrice bit into a plump doughnut filled with sweet yellow custard. "God, I love these things. Of course I'm going. She's been bending my ear with the planning phase for over two years, so I bloody well deserve a sit-down meal, some fizz and a spoonful of trifle. Are you?"

Ranga opened his palms. "I wouldn't dream of missing it. She's the nerve centre of this place and I think we're all very fond of her. Latte macchiato?"

"That would be just the ticket. Thank you." She raised her voice above the buzzing of the machine. "You didn't get me in here to discuss wedding outfits. What's this about? We had the weekly stand-up yesterday so this is either a problem or an issue and I'm not wild about either."

Ranga sat down, set their coffees on the table and selected a sticky croissant, still wearing a relaxed smile.

"No problems or issues. But something interesting has come to my attention and I wanted to share it with you before you leave for Portugal."

"Something interesting?" Beatrice brushed sugar crystals from her mouth, leaving most of them on her knuckles.

Ranga bit into his croissant and chewed. Impossibly, the man made no mess apart from a few crumbs on his napkin.

"Gossip. Nothing more. Word is there's a book. Creative nonfiction, thinly disguised facts, whatever. But it could expose, embarrass and possibly even indict senior officers across the continent. It's due for release this year."

"How bad? Who's behind it? Can it be stopped?" Beatrice put down her pastry.

"That's the difficulty. You see, we don't know. All we have is rumours and conjecture. No one can get close enough to find out who, when or exactly what. However, you'll be mingling with all the likeliest suspects for almost a week. My advice would be to say nothing but keep your ears and eyes open. Ask the right questions. Sniff the wind and follow your nose."

"That's not much to go on."

"I know, but it's all I have," Ranga opened his palms. "Someone or someones in the senior ranks of international law enforcement has hired the services of an expensive legal firm for personal reasons. We wouldn't normally take any notice. It's not an unusual occurrence, but it seems the same lawyer is in correspondence with a fairly well-known publishing house. Preliminary enquiries, through mixture of deceit and flattery, seem to show these legal checks are related to the imminent publication of a ghost-written book. But everyone involved is close-mouthed and cautious. Which gives even greater cause for concern."

Beatrice looked into Ranga's eyes. "How would you play it?"

"How I'd play it is probably not relevant. Whoever is writing an exposé must have quite an ego. In your shoes, I'd be unimpressed and under awed."

"Give them room to show off and let them come to me?" She returned her attention to her doughnut.

"Precisely. And I will be doing the same. We don't know

whether this individual or partnership is internal. I am going to be observing your potential replacements very carefully, as it could just as easily be one of them. We have at least five internal candidates who want to be sitting in your chair when you finally retire – three of whom you know personally. So while I send you on useful collaborative missions to benefit the force as a whole, this conference being an example, your shoes will be tried on for size. The job continues as usual and you hand over the baton for a few days every couple of months. Then we evaluate their performance and make a decision as to your worthiest successor."

Logical. Inarguably astute management practice. And now that she had a secondary mission to fulfil she was less disgruntled about spending a residential week with a bunch of Euro-stiffs attending workshops with titles like 'Data-transparency: ingress, egress and mining'. She'd been dreading it. The worst bit would be the fact it was 90% men all itching to wield ego-sabres over canapés.

"Really Sven? We vastly prefer sequential presentation over simultaneous in witness ID. Have you read the study by... blah, blah, bloody blah."

But if she was covertly gathering information on them at the same time, the tedium would at least be alleviated a little. Ranga wouldn't exaggerate just to pique her interest, she knew him better than that.

She ate. Ranga drank. Pigeons purr-cooed on the guttering above the huge glass vitrine.

"So I spy on my peers while you spy on our colleagues?"

Ranga's face creased into one of his good-natured smiles. "Spy might be too strong a word. What we need to remember is that information is power. You are a perspicacious judge of character and that is an extraordinary skill. I want to know everything you find out, but in particular I want your opinions... but there is one small catch."

Beatrice sighed. "You want me to sleep with them all and tape their pillow-talk."

Ranga smiled again. "Not quite, but you might be better placed to judge if you spend at least one evening in their company as well as the daytime activities. Now before you erupt, I know you're mixing business with pleasure on this one. But if you flew out earlier, on Friday, you could go directly to the venue, attend the opening night dinner and stay overnight. Then join Matthew, Adrian et al on Saturday. You would get two days in lieu as compensation. Am I being unreasonable?"

Beatrice thought it over and shook her head. "Suppose not. You're just as devious as Hamilton was, aren't you? "

"Perhaps. But he was by far the better actor. So you'll go for Friday evening? I want the best pair of ears I've got on the ground from the outset."

Beatrice lifted her shoulders as high as they would go and dropped them with a sigh. "You can dispense with the flattery. I'll go. But I should make you tell Matthew."

Ranga grinned. "There is one piece of good news. One of the delegates is an ex-colleague of yours. Do you remember Xavier Racine?"

Chapter 3

Catinca burst through the doorway of Harvey's Wine Emporium just before five o'clock, still sporting the Frida Kahlo look. That made it almost a whole week now, but the look definitely suited her. She wore a white peasant blouse with an embroidered collar, a voluminous yellow skirt and black leather clogs, her hair was plaited and rolled on her head, with three silk roses in her crown. Over her arm hung a scarlet shawl and a tote bag printed with wildly coloured parrots.

Adrian greeted her with an affectionate smile. "You can't just come into a room like a normal person, can you? It always has to be an entrance. But you're looking good. As always."

"Feeling good an' all. Done my application to remain today."

"You're definitely not going back to Romania?"

She gave an emphatic nod. "Staying here, if they let me. Got meself nice flat, decent man and the job's not too bad."

Adrian reached up for a high five. "From an employer's point of view, I am relieved. I really want to keep you."

She smacked his palm. "Cheers! You all ready for Portugal?"

"I've been ready for approximately three weeks," he admitted. "The final item, my mobile boarding pass, arrived an hour before you did. The big question is are *you* ready?"

Catinca cackled and bustled off into the office to deposit her things. Her voice carried back into the shop.

"I gonna do a top job while you is gone. So good you want go away every other week, mate. Plans coming out my ears!"

The bell rang as a young couple entered the shop. They held the door open for three women following them in.

Adrian readied himself for rush hour, reminding himself to check exactly what 'plans' Catinca had for his beloved business. She emerged from the back room and made for the group of women just as he offered assistance to the browsing couple.

"Good evening. Were you looking for anything in particular?" he asked.

"Wotcha ladies! What you after? Bookclub or hen night? Come on then, Catinca gonna sort you out."

An hour and a half later the rush hour had died down and the heat of the day subsided as a golden sunset bathed the street outside. Adrian was laminating his DO NOT FORGET document for Catinca when the sound of a car horn tooted twice outside the shop. Catinca dropped the calligraphy chalk she was using on the blackboard and rushed to the window.

"Is Will! With new Audi! God, I love your boyfriend!"

Adrian stayed behind the counter, serving customers and shaking his head at the sound of Catinca's oohs and aahs from the street. The car pulled away with the top down and Catinca in the passenger seat waving back at him, her mouth set in a wide grin. Will would probably drive her round the block at least. Adrian gave an indulgent laugh. His assistant's enthusiasm would please Will, because try as he might, Adrian couldn't really see what the fuss was about. If it started when it was supposed to, didn't break down, was an inoffensive colour and emitted no attention-seeking roars on city streets, it was a perfectly acceptable means of transport. Not a source of breathless joy.

But Will wanted appreciation of the upholstery, the fuel consumption, the range of instruments at the driver's disposal and even the non-slip drinks holder. And that was before he'd even started the thing.

Within ten minutes, Catinca was back, face glowing. "That is one sexy beast! And not just talking about the driver!"

Adrian laughed, a little demob happy, and handed Catinca his list. "Here. Be good. Be creative. Be careful. Any problems, call me. And thank you so much for giving me a whole week with my wonderful man."

"Awww!" Catinca grabbed him in a hug and squeezed. "Have a great time, maties, I mind the shop so don't worry. I offer to mind his car, but he's not very trusting. Probably 'cos he's a copper. Go, have fun, bring me a present! Go now! He's on double yellows."

Adrian went, and jumped into the car beside Will with one last look back at the shop. He waved goodbye to Catinca, who was miming heart pumps in the window.

"She loves it. And you." Adrian leaned over for a kiss.

"Course she does. The girl's got taste." Will drove along the street and waited to join the main artery, still clogged with traffic at the tail end of rush hour.

"You can't really appreciate it when all we do is stop-start. The real test will come when we're cruising down a motorway. That's when you'll notice the smooth handling. Travelling will be a pure pleasure," said Will, raising his hand to thank a driver who let them out.

"Does it have a radio?" asked Adrian, his mind on whether he'd mentioned fire alarms to his assistant.

"It has every means available of playing any sound. Can you imagine? Roof down, music playing, wind in our hair and sun on our faces."

"Something to look forward to when we get back. I always feel deflated after holidays," Adrian said.

"Do you? I love coming home. But I'm looking forward to this holiday more than I did Mauritius, you know."

Adrian looked across at his partner, unable to resist his enthusiasm. "Me too. Though I doubt the weather will be quite the same."

"Don't care. Good company, fine food..."

"And when we get back, a new toy to play with. Are we going

out for dinner tonight? I think we've pretty much emptied the fridge."

Will reversed into a parking space opposite the flat and turned off the ignition, grinning at Adrian.

"As we'll be eating Portuguese salads and fish for a week, we could be forgiven a pie and a pint tonight."

"I'm sure we could," Adrian reached for his seatbelt and spotted a familiar figure crossing the road. "There's Beatrice! Shall we ask her to come too?"

"Of course. If you'll forgive us a bit of police gossip."

"As if I have a choice. Hang on a minute, she's got a face like a wet weekend. Let's go and see what's wrong."

Any hopes Will might have had of the Audi garnering a little more admiration from Beatrice were soon dashed.

"It's very nice," she said, patting the bonnet. Adrian gave up on the car and ushered Beatrice into the building, through the front door of his own flat and straight to a stool in the kitchen. By the time Will joined them, Adrian was adding a slice of cucumber to three gin and tonics.

"I have to travel to Portugal earlier on Friday to be there for a welcome dinner." Beatrice blurted out. "So I can't fly with you and the others. Not only that but because I've been given extra duties, I'll have to attend workshops on the Saturday. So our first weekend is going to be severely hampered. To be honest, it's a bloody pain."

"That's a shame. But if you can't get out of it, we'll just have to make the most of the time you do have. Cheers!" Adrian raised his glass and his eyebrows at Will, a silent signal to join in with the positive spin.

Will picked up his cue. "Cheers! I don't suppose you can tell us what the extra duties might be?"

"Not really. We have some intelligence which I am supposed to explore, basically." Beatrice screwed up her nose. "It's pretty vague."

"Well, look on the bright side. You get to spend an extra two days with some seriously big fish. I'm a bit envious, actually. Am I allowed to pick your brains every evening?"

Beatrice chinked her glass against theirs. "Cheers and thank you for being so upbeat about this. Matthew and the girls won't take it so well, I'm sure. Yes, it would be a golden opportunity to network and make contacts for someone keen to pursue a career with the police. But for me, it's a curate's head. I'd send you instead if I could, Will. For someone intent on retirement like myself, it will be an exercise in gathering information and making space for Ranga to trial run a replacement."

Will opened a packet of pistachio nuts and poured them into a bowl. "Do you know who the Super has lined up for the job? Sorry, you don't have to answer if it's confidential."

Beatrice peeled apart a nut. "All Ranga said was three of the five are known to me. I assume he means our existing DIs – Cooper, Bryant and Whittaker. By which I mean Dawn, not her husband. That would be politically awkward, having one's ex as line manager. I suspect they may be looking at a sideways transfer from LTP or another force."

"The Thames Valley DCI is keen, I hear. But with so little inner-city experience, I can't see it happening."

Adrian yawned with great ostentation. That was the only downside of his partner and neighbour being in the same line of work – talking shop.

"DCI Stubbs, DS Quinn, let me read you your rights. Next week, you are allowed half an hour over aperitifs to discuss police politics and that is your daily ration. Do I make myself clear?"

"Sorry," Beatrice held up her hands. "It is a bad habit. Blame Will for encouraging me. I promise I'll try and behave next week."

Will laughed. "Me too. Beatrice, have you got plans for dinner? Adrian and I were thinking of heading over to The Morgan Arms for something to eat."

She grimaced. "I can't, much as I'd love to. I have to phone

Matthew and break the news. Then I need to pack and do my homework for the course. The Morgan Arms...is that the one that does those pies?"

"'Fraid so," Adrian pulled down the corners of his mouth in a moue of regret and Beatrice sighed before draining her drink.

"Life is *so* unfair. Thank you for the gin. I feel slightly fortified but still awfully hard done by. Enjoy your dinner and I'll see you in Portugal." She kissed each of them on the cheek, heaved up her briefcase and trudged towards the front door.

Once the door had closed, Will indicated the bottle of Sipsmith's.

"If we have another, I can't drive. Shall we walk to the pub instead? Or would you prefer to stay in and get a takeaway?"

Adrian used his fingertips to push his glass towards Will. "Of the many reasons why I love you, the fact that Action Man occasionally indulges my inertia is one of my favourites."

Chapter 4

All things considered, Matthew took it very well. Beatrice's biggest concern – that police work always taking precedence over her private life – was not even mentioned. Weekends with Matthew and his daughters were a regular occurrence. To Beatrice, Marianne and Tanya were more like good friends than anything resembling step-daughters, and Tanya's son Luke, now five, was a sociable, well-behaved child, comfortable with adult company.

But this would be the first holiday they had ever spent together, and they'd been planning for months. Their first time abroad as a family. The first time with the additional company of Adrian and Will. Her neighbour and his partner were both urbane and social, yet the connecting factor was Beatrice, who would be absent for the first two days, leaving poor Matthew to hold the fort.

"I'm really sorry about having to do this. I feel rotten about arranging it all then leaving you to provide the social glue," she told him.

"Not to worry. Marianne's had to reschedule their flights too. She and her new chap will arrive for Saturday. Something to do with his work. So we'll be an advance party setting up base camp. Tanya and Luke won't mind and I assume you've already told Adrian and Will. We can take care of ourselves for the first day and you'll be with us on the Saturday evening. We can manage,

Old Thing. Then when we all fly home, you and I can have a few extra days to ourselves. We'll have to think about how best to use our time together."

"Practising?"

He was silent for a moment. "Yes. Practising sounds like a very good idea. Stay home, garden, potter and get used to having each other about." He snorted a laugh.

"What's so funny?"

"That it's taken us twenty-five years to try cohabiting. Marianne and Liam moved in together just two months after they met."

"I thought his name was Leon, not Liam."

"Is it? Perhaps you're right. I'd better check that before we get to Portugal."

"Matthew, do you mean to say you haven't you actually met him yet?"

"Yes, I have, if more by accident than design. I was in the ironmonger's in Crediton on Tuesday, getting some grouting for the downstairs bathroom. Walked out the door and bumped right into them both. He – Leon, Liam, whatever – was charming. Respectful, polite and jolly well turned-out, in my opinion."

Considering the way Matthew dressed, Beatrice had a broad interpretation of 'well turned-out'.

"Look forward to meeting him myself. She seems quite smitten."

"Yes. She is."

Beatrice picked up on the reserved tone. "You just said you liked him."

"I do, judging on the little I've seen. It's just... I wish her absorption with him left a little more room for the rest of us. She's not seen Luke or Tanya for over a fortnight now and I've hardly spoken to her. She came over here once but only to drop off her cat. I'm actually surprised she agreed to come on holiday with us, to be honest. She seems to have no time for anyone else."

"That's just the heady rush of young love," Beatrice said. "The honeymoon phase. It'll wear off. And to be fair, Marianne was overdue some romance in her life."

"You're right, I'm being selfish. I'll be on my best behaviour next week and I'll cook for us all on Saturday evening. You'll definitely be able to join us by then?"

"Yes. I'll get a taxi from the conference and be there as close as I can to dinnertime. Matthew, I really am sorry about this. Genuinely sorry and not just pretending because I'm a bit excited about the alternative. I wish I didn't have to do this and could spend the time with all of you instead."

"This is where I could say something about having the rest of our lives together but that might put you into a flat spin so I'll simply say, I know."

Chapter 5

On the flight to Porto, Beatrice studied the conference programme in order to manage her expectations. A key event in the law enforcement calendar taking place from Friday to Friday, this would be the fifth and last time she'd have to attend the European Police Intercommunication Conference, or EPIC.

EPIC, for pity's sake. She loathed these cutesy acronyms. This one was bound to provoke police websites across the continent into endless bad puns and tired headlines.

Think positive, she muttered to herself. She spent a while checking the various workshops on offer, entering her options and wondering whether she'd made the wrong choices. Then she read the list of participants, checking ranks and positions and looking for names she might recognise.

At least there would be one friendly face – Xavier Racine. She smiled. Four years earlier, after an extended break, she'd got back into the saddle with an assignment in Switzerland. It wasn't the easiest case, but she'd respected and enjoyed working with her international team in Zürich. Xavier Racine was intelligent yet endearingly shy, and worked as part of a specialist task force. She remembered a few details about the young man. He was eager, clumsy, prone to blushing and one of the top ten marksmen in the country. She'd grown very fond of him and had even put in a word with his superior.

She had no idea whether that had made any difference or

not. But here, near the end of the list, was a photograph of Herr Xavier Racine of Swiss Fedpol – a little older with a receding hairline, but the same freckles and awkward grin. He was a speaker, no less, leading a workshop she'd never have thought of attending – Markers of Terrorist Activity in Online Communications. Perhaps it was not too late to change her mind.

The second factor to lift her gloom was the location itself. Gerês College of Hospitality promised five-star cuisine, an expansive wine cellar and silver service to train its students before they graduated to take roles at key hotels, discreet homes, yachts and private jets across the world. Its grounds and 120 rooms looked luxurious and Beatrice even considered for a moment the wisdom of travelling to and from their holiday villa each day. She was extraordinarily partial to a nice hotel room and the sense of freedom that came with it. At least she'd have one night to experience its comforts.

Maybe the week would be rather more enjoyable than she'd first thought. Certain names on the list of speakers and attendees she recognised, including Commander Gilchrist, a high-profile UK senior officer charged with the task of promoting European police cooperation. A regular on various news sites with his white smile and reassuring wrinkles, Gilchrist was the popular face of international law enforcement. Beatrice found his approach informed and wise, if a little media-flashy. Still, she could not deny looking forward to meeting the man in person.

A car collected her from Aeroporto Francisco Sà Carneiro and drove her north. She gazed out at the terracotta roofs, window shutters, dusty summer foliage and roadside hoardings with a familiar sense of excitement. She was back on mainland Europe, where things were just a little different and always unpredictable.

The taxi crossed various bodies of water, each reflecting the afternoon sunshine and deep blue sky as they entered the natural park and drew nearer to their destination. Buildings became scarce and the terrain grew more mountainous and verdant. If a moose or a wolf had strolled out of the forest, Beatrice wouldn't have been in the least surprised.

Low sun hit the fields surrounding Gerês College of Hospitality as the car rumbled up the drive to the grand-looking castle. The facade was slightly marred by damage to the uppermost stonework, where part of the crenellations had crumbled, leaving a gap resembling a missing tooth. Red and white plastic tape secured the area but detracted from the charm of the building.

She tipped the driver and pulled her suitcase behind her into an equally impressive portico lined by blue and white tiles depicting scenes of country life, reminding her of her mother's willow pattern crockery.

She checked in, received her welcome pack and made her way to a first floor room without seeing anyone she knew. Large, modern and practical, the room had all the necessaries, including a mini-bar. The most luxurious element of all was the view. She stepped out onto her balcony and soaked it all in.

Below, a terrace stretched the breadth of the building, and in its centre a few steps led down to a tidy lawn which sloped away towards a lake. A path meandered through the shrubs between cerise bougainvillea and blousy pink camellias. To her left, another path led under a walkway of climbing roses to a sort of temple, complete with white marble columns. The perfect place for a wedding.

Beatrice sighed, opened a bottle of water and dithered. Once she left her room, she would be exposed and forced to find a conversational partner or fake a certain business-like air by muttering into her mobile. She wandered back to the balcony, watching small groups and pairs stroll the grounds in the summer sunshine. She would much prefer to stay indoors alone. But how could one gain intelligence without actually talking to people?

The pressure of enforced sociability hemmed her in. She paced the room and rehearsed casual introductions while inwardly wishing she was back in her intimidating office in Scotland Yard. The ring of the room telephone startled her.

"Hello? DCI Stubbs speaking."

"DCI Stubbs, hello! This is Xavier Racine from Zürich. Do you remember me?"

"Xavier! Of course I remember. I was so pleased to see your name on the list of participants. How are you?"

"Thank you, I'm very well. I'm calling to see if you would like to join me for a drink before dinner?"

Relief flooded through her. "I would love to. Shall we say in ten minutes, on the terrace?"

"Perfect. See you then."

Beatrice replaced the phone and began digging through her case to find her hairbrush.

He'd barely changed at all. A few fine lines formed a delta at the corners of his gentle hazel eyes, his hair had receded but it was still the same copper colour, and his eager smile radiated from a clean-shaven face. She held out her hand and he took it in both of his.

"Beatrice! So good to see you again! Oh, can I still call you Beatrice now you are DCI?"

"Of course you can. It's lovely to see you too. You don't look a day older since the last time I saw you."

"Thank you. You actually look a lot better than last time I saw you. Shall we sit here?" He indicated a table beneath the green and white striped awing." I ordered us a bottle of white wine and sparkling water. If I'm not wrong, your preferred drink is a spritzer?"

"You are not wrong. So how's life in Zürich? Do you still work with Herr Kälin?"

"No, he retired last year. Before that we worked closely together. He was a great support to me and recommended me for promotion to Fedpol. That's why I'm here. And you are now Detective Chief Inspector! Congratulations!"

"Acting DCI. I plan to retire at the end of this year."

"So soon? That's a shame. For the Metropolitan Police, I mean. Ah, the wine."

Beatrice watched him as he tasted the Chardonnay and thanked the waiter in Portuguese. She revised her opinion. He *had* changed. There was an assurance to him now which had been absent four years ago. All that gauche awkwardness had disappeared, leaving a confident, measured man comfortable in his own skin. She noticed the gold wedding band.

"And you got married!"

He smiled, a touch of the old bashfulness surfacing.

"Yes, last year. I still can't get used to saying 'my wife' but it's the best decision I ever made. What about you?"

"Still happily unmarried, but I'll be moving in with my long-suffering partner at the end of the year. It's about time, really. We've been together over a quarter of a century."

"That merits a toast. To success, professional and personal!"

"Success!" Beatrice beamed as they touched glasses and drank.

"I see you're a specialist in spotting terrorist activity now," she said.

"Specialist? Well, I hope to share some techniques. I've been training in Germany and want to pass on what I discovered. Will you be at that workshop?"

"Of course I will. Even if I wasn't interested, which I am, I'd come along anyway to support you. Which other sessions are you attending?"

"My priority is to attend everything by Samuel Silva."

"Who's that?" asked Beatrice.

"A Portuguese psychologist who works for the Lisbon Intelligence Unit. He's developed an exciting new profiling tool to assess levels of sociopathy in social media behaviours. It could be helpful in monitoring potential domestic incidents."

"Home-grown terrorists?"

"Yes, but more of the individual variety than organised cells."

"I see," said Beatrice. "More Brevik than Brussels."

"Exactly," Xavier nodded, his expression serious.

They chatted about the week ahead and strayed into police 'news' – which a casual observer might have construed as gossip – as they emptied the bottle. Shadows lengthened across the table and the cooling dusk attracted mosquitoes enough to eventually drive them inside.

In the dining-room, eight tables of six were laid out with sparkling glassware and floral centrepieces. It looked more like a wedding than a conference of senior police officers. On the stage sat the bigwigs, with Commander Gilchrist at the centre, and suddenly Beatrice was reminded less of weddings and more of school assemblies. There seemed to be no seating plan so Xavier led Beatrice to join a group of three on the second table. She was relieved to see another woman amongst them. Xavier made introductions and the reason for his choice became clear.

"Good evening, may we join you? My name is Xavier Racine from Swiss Fedpol and this is DCI Beatrice Stubbs of the London Met."

A tallish chap in a tweedy jacket stood up. "Please do. My name is Samuel Silva of the LIU. This is my colleague André Monteiro and we have just introduced ourselves to Agent Cher Davenport of the FBI."

The Monteiro boy stood up for the handshakes. Beatrice tried not to gawp at him, as he really did appear to be no more than fourteen years old. The American lady remained seated and Beatrice realised she was in a wheelchair. Her sleek fox-red hair framed an open, bright face with a broad smile. Like Xavier, she had freckles. Unlike Xavier, she had pretty green eyes.

Silva had a friendly demeanour, a wise expression and a touch of grey at his temples. Xavier took the seat next to him and the two immediately fell into animated conversation. Beatrice sat the other side of Xavier, opposite the FBI agent, with a space between herself and the Portuguese lad.

"Can I get you some water, DCI Stubbs?" asked Monteiro.

Beatrice smiled. A teenager he might be but he had excellent manners and the hint of an American accent. "Yes please. And seeing as we're going to be colleagues this week, shall we use first names? You can call me Beatrice."

Cher Davenport's face broke into another wide smile. "That is exactly what we were just saying. So: Cher, Beatrice, André, Samuel and Xavier."

"And Roman."

A deep voice came from behind Beatrice. She turned to see a surfer-type with tanned skin, blond hair in a ponytail and a neatly trimmed beard. He looked around the table with a half-smile, his steady eyes the colour of dawn.

"Hello everyone. Roman Björnsson from the Icelandic *Víkingasveitin*, or Viking Squad. Can I sit down?"

Dinner, despite Beatrice's reservations, turned out to be thoroughly enjoyable, in terms of both food and company. She and Cher bonded instantly, in firm agreement that the gender imbalance in senior international law enforcement and intelligence was an embarrassment for all concerned.

Fishcake on a lake of beurre blanc accompanied by a Pinot Gris was their first course, during which she grilled the Viking on Icelandic culture. An easy-going, relaxed young man with a ready laugh, he answered all her queries with good humour and batted several more in her direction. Their conversation attracted André's attention. He added his opinion on how a country's cultural outlook affected its policing, offering his training experience in Brazil as an example. That explained the American accent. His voice and opinions were mature and Beatrice wondered if his boyish looks had deceived her.

Roman asked André about the effect of differing climates, citing long, dark Reykjavik winters and corresponding crime statistics. By the time the pea, asparagus and nettle risotto arrived, the whole table was in lively discussion. The staff made sure the diners' glasses stayed filled and the noise of cutlery, crockery and chatter rose to a boisterous rumble.

The conversation turned to national legends, and Beatrice had just finished regaling her party with the story of the Beast of Bodmin Moor when Commander Gilchrist stood up on the raised podium and switched on the microphone. There was a brief squeal of feedback and the hubbub hushed to an expectant silence.

"Good evening ladies and gentlemen, and welcome to Gerês College of Hospitality. I hope you all enjoyed this evening's meal. I think you'll all agree with me, these young people have a great career ahead of them. If I were the judge, I'd give this restaurant five stars!"

Enthusiastic applause rang out and heads nodded in assent. Gilchrist joined in the clapping, directing his approving smile in the direction of the kitchens.

"This week is going to be EPIC!" he said, and Beatrice sighed at the early onset of the puns. "I'd like to start by thanking all of you for giving up seven full days to attend this exciting event. In unprecedented circumstances across Europe, closer cooperation matters like never before. Many of you have left crucial posts and travelled significant distances to better your police manage-ment skills and align practices. This marks each of you as a true leader in the field."

He patted his hands together and rotated in a semi-circle, as if to applaud them individually.

"Gathered in this room are some of the finest senior police officers on this continent, not to mention lecturers representing another three: America, Asia and Africa. This week will see a packed programme of cutting-edge technology, superlative exemplars of best forensic practice, game-changing advances in psychological research and theories on detection as prevention, alongside some of the grassroots work done in community and social cooperative projects. We'll learn from each other, network and connect, build relationships and get back to basics.

"We're a relatively small group, but I want us to share our learning widely. In addition to feeding back to your own teams at home, it's essential to involve our colleagues across the globe. This year, the tech boffins have made that possible, via a brilliant new app called BluLite! In your welcome pack, you have instructions on how to download BluLite, which will enable you to add content to our exclusive international video-platform! Please download the app, use it according to the professional guidelines and spread your EPIC experiences on our unique intranet. You could start right now!

"Taking a week out from those whom we strive to serve, we must remember why we became police officers. I am quite sure we're all going to come out of this week tested, challenged but above all improved. I wish you all an unforgettable and EPIC week!"

Beatrice and her colleagues clapped and smiled, as did every other table, but she caught the Viking's eye roll and André's complicit grin. Xavier excused himself and made for the bathroom. To Beatrice's surprise, Samuel Silva slid into his seat.

"I understand the hierarchy at the Met is undergoing some changes," he said with a diffident air. His expression of genuine interest and his attentive listening manner led her to go into rather more detail than usual, encouraged by his gentle questions. Their superficial small talk soon became a serious and frank conversation about fears for the future.

Xavier returned and held out a palm to indicate the seating arrangement was fine with him. He took the empty seat next to Cher. Their conversation sounded interesting but Beatrice was drawn back to Samuel Silva's unassuming yet perceptive eyes.

Sotto voce, he enquired how she felt about retiring.

"Truthfully, I feel dread and anticipation in equal measures. I worry about getting bored in retirement and maybe even missing the pressures of this job. I worry about my partner finding me far less interesting when I'm attainable. I worry about what I'm going to do with all that free time." She gave an embarrassed shrug. "My worries are most people's dreams."

"None of us can truly envy or pity each other because we

are not wearing each other's shoes." Samuel sighed. "I was just talking to Xavier, who admits nerves about his upcoming presentation and wishes he had my speaking ability. Whereas I can address 200 international police professionals with confidence but confess pure terror at something the rest of the world takes for granted – becoming a parent."

He looked a little old for a first time father, but Beatrice was poor at judging ages. She sought a diplomatic reply. "Is that a recent development?"

"Yes. I left everything too late," he confided. "I was forty-five when I met my wife and we knew we were unlikely to conceive a child. But now, after two years of red tape, we just succeeded in adopting a little Romanian girl. She's two years old."

"Congratulations! That is a huge step."

"Thank you. It is. A first-time father at the age of fifty-two, I don't have the blind braggadocio of a young man. My job makes it worse. An entire career studying sociopathic behaviours and their consequences tends to test one's faith in humanity. On top of that, I have the added pressure of leaving them alone to come to places like this. I'm sorry, I shouldn't have said that. It was rude of me."

"Not at all. It makes perfect sense," said Beatrice. "You found something you thought you never would. Then to experience the emotional wringer of the adoption process, to bring her home after so long and have that precious little life in your care, no sane person would wish to be anywhere else but by her side. What's your daughter's name?"

His face creased into an expression of such heartfelt gratitude that his eyes almost closed. He slipped out his phone and showed her pictures. Marcia in the hospital, Marcia with her new parents, Marcia on the balcony with views of Lisbon's castle beyond, Marcia sleeping, her tiny fists beside her head.

Beatrice could see his point. "I'm not a baby person as a rule, but I have to say she is completely adorable. I'm not surprised you're in love. How did you..."

"And here I see some familiar faces!" Commander Gilchrist placed his hands on the back of Cher and André's chairs, as if he was Jesus at the last supper. "Silva, you old rogue! It's been years."

He reached across and shook Samuel's hand before flashing his teeth at the whole party. "Silva and I used to go to the football together. Then I think he got sick of England winning! Now, Acting DCI Stubbs I recognise. Holding the fort for Jalan, I believe."

Beatrice smiled as they shook, aware there was no need to reply.

"Monteiro Junior! How's your father doing?" He loomed awkwardly over André to offer his hand, forcing Cher to lean sideways in case she got an elbow in the face. "So, who's doing the introductions?"

Xavier stood up. "Good evening, Commander. My name is Xavier Racine from Fedpol, Switzerland, and this lady is Agent Davenport of the FBI. Here is Roman Björnsson of Iceland's Viking Squad. Pleased to meet you."

Beatrice watched Gilchrist turn his spotlight on each, throwing out a charming compliment or brief mention of common interest, to make everyone feel included. The man was a professional, she recognised.

He stood back and drew out his phone. He filmed the table, introducing each delegate and signed off his mini-reportage with his signature speech. "Good to meet you all, and I hope you'll learn a great deal from this EPIC experience. You're going to work hard, but this week will reignite your passion. That much I guarantee. Enjoy your dessert and coffee and see you all bright and early in the morning!"

He saluted and moved on to the next table. Beatrice and the Viking locked eyes. His smile was brief yet sardonic, and made him all the more interesting. The week ahead was beginning to develop quite some potential.

Dessert was a sorbet of melon and port. It was delicious, but no one at the table felt the need to film or photograph it and share the results online with their colleagues. After coffee, Roman suggested an after-dinner drink in the bar. André, Cher and Xavier agreed with enthusiasm, but Samuel demurred.

"That's kind of you, but I want to prepare for my lecture in the morning and call my wife. So I'll thank you all for such an enjoyable evening and go back to my room now."

Beatrice folded up her napkin. "Me too. I need to find out if my friends made it to the villa and get my beauty sleep. As Samuel says, you've been very good company. The rest of the week has a lot to live up to."

"Not if you always sit with us," said Roman, to general laughter.

Xavier and André stood as Beatrice rose from her seat and said her goodnights.

In the foyer, Beatrice and Samuel stopped for a moment.

"It was really interesting to talk to you, Beatrice. I hope we can manage another conversation together over the next week."

"So do I," said Beatrice, with genuine sincerity. "I'll be at your seminar tomorrow and will probably want to pick your brains. Thank you for the pleasant company over dinner."

"How about having breakfast together? Not tomorrow – I promised the Commander my undivided attention. He wanted to have lunch today but I always eat my midday meal in my room. It's the only chance I have to call my wife and talk to Marcia. Any other morning I'm free?"

"I'd be delighted. Let me check which night I'll be staying again and we can fix a date."

As they stood there, Roman and Xavier headed towards the bar, the tall blond inclining to listen to the shorter redhead. Behind them, André walked beside Cher's wheelchair, laughing at something she said.

Beatrice grabbed the chance to ask her burning question. "Your colleague is a charming young man. Such maturity for one so young. How old is he, exactly, if it's not impolite to ask?"

Samuel chuckled. "Exactly? He will be twenty-six on

September the fifth. Between you and me, Beatrice, André is not just a colleague, he's also my godson. His father is my oldest friend."

They watched as the foursome settled at a table by the window, André solicitous over Cher's comfort.

"Well, you should be very proud of him. He's a credit to you."

"Thank you. I am proud. I'm a very lucky man. Goodnight Beatrice."

"Goodnight Samuel. Sleep well."

Chapter 6

Considering his usual allergic reaction to children, Adrian would go as far as to say he didn't actually mind Luke. A quiet, introspective child, he listened to conversations and asked thoughtful questions of his mother and Matthew. Luke had met Adrian before but this was the first time he'd been introduced to Will. He tucked his cuddly dolphin into his armpit and shook hands, but regarded the newcomer with watchful eyes until his attention was claimed by the complexity of the security procedures at the Queen's Terminal at Heathrow.

Luke followed his mother's instructions and cleared the checks with ease. The only hold-up was Matthew, who had forgotten to remove his belt, keys and phone. Tanya shrugged and shook her head at Adrian and Will as Matthew submitted to a hand-held body scanner.

Once in the departure lounge, Matthew, Will and Luke went in search of a vantage point to view the planes taking off and landing, while Adrian and Tanya made a bee-line for the Duty Free. On the escalator they had to stand and wait as a family of five had clearly never heard the Stand on the Right, Walk on the Left maxim. The father carried a baby and travel bag, while two knee-high children held their mother's hand and blocked the entire space.

Adrian suppressed his impatience and bounced his right leg as the steel staircase bore them upwards. In front of them, one of the children was trying to pull free of its mother while the other trotted a plastic toy along the handrail. Adrian took a deep breath but chose not to make a comment. After all, the children were not that much smaller than Luke.

A sudden shriek jolted his senses. One child had lost its grip and its toy tumbled downwards. Immediately, the kid tried to clamber onto the handrail. The mother panicked and let go of the struggling one to grab the potential jumper with both hands. The released child bolted past his father, racing for the top of the escalator, but tripped and fell forwards onto his hands and knees.

Adrian saw the tiny fingers approaching metal teeth, heard the screams of the parents and acted without a rational thought. He ran past them and scooped up the child, but its weight overbalanced him. With the force of fear and shock, he got to his feet before the stairway ran out and stumbled onto the steel platform, the child held firm in his protective grip.

Adrenalin pulsed through him long after he'd returned the child, shaken the hands of the parents and various onlookers, and even posed for a photograph, ruffling the boy's hair as if he were Jimmy Stewart.

When they finally got away, Tanya took his arm with a squeeze. "You, Adrian Harvey, are a class act."

"With torn Paul Smith trousers and a massive bruise to wreck my tan."

"It's not a bruise, it's a mark of bravery," said Tanya. "Come on, we should be able to get all the ingredients for the perfect martini and a great big bottle of champagne to toast our hero."

"Hero, schmero. But I never say no to some classy sparkles. How about I get the gin and you choose the vodka? Let's make it quick because Will is obsessed about getting to the gate early. As for the rest, I'm sure Portugal has shops."

"Yep. Or we can get Marianne to bring anything we've forgotten when she flies later."

With practised efficiency, Tanya selected a litre bottle of

Grey Goose and a bottle of Mumm, while Adrian dithered over a bottle of The Botanist or Hendricks.

"Why didn't she come with us this morning?"

Tanya shrugged once more. "Because Leon had to work, and she can't do anything without Leon."

Adrian opted for the Hendricks, added a chocolate selection for Luke and they moved to the till. "Well, it's always nicer to fly together."

Tanya snorted. "If you've got the cash to chuck away on rescheduling two flights, I'm sure it's much nicer."

"Look at it this way. At least we get the pick of the bedrooms before they arrive."

Tanya flashed him a wicked grin and showed the cashier her boarding pass.

Eight people, two cars. They could have hired a people carrier, but two separate vehicles were actually cheaper and allowed for more independence. So Tanya took the wheel of the Peugeot estate while Will assumed control of the Fiat Panda.

"Bit of a comedown from the Audi," observed Adrian.

Will buckled his seatbelt and adjusted the mirror. "Yes, but imagine how happy I'll be to get back to it next week."

They ignored the motorway and took the coast road north, passing through quiet villages with beachside bars, black-clad old ladies and the occasional chicken scratching in the dust. After one ice-cream stop and two bathroom breaks, they turned inland and soon found themselves in the national park area of Gêres. Adrian could see why it was protected. For almost an hour, he said nothing more than "Wow!" and "Look at that!".

Lilac mountains soared into a cloudless sky around midnight-blue lakes. The landscape alternated between rocky cascades and dense forests or sudden bursts of flowering shrubs which erupted like fireworks alongside the winding road. Best of all, other vehicles were scarce and they encountered remarkably few people apart from occasional clusters of old men sitting outside tiny cafés, smoking and squinting at them as they passed.

The GPS told them they were approaching their destination.

"I am officially excited!" said Adrian, almost bouncing in his seat. The square sand-coloured house had its own driveway off the main road and sat on a terrace above a shimmering green lake. Will parked up in front of the main house. Between it and a small outbuilding to the left, Adrian spotted a trapezoid of brilliant blue.

"Swimming-pool!" Pointing with a chocolatey finger, Luke jumped from the Peugeot before Tanya had switched off the engine.

Will threw the keys over the bonnet to Adrian and called to Luke. "Race you!"

Luke took off immediately and the two disappeared around the corner. By the time Matthew, Tanya and Adrian caught up, the pair were exclaiming over the range of pool toys available in the little cabana.

Tanya and Adrian followed the terrace that surrounded the villa. It was a heavenly spot. The house jutted out towards the lake, meaning two sides enjoyed a lake view. The mountainside tumbled away below them, strewn with orange and purple flowers, boulders and occasional thickets of trees. On the opposite bank, less of a village and more a scattering of houses clustered around a little harbour. Cicadas chattered away in the foliage and a breeze brought the faint scent of lemons.

"This is gorgeous!" Tanya breathed.

"Perfection," Adrian agreed. "I plan to lie on that sun lounger with a chilled martini always in reach, working on my tan until I get too hot, then a cool swim, a lazy lunch and back to it."

"If Action Man will let you."

"Good point. He'll sit still for a maximum of half an hour before suggesting a hike, or a quick water-ski round the lake, or an exploration of the nearest village."

Matthew eased off his jacket and came to stand beside them.

"I say. This looks jolly nice. Let's take the bags in, explore the house and open a bottle of something local. I have a feeling this will be a most relaxing week."

Chapter 7

Towards the end of Samuel Silva's seminar on Common Psychological Factors linking Mass Shootings, Beatrice's stomach began rumbling, growing increasingly louder until she drew amused glances from those around her. When Silva had finished answering a question on gun licensing, he checked his watch, apologised for over-running and announced lunch. Beatrice shoved her notes into her bag and got to her feet. Cher Davenport, sitting beside her, made a suggestion.

"Beatrice, you wanna steer me out? People always make way for a wheelchair and that way we get to the front of the lunch line."

"Brilliant idea. I'm starved."

"Yup, I kinda guessed."

They took full advantage of the salad buffet and chose to eat on the terrace in the sunshine, Cher carrying both their meals on a tray in her lap. Sharing their thoughts on Samuel's excellent talk led naturally to a conversation on US gun control, a subject on which Cher was well informed. Xavier arrived with a plate piled high and immediately joined in the discussion with some facts on Swiss gun ownership.

"And as Samuel mentioned," he said, "the American culture surrounding weapons couldn't be more different."

Cher nodded, waving a celery stick to emphasise her words.

"Damn right. He totally nailed it by looking at the issue from the prevailing cultural values perspective. The right to bear arms for self-protection is individualism in a nutshell. Where is Samuel, by the way? I have a whole bunch of questions I didn't get chance to ask. We shoulda invited him to join us."

Xavier swallowed a mouthful of bread. "I did. He said he was going to have lunch in his room so he could call his wife, but he'd catch up with us later. And it won't be long before we can all read his book."

"He's writing a book?" asked Beatrice, flapping open a napkin to disguise her curiosity.

"Sure," said Cher. "He told me about it last night. But if you've heard the same stories I have, we're not talking about *that* book. Samuel's publishing his research, that's all."

"Ah," said Xavier. "So this mysterious soon-to-be-published novel is already common knowledge?"

Beatrice shook her head. "Is it? Unless you two know more than me, the problem is exactly that. The knowledge we have is far from common."

Xavier and Cher shook their heads.

"Nope," Cher replied. "All I got was the order to watch and listen. So let's cut to the chase. Either of you two writing a fictional exposé on senior police officers?" Cher pointed her fork at them in turn.

"To be honest, I have no idea where I'd find the time," said Beatrice.

"It's not me. Telling stories is not my strong point," said Xavier.

"Well, that makes life easier. Which workshops are you two attending this afternoon?"

Beatrice consulted her participant pack. "Multiracial and Interfaith Cooperative Projects, as one of ours will be on the panel, talking about our own Operation Horseshoe. Then I want to catch the International Team Management session. Cher?"

"Presenting this afternoon. Oh wow, the nerves just kicked

in. Bathroom break. I'll be right back. Don't let anyone steal my salad!"

She wheeled herself rapidly across the terrace and into the hotel.

"What about you, Xavier? Your workshop isn't today, is it?"

He shook his head. "Tomorrow. I'm trying not to worry about it. I've given this talk to hundreds of trainees but now that I have to address peers and senior officers, I'm having nightmares. Still, this afternoon I'll be at Cher's seminar on Hostage Negotiation then I can't decide between..."

A burst of laughter from a nearby table made them both turn. Gilchrist joined in the amusement and inclined his head to accept the approval. Behind him, Beatrice spotted the Viking emerge from the French windows.

So did Xavier. He waved an arm. "Roman! Come and join us!"

The Viking's face broke into a crooked smile as he loped towards them.

"You're late for lunch," Beatrice observed. "Did your session run over as well?"

"No. I slept in this morning, so I had to go to my room before lunch and take a shower or stink all afternoon. That's the danger of having 'just one more' with certain people." He took a bite out of a chicken drumstick.

Xavier laughed and pulled an innocent face.

"Have you seen André today?" asked Beatrice.

Roman nodded and swallowed. "Just now. I passed him in the corridor. He already had a lunch appointment. Is anyone eating that bread roll?"

"Hands off, Blondie." Cher took her place and reclaimed her tray, a faint blush suffusing her cheeks. Beatrice was not surprised. He was a rather striking Viking.

"I was just telling Beatrice how you, Xavier and André led me astray last night," Roman said, gnawing on his chicken.

Cher affected outrage. "I don't recall Xavier or myself

proposing a round of schnapps! Still, it was an educational evening."

"Ah yes," said Beatrice. "The bar is often underestimated as a seat of great learning. If I was twenty years younger, I might have joined you."

Cher threw her a sardonic look. "C'mon Beatrice, you're not milky drinks and slippers just yet. Why not join us for a glass or two tonight?"

"I would love to, but part of the quid pro quo for my attendance this week is the chance for a semi-holiday. A group of family and friends are staying nearby, so I'll divide my time between business and pleasure. Nevertheless, one night this week, I'll certainly stay for a snifter. And undoubtedly drink the lot of you under the table."

"Now that I would like to see!" Gilchrist materialised as if from nowhere and joined the conversation with his normal self-assurance. He clapped a hand on Roman's shoulder. "I'd say you young fellas would give her a run for her money, eh?"

Roman turned to address the Commander, subtly removing his shoulder from the other man's grip. "Perhaps when I've fully recovered from last night, sir. Did you have a successful morning?"

"Superlative. I popped in on the human trafficking workshop and then caught most of the forensics lecture from Oyekunle over there, before having to deal with the usual admin headaches before lunch. Extremely pleased with the live streaming via BluLite. This is the wonderful thing about social media. Immediacy and inclusivity. How is everyone's day going?"

There was a general murmur of positive noises, which appeared to please Gilchrist. "Excellent. We're off to an EPIC start. Agent Davenport, I will make every effort to be at your talk today. You of all people know what it means to take one for the team."

Cher seemed at loss to respond, but Gilchrist didn't wait. "DCI Stubbs, your room is booked for the entire week, so whichever night you plan your 'snifter', you have somewhere to stay. We're neighbours, in fact. I'm in Room 1101. I wanted Room 101 but that was the closest I could get!"

Everyone laughed, even those who clearly didn't get the reference.

"Enjoy the afternoon, one and all." With that, he sallied forth to join another party, soon eliciting a round of polite laughter. The man really was a pro.

"He reminds me of someone," said Cher, following her eye line. "An actor, perhaps. Or a newsreader."

"I know what you mean. He has that way about him. Very slick, very practised. Like a politician," said Roman.

"I wish I could do what he does," said Xavier, a touch of wistfulness in his tone.

"Really?" asked Beatrice. "I wouldn't want his job for all the peas in China."

"Not his job, at least not for another ten years. I mean his ability to talk to everyone, to be so comfortable with crowds and at ease when he's the centre of attention."

"I suspect that's exactly where he wants to be," said Beatrice. "Anyway, Xavier, you have something much more valuable."

"What is that?" Xavier asked, with a puzzled look.

Roman got there before her. "Sincerity."

All three of them nodded and Beatrice was delighted to see two spots of pink on the Swiss redhead's cheeks.

While it was a familiar feeling to learn something useful at events like these, it was rare to feel an emotional surge of pride during a workshop on community projects. However, hearing to what various forces had achieved by listening to religious leaders and encouraging dialogue delivered exactly that. Beatrice grew oddly fond of the human race, a sensation she seldom associated with her job. All the initiatives were encouraging and inspirational. None more so than when her own colleague, Dawn Whittaker, appeared on the screen from London to explain the aims and achievements of Operation Horseshoe, Scotland Yard's interfaith initiative.

When she'd finished, Beatrice slipped her phone from her handbag to try this BluLite thing. She couldn't make it work and found the whole thing rather intrusive, so she reverted to text message and sent an exclamation-filled pat on the back to Dawn. Two missed calls from Xavier with voicemail alerts made her frown. There was no way she could listen to messages in the middle of a lecture. The next speaker ascended the podium, a heavyset man who began describing the intercultural challenges of dealing with the refugee crisis off the coast of Greece.

She sent a quick text to Xavier.

Something wrong?

The phone vibrated almost instantly.

Silva AWOL. You saw him this morning?

Beatrice sensed heads turning her way in disapproval as she typed a hurried reply.

Yes. Session overran – maybe asleep?

Then she put the phone in her bag and returned her attention to the Greek chap, who was introducing a collaborative venture between NGOs, police and the Refugee Council.

Only when the applause had died down after the moderator's summation did she pick up her mobile again. There was one message.

Silva found in his room. Not asleep. Dead.

Chapter 8

A loud report, a splash and burbling laughter woke Adrian from a light doze. He lifted his head and shielded his eyes. Will had dived from the board, swum the length of the pool and surfaced underneath Luke's lilo, toppling him into the water. Adrian watched as Luke attempted to clamber back on, impeded by his water wings. He spluttered giggles as Will circled him, swimming one armed, with the other hand vertical above his head, presumably to indicate a shark's fin. His menacing noises were no more than bubbles under Luke's squeals.

By eleven, the heat had become too strong to lie on the loungers, so Adrian and Matthew moved to the shade of the cabana, sighing with contentment, reading their respective publications and sharing smiles at the energy of the two in the pool. True to his promise, Will had agreed to stay at the villa for their first day. Sitting still, however, was impossible. He swam, dived, played Swing ball with Luke, harassed Adrian into a game of volleyball and helped Matthew with the crossword.

Tanya had left after breakfast to collect her sister and Leon from the airport. If all went smoothly, they would be back in time for lunch. Thinking of Tanya reminded Adrian of her stern words on sun protection.

"Luke? Luke! What did you do with your hat? Your mother's going to kill me. Will, come out of there and let's get some sun cream on him. It's all right for you, with skin like a saddle, but Mr Blonde here will turn into Mr Pink if we're not careful."

Like a pair of obedient otters, they hauled themselves out of the water, leaving wet prints on the tiles as they came towards the cabana. Adrian held open a towel for Luke to run into, wrapped it around him and pressed his nose with a firm finger. The skin turned white for a second then back to pink.

"As I thought. Already glowing. Sun block this afternoon. You don't want to spend two days in bed with heatstroke, do you?"

Luke shook his head vigorously, sprinkling droplets onto Matthew's paper.

"Where's Mum? I'm hungry."

Matthew folded his copy of The Times. "I was just thinking the same thing. They should be here within the hour, so let's make a start on the food. No reason you can't have a banana to keep you going, Small Fry. You and Will have used up quite some energy this morning."

"I could hardly keep up with him. He's a natural in the water. Can't wait to get into the sea tomorrow," said Will. "Right, I'll put some clothes on and set the table."

The four of them were in the kitchen – Adrian assembling the salad, Matthew baking whole trout, Will slicing bread rolls and Luke eating them – when a horn sounded outside.

"Mum!" Luke dropped his bread and rushed to the front door.

Matthew wiped his hands and followed, but Adrian motioned to Will to hang back. He didn't want to overwhelm Marianne's new boyfriend as soon as he arrived. They continued preparing the food and Adrian took the opportunity to steal a kiss from his incredibly sexy man. A whiff of burning came from the oven and Adrian checked the trout. Skin already blackened, but just about salvageable.

After rescuing the fish, they went to greet the new arrivals. Adrian followed Will out for hugs and handshakes but stopped in the doorway and stared at Marianne. Last time he'd seen her, she was pasty and overweight, hair scraped back, with an aggressive attitude. Not anymore. Her smile was broad, highlighted hair glossy and her summer dress indicated a curvaceous, healthier figure.

"Adrian! Look at you!" She held out her arms for a hug.

Adrian obliged then stood back to admire Marianne's transformation. "Look at me? What about you? You look amazing, Marianne! What have you done?"

She gave a delighted laugh. "Ain't love grand? Meet Leon. The guy who changed my life."

Adrian had a lifetime's experience assessing men. In the time it took to smile, reach out a hand and say 'Pleased to meet you, Leon,' he had made several not entirely conscious judgements.

Average height, a looker in that backroom-of-a-dirty-club sort of way, a stylish dresser who tried to look careless, black hair falling over one eye and a day's growth of stubble on his angular jaw. Handshake firm, smile less so.

"I took a risk, Adrian. Knowing your profession, you'll be even more critical about wine than Matthew." He held out a bottle wrapped in green tissue paper. "So I thought I'd bring a Touriga red. Going local kind of thing."

"Touriga? That's very thoughtful. We'll enjoy it this week. How was the trip?"

Marianne interrupted. "Apart from getting up at stupid o'clock, fine. Can we dump the bags and then eat? I'm itching to get in the pool."

Tanya, Luke and Will took the arrivals upstairs while Adrian set out the salads. Matthew was deliberating on which white wine would go best with the trout when Will came back into the kitchen.

"Might have to rethink the rooms. Leon is less than chuffed at sharing a bathroom with Tanya and Luke. Shall we offer to swap? I really couldn't care less."

Matthew grunted. "First come, first served. They'll have to lump it. *Vinho verde*, with lunch, I thought. We have three bottles of this. What do you say, Adrian?"

"I say yes to wine and no to swaps. I've unpacked now anyway. I think we'll just serve the trout as they are and call them peasant-style. Bit of blackened skin never hurt anyone. For future reference, it seems that oven cooks on max regardless of setting. Will, look in that drawer for a fish slice, would you?"

Lunch was polite and chatty, with everyone trying to make Leon welcome. Skin removed, Matthew's fish was delicious and the wine slipped down easily as the party relaxed, aided by Luke's happy chatter. Tanya's expression relaxed, Will's cheeks bloomed and Marianne babbled away like a bride at the top table.

"Did you see that little village with the fabulous church?" asked Adrian.

"Yes! I made Tanya stop so I could get a photo. And that dinky little square!" Marianne exclaimed.

"Looks like we have a bit of everything." Will said, extracting a bone from his teeth. "Mountains, villages, countryside, interesting cities within driving distance and the seaside."

"Yay! Seaside tomorrow!"

Will joined in Luke's excitement. "Yay! Seaside tomorrow!"

Tanya reached over and kissed her son's cheek.

Just before dessert, Leon admitted with endearing shyness the reason they had not been able to fly on Friday.

"Yes, sorry for the delay. My boss asked me to come to a meeting. I was a bit concerned, to tell the truth, but in fact, they offered me a promotion."

Marianne glowed with pride.

"A promotion! That's worthy of a toast, I'd say!" Matthew topped up all their glasses and they offered congratulations.

"Great news!" said Will. "What line of work are you in, Leon?"

"Consulting. A business advisor, basically. I just got made partner in the firm, which means a better salary and more civilised hours. More time for life." He exchanged a loving glance with Marianne.

"Exactly. Just what we all want," said Matthew.

Tanya swigged from her glass. "Too right. Though Beatrice's promotion has had the opposite effect. I can't wait till she's retired and we can actually spend more than one meal at a time together."

"Beatrice is a police officer, I hear," said Leon, folding his napkin neatly into a triangle.

Will raised his eyebrows. "Bit more than a police officer. She's an Acting DCI with the London Metropolitan Police. A senior detective with years of experience whom I would love to have as my boss."

"You're out of luck there," said Matthew. "She'll be retiring at the end of the year to become my boss instead. Now who's for some cheese and quince jelly? Luke, do you want ice-cream instead?"

Tanya and Matthew gathered the plates and Leon addressed Will. "When you say you'd like Beatrice as your boss, I'm assuming you're police too?"

"Yeah. I'm currently a DS, but aiming for promotion by the end of the year. I want to be an inspector. Just like Beatrice Stubbs, but with better hair."

Marianne and Adrian laughed loudly, both cuffing Will for his cheek. Leon looked bemused.

"You'll see when you meet her, Leon. She has the most unruly mane," Adrian explained. "She'll be here this evening – so whatever you do, don't stare."

Leon gave a brief smile. "I look forward to meeting her and promise to be discreet. One thing I meant to ask, the garden flat. Do we have access?"

Tanya returned with a platter of cheeses, grapes and a solid-looking jam in one hand and a basket of crackers in the other.

"Cheeseboard! Yes, we have access. The house can accommodate ten if we want. But we thought we'd all stay together in the main house."

"Can we have a look at it after lunch?" asked Leon. "Don't mean to be rude, but I do need a bit of space. As an introvert, I like to have a bolthole where I can decompress. "

Tanya blinked. "Sure. I'll find the key and it's all yours."

"That's very kind. Marianne and I would be most grateful."

"Knickerbocker Glory!" Luke marched into the room carrying a ludicrously ornate dessert of multi-coloured scoops, glitter and Smarties, topped off with a lit sparkler.

Tanya covered her eyes. "Dear God, Dad, you are a Health and Safety nightmare."

Will stood up to applaud. "All the best granddads are."

Adrian beamed at the party as the sun streamed across the table, lighting Luke's dessert with a honeyed glow. Birdsong trilled from Matthew's mobile. He took the call out on the patio.

While Marianne, Will and Tanya argued over regional British cheeses, Luke finished his dessert and ran upstairs to change into his swimming trunks. Adrian asked Leon his opinion on European holiday destinations and found him well travelled and informed. The chatter died when Matthew returned through the French windows, his face drawn and concerned.

"Bad news, folks, I'm afraid. Beatrice is going to be late, if she gets here at all tonight. Seems one of her colleagues has been shot."

Chapter 9

Beatrice quite literally couldn't believe it. Everything about the situation seemed unreal. When Gilchrist gathered all the participants into the dining-room to give a briefing, his demeanour was completely inappropriate.

"Good afternoon one and all. As you all know, we lost a dear colleague today. What you may not know it that the sudden death of Samuel Silva was not an accident. He was shot in the head at close range. Next of kin have been informed and the local police will be in charge of the murder investigation. I would like you all to assist in any way you can, but as civilian witnesses. Regardless of our profession, we cannot interfere in the Portuguese jurisdiction."

Beatrice saw the same concerned, shaken expression on the faces of her colleagues. No one spoke, waiting for Gilchrist to continue.

"Those of you planning to attend the Briefing the Press session will be able to learn on the job via a real-life example, or perhaps I should say real death? I will be making a press statement tomorrow morning and must ask you all to keep the event quiet until then. Please tell no one what happened until we have formulated an official response. I apologise for the disruption to your schedules this afternoon and hope you understand. However, I encourage you to put the incident behind you and concentrate on making the rest of the week an EPIC success.

One final reminder regarding the BluLite platform. I would like to see far higher usage of the app to share your experiences, today's sad loss excepted. Now, afternoon tea will be served on the terrace before the final sessions of the day. Thanks to all of you for your patience."

Judging by the bewildered expressions of those around her, Beatrice wasn't alone in finding his tone a touch too convivial. Conversations ebbed and flowed around her as she tried to make sense of it all. An idea took root. It was quite absurd but she found it hard to shake. She retreated behind a large flower display to give herself a moment to think.

She had seen no body. None of them had. Apparently it had been removed to the pathology lab and Scenes of Crime Officers now occupied the room. Without the evidence of her own eyes, she really couldn't conceive of that gentle, diffident man having gone, leaving his poor wife and their new baby daughter alone. Beatrice squeezed her eyes shut. It was too much to bear.

Several peculiar circumstances gave her cause for concern. A murder at a country house amidst a bunch of strangers who happened to be police detectives? It was ridiculous, exacerbated only by the fact that said country house hotel was a hospitality college, or to look at it another way, a school for butlers.

The final element of the sense of farce was Gilchrist's near glee at the drama of it all. As if the entire thing was an elaborate set-up to test their mettle as detectives setting out to solve the case of the murdered psychologist. At that moment, in the gap between her flowery screen and the wall, she spotted a black-clad figure at reception. She narrowed her eyes. *Enter a priest? Who wrote this script?*

"Would you like a cup of tea?"

A waitress holding a tray full of cups and saucers peered around the foliage. Behind her stood a man with a large china teapot.

Beatrice emerged from her hiding-place with as much dignity as she could manage. "Yes, please. Milk, no sugar."

"Certainly, madam. On the table by the staircase, you will find a selection of cakes and sandwiches for afternoon tea. Dinner will be about half an hour later than expected this evening."

"Oh, I'm not staying for..." She stopped, aware of her mood and her preoccupations. She would be terrible company for Matthew and the others, and what a way to meet Marianne's new boyfriend. She'd be better off staying until things calmed down. "Actually, yes, I am. Thank you very much. Can you tell me something? Is that man..." she gestured at the priest, "staying at the hotel?"

"No, madam. This week, the hotel is for the exclusive use of EPIC, the police convention. We are at capacity."

"I see." Beatrice watched the man pour the tea and a thought occurred. "Capacity? But there can't be more than sixty of us. It says in the brochure you have 120 rooms."

"That is correct, madam," said the girl, handing her a teacup. "But currently, the top two floors and roof terrace are undergoing refurbishment because of extensive storm damage this spring."

"Thank you. So if he's not staying here and the body's already gone, what do we need with a man of the cloth?"

"The priest is here to bless the room where... where it happened."

Beatrice thanked the girl again and made her way to the cakes. After a scone and a slice of sponge, she went to reception where a clerk confirmed her room was available all week. She was on her way upstairs when footsteps pounded up behind her. Roman, taking the stairs two at a time, pointed a finger at her.

"Where have you been hiding? We were looking for you."

"A secret place. Who's looking for me?"

"Me, Cher and Xavier. Which secret place?"

"I'm not telling you in case I need to use it again."

Roman's lip curled into a half smile. "I see. And where are you going now?"

"To my room. I'm staying here again tonight. Shall the five of us have dinner together?"

"That's why we were looking for you. We thought we might get away from here and eat in a local village. Xavier is trying to find a taxi service with wheelchair access."

"That's a good idea. I don't want to inflict myself on my friends after what's happened, but I do want to talk about it with people who understand. Are we allowed to go off campus, do you think?"

Roman snorted. "Who's going to stop us? Let's meet on the terrace at six-thirty and make our getaway. By the way, we are only four. André has gone back to Lisbon."

"Of course. Samuel was his godfather. That poor boy."

"Beatrice, are you OK?" Roman's expression invited confidence.

"Not sure yet. What about you?"

"I feel bad. About Silva and about this whole situation. Something feels wrong in here." He pressed a fist against his stomach.

Beatrice looked into his grey-blue eyes. "I know exactly what you mean."

A wheelchair-friendly taxi at such short notice was too much to expect. Roman dismissed the issue as insignificant and asked Cher if she would object to being carried. After some consideration, she decided she would not mind. So at six-thirty, four guilty-looking detectives convened on the terrace while most of the other participants were preparing for dinner. When the cab pulled up in the driveway, Roman scooped Cher into his arms, Beatrice opened the back door of the taxi and Xavier folded the wheelchair into the boot. Within two minutes, they were on the road, with as much relief as if they'd just pulled off a heist.

Xavier, in front, gave the driver the address in what sounded like flawless Portuguese and they drove along a road that paralleled the river towards the town of Ponte de Barca, its dusk lights twinkling in invitation. The atmosphere had a peculiar charge, as if each was silently acknowledging the fact that together they had formed a discrete, complicit bond of trust. Beatrice looked backwards on several occasions, but they had not been followed. She shook her head. Why on earth would anyone bother?

The arrival of four *estrangeiros* would inevitably have attracted attention in the small town, and they certainly looked like an odd collection of foreigners. But while Beatrice and Xavier drew only mild curiosity, the tall long-haired blond guiding a pretty redhead in a wheelchair invited open stares. The waiter showed them to the table, rearranging the seating to give Cher sufficient space.

As the waiter distributed the menus, Xavier gave him a brief instruction. He nodded and hurried off. No one spoke for a moment, a self-consciousness hanging over them, not helped by the unashamed observation of the other diners.

Beatrice and Cher spoke at the same time.

"Why is your Portuguese so good?"

"You guys deserve an explanation."

Beatrice held up her hands. "Sorry. You go first."

Cher smiled. "Thanks. And I agree, I want to know Xavier's secret too. No, what I was going to say is you're all being very cool in accommodating me, and I'd like to explain the wheels."

"You don't owe us any kind of explanation," said Roman.

She bumped his shoulder lightly with her fist. "I appreciate that. But after Gilchrist dangled it out there, I wanna give y'all the full picture. So here goes. Until 2007, I had a pretty good pair of legs. I used to play tennis in summer and ski in winter. In the fall of 2007, I was on patrol in Boston. My unit was called to assist in an armed robbery and siege situation at a print factory. We secured the area, released the hostages and moved in to make the arrests. It all went well until one guy panicked. He was hiding behind a curtain, can you believe? He shot me twice in the lower back. I was wearing body armour, so if it had been higher up, I'd have escaped with a nasty bruise. But his aim was off and one bullet shattered my pelvis while the other penetrated my spine."

Beatrice sensed rather than saw the collective wince.

"The result was Brown-Séquard syndrome, where only half the spinal cord is affected. So after a year and a half of rehab, I have as much of my muscle function back as I'm gonna get. On the bright side, I love the office job. I get to use a whole bunch of other muscles." She tapped the side of her head.

There was a moment of silence, as the group digested the information.

"I'm sorry you had to go through that, Cher," said Xavier. "You are a very strong woman, and thank you for sharing your story with us."

"Well said," Beatrice agreed. "I'm so pleased that horrible incident didn't put you off the police force. You're an asset we could ill afford to lose."

Cher smiled. "I had no choice. No way would my boss let me give up. She pushed me all the way up that hill. Amazing woman. You know what, Beatrice? When I first saw you at dinner last night, you reminded me of her."

"I'll take that as a compliment," Beatrice replied, smiling.

"Cher," said Roman. "Can I ask a question?"

"Sure."

"From what I know about spinal injury, especially if only partial damage is done, patients still have a certain amount of feeling in the affected area. So they can control bladder and bowel movement, enjoy a good sex life and live independently of carers. Tell me if I'm getting too personal."

Cher and Xavier blushed, and Beatrice's own ears got a little warm.

Cher took a deep breath. "Pretty close to the bone there, Roman, but hey, we're amongst friends. Truth is, it depends on the person. I can only speak from my own experience. I live alone and since my apartment's been adapted, I manage just fine. I can go to restaurants and fly and stay in hotels and use the bathroom same as anyone else. As for my sex drive, same as it ever was."

Roman locked eyes with her. "Thank you for being so honest."

"You're welcome."

Sex, violence and bowel movements all before the aperitifs? Beatrice was casting around for a light-hearted remark to break the tension when thankfully, the waiter arrived. Xavier examined the bottle he was shown and gave his approval. The waiter pulled the cork and started pouring sparkling wine into their glasses.

Xavier glanced around the table. "I hope you don't mind, but I ordered a bottle of Espumante. I thought we should raise a glass to say goodbye to Samuel Silva."

"Oh what a lovely idea," said Beatrice. "And let's spare a thought for his wife and their new little girl."

Cher's face paled. "They had a new baby?"

Beatrice bit her lip and nodded. "Just finished the adoption process. He showed me the pictures. A two-year-old called Marcia."

Cher pressed the bridge of her nose and closed her eyes.

Xavier went to stand, changed his mind and lifted his glass instead. "To Samuel Silva, an extraordinary man, police officer, husband and father. None of us who ever met you, no matter how briefly, will ever forget you. To Samuel, may you rest in peace."

Beatrice, Cher and Roman tilted their glasses to his and repeated, "To Samuel, may you rest in peace." They all sipped and stayed silent in thought for a moment, the waiter sensitively keeping his distance.

Somehow, Xavier had become the natural leader of the foursome. He suggested they choose the set menu and get down to business. Everyone fell in with his plan and the waiter was despatched for four orders of *Arroz de Marisco* and a bottle of Dão.

Beatrice offered around the bread rolls, helped herself and started buttering.

Xavier began. "I can't speak for anyone else, but Samuel

Silva's death has affected me deeply. Not just the shock of such a sudden and brutal death, but the situation, the environment and the circumstances. To me, this whole situation feels very bizarre."

"That's pretty much what I thought," said Beatrice. She relayed the thoughts that had occurred to her whilst concealed behind the flower display. No body, the artifice of the crime, a country house full of butlers. Shaking her head, she laughed with more disbelief than humour. "If I didn't think this was ludicrous, I'd honestly suspect hidden cameras. I feel as if we're in a reality TV show and Gilchrist is our puppet-master."

Cher was nodding energetically. "Yup, there was something weird about his reaction. Where was the shock? Where was the grief? Goddamit, I only met Samuel yesterday and I'm hurting. You know what I think about Gilchrist's speech? It was rehearsed. I don't know if it comes across that way because he's so media-savvy, but his reactions were not natural. And as you say, Beatrice, no one saw a body."

"I did," said Roman.

Everyone stared at him, awaiting an explanation.

"He was on the first floor, same as me. When I tried to go back to my room this afternoon, the corridor was taped off. I was explaining to the uniform that I only wanted to drop off my computer when a gurney came past with the body bag."

Beatrice hesitated. "Seems a stupid question, I know, but could you be sure it was Silva?"

Roman shook his head. "No. Those Portuguese cops are way too efficient. They didn't leave a hand hanging out with a distinctive signet ring on a finger, and they didn't drop his ID card as they passed. All I can say is it was a body of similar height to Silva, coming from the direction of his room, where he was reported as shot." He shrugged, but offered a crooked smile to temper his sarcasm.

The waiter brought the wine and a bottle of sparkling water. As Xavier thanked him and received a gracious smile in return, an idea occurred to Beatrice.

"Xavier, you didn't answer my question. How come you speak such good Portuguese?"

He looked up from tipping oil and vinegar onto his side plate. "My wife Yasmin comes from Florianópolis in Brazil." He tore off a piece of bread and dipped it in the oil-vinegar mixture. "She taught me how to mix *caipirinhas* and make *feijoada* but I still can't dance the samba. Portuguese is not so different from Italian so I picked it up quickly."

"You speak Italian too?" asked Roman.

Xavier shrugged, apparently modest about his linguistic abilities. "I'm Swiss. We have three languages."

Cher narrowed her eyes at Beatrice. "Are you thinking what I'm thinking?"

"If you mean that the four of us should work this case as a private investigation without bothering the local police, using Xavier's language skills to find out as much as we can, then I'd say yes."

Cher looked at Roman. "What do you say?"

"I can't offer any relevant language skills, but I think four detectives at our level could combine a lot of intelligence, ability and a very healthy disregard for protocol. Yes, I want to be a part of this, if you'll have me."

"So that's settled then. Now we just need a game plan," said Beatrice.

Xavier pulled a notebook from his jacket. "I already wrote down a few ideas, just in case."

"You planned this all along, you dog!" exclaimed Cher, with a broad smile.

"As I always say," said Xavier, with mock dignity, "be prepared for the worst, but hope for the best."

"I'll drink to that," said Beatrice, triggering another hasty toast before they had to clear space on the table for a huge gleaming tureen borne by two waiters. The smell of saffron, spice and fish enveloped them and Beatrice saw the appetite for food and investigation dancing in everyone's eyes. With the help of this unconventional team, she would find out exactly who was behind the death of Samuel Silva and see justice served.

For Marcia's sake.

Chapter 10

When it came to cars, Adrian seemed to be missing the point once again. The debate over breakfast was all about who should travel in which vehicle.

Will phrased his claim as an offer. "How about I drive the Panda for our trip to Braga and take Leon and Marianne as passengers?"

"If it's OK with you, I'm happiest behind the wheel," said Leon. "Maybe I could drive Marianne and Matthew in the Peugeot while you take Tanya and Luke in the back seat."

"Wait a minute." Tanya frowned. "Why is it only blokes have access to car keys? I've driven the Peugeot so far and don't see why I should be relegated to passenger status just by the arrival of another man."

"I want to go with Will!" said Luke.

Matthew stirred his coffee. "Personally, travelling in the back seat is not a pleasant experience for me. I get queasy and there's never enough leg room. I don't mind who drives but I would put in a request for the front passenger seat."

Everyone had strong views on the subject apart from Adrian. So long as they went somewhere nice and considered cars as nothing more than a means of getting there, he was happy.

Bored of the discussion, he took his coffee onto the terrace. The sun was beating down already, heating the tiles and warming Adrian's skin. Far below, boats puttered across the lake and a riot of birdsong populated the shrubs. He drank his latte in peace and inhaled the herby scents of nature. He wished Beatrice was here.

Eventually they struck a compromise. Leon would drive the Peugeot to Braga, Will would drive it back. Tanya would chauffeur her father and son in the Fiat. In the spirit of cooperation, they cleared the breakfast detritus and got into their respective vehicles.

In the back seat of the Peugeot, Adrian rested his hand on Will's thigh and gave him a 'you OK?' look. Will smiled and leaned over for a brief reassuring kiss.

"No snogging in the back seat!" said Marianne, laughing at them through oversized sunglasses.

Leon opened the window. "Tanya, you follow me. Shouldn't be difficult to find, but we've got a satnav."

Tanya's mouth opened to respond, but Luke was cavorting around, pulling faces and distracting her attention.

Adrian spent the entire drive oohing and aahing at the views. Thankfully, for fear of losing Tanya, Leon had slowed to a pace more suited to holiday driving, so they could enjoy the constantly surprising landscapes of the national park. Will read out historical facts from the guidebook and details of the protected species in the park.

"I'd love to see one of those Minho horses. But if they're that rare, it's probably unlikely," said Adrian, while trying to capture the scenery on his phone.

"I expect they're much like Dartmoor ponies. You only ever see them at a distance," Leon answered.

The tourist board had helpful signs warning motorists of upcoming photo opportunities, and Adrian persuaded Leon to stop at every one. He and Marianne were the first out of the car, but for different subjects. Adrian wanted sweeping views, details on lichen on rock or a sunbathing lizard. Marianne wanted pictures of herself and Leon in all variety of affectionate poses.

When Will was unavailable, she took selfies. Leon didn't seem to mind.

"Here, let me take one of you two," he offered, as Adrian snapped a shot of Will against an oak tree.

They posed for the camera and Marianne came to look at the result. "Aww, you two. You're so photogenic, it's sickening."

The sound of a chirpy horn tooting made them look round. The Panda whizzed past, hands waving from within. "Eat my dust, suckers!" yelled Tanya, as the car sped up into the bend.

"She's such a tomboy," said Marianne.

Leon returned Will's phone. "I hope she doesn't get lost. She's supposed to follow me."

"Don't worry about Tanya. She's a terrific driver," said Will. "Right, let's get on or we'll be the ones left behind."

"Oh my God! Is that a salamander?" Adrian gasped. "One sec, I have to get a shot of this."

Will rolled his eyes, but Leon merely grinned, leaning against the car. "Take your time, Adrian. We're on holiday."

Braga had the most divine architecture. Literally. Austere yet ornate, the whitewashed buildings and towering edifices were designed to invoke a higher presence. Stone crucifixes, arches, turrets and clocks threaded a motif of religious piety through the streets. They wandered past so many churches in sparsely populated squares that Adrian wondered where all the worshippers came from.

As always with a group of disparate people with differing interests, it was a stop-start progression around fountains, cafés and beautifully decorated buildings. The souvenir shops appealed to everyone, and even Matthew found something local for Beatrice. The heat intensified towards mid-afternoon and Adrian understood why so few locals were on the street. Everyone must be enjoying a siesta after lunch.

"I'm hungry," said Luke.

Matthew glanced at his watch. "Good heavens, it's half past

two. Yes indeed, we should set about finding a place to eat."

"Is it that late already? We've probably left it a bit too long," said Will. "My guess is most places have finished serving lunch by now. We might find a chain or something still open."

Leon agreed. "If we'd got here by twelve, we might have had a chance. But we didn't bargain for so many photo opportunities!" He nudged Adrian with a wink and a smile. "Sorry to put a dampener on things, but we'll be lucky to find a local restaurant still open and prepared to seat such a large party."

"Don't they have a McDonald's?" Luke asked.

"I never eat junk food. Sorry. We can do better than that." Leon gestured to a nearby café with empty tables and drawn curtains. "Sit down in the shade for a moment and I'll have a scout around." He strode off up the nearest alley.

Assuming the restaurant was closed, Adrian was surprised to see a weary-looking waiter emerge from the front door once they had rearranged tables to suit their party of six and a half.

"Food finish. Drinks only. Coffee? Beer? Water?"

Marianne counted heads. "Six bottles of water and a Coca Cola, please."

"With gas?"

Marianne's forehead creased. "With what?"

"He's asking if you want still or sparkling water," said Will. He spoke to the waiter. "Four waters, two with gas, two no. *E duas cervejas, por favor. Obrigado.*"

"Where did you pick up the lingo?" asked Adrian.

"It's just a few phrases from the guidebook. How are you feeling, Matthew?"

"I'll perk up as soon as I get some food inside me. Luke and I are very similar in that way. Feed us regularly and we are docile as lambs." He brushed the hair from Luke's forehead, which flopped right back into his eyes.

When the drinks arrived, Adrian appreciated Will's choice of beer over water but regarded the bowl of small yellow pods which accompanied them with some suspicion. Will asked the waiter what they were but couldn't really understand the reply. The man demonstrated by picking one up, squeezing to release it from its skin and popping it in his mouth. He smacked his lips and winked at Luke, who naturally wanted to try one as soon as the waiter had returned inside. Tanya gave her permission.

"Are you sure that's a good idea?" asked Marianne. "You don't know where they've been."

"I'll volunteer as taster," said Will, copying the waiter's movements and chewing cautiously. "They're nice. Salty, like soybeans. Probably make you want to drink more."

Luke and Matthew followed his lead and soon everyone was snacking on the odd little pods, leaving the carapace of skins around the bowl. The restaurant door opened and a short, white-haired man in a light blue suit approached the table, bearing another two bowls. His face was lined and brown, and his blue eyes sparkled under wild eyebrows.

"Good afternoon, my friends. I see you like our *tremoços*. Here, I bring you another bowl and some potato chips. Are you hungry? Would you like some proper snacks?"

Will spoke. "You are open for food? We thought it was drinks only."

"We are open. Restaurant service finish at two but we can make toasted sandwiches, salads, fishcakes, French fries or our special, the *francesinha*."

Marianne began to refuse. "Thank you, but we have plans to..."

"What's a *francesinha*?" Tanya asked.

The old man made a face of exaggerated disbelief. "You never tried a *francesinha*? What are you, vegetarian?"

"No, I just don't get out much." Tanya cast a meaningful glance at Marianne, who made a show of looking up the street for Leon rather than meeting her sister's eyes.

Their host was in his element. "Imagine the king of sand-wiches. A slice of bread. Piled on top you have pork, chorizo, bacon, steak and another slice of bread. Cover the whole thing with spiced cheese sauce and a fried egg. If this is your first, young lady, I will make it myself. It is an experience you will never forget."

"Oh God," moaned Adrian. "Carbohydrate City here I come. I want one so badly it hurts."

"Me too!" Matthew and Luke spoke simultaneously.

They ordered six full *francesinhas*, with three bowls of chips on the side and a salad for Marianne. She sent Leon a message to announce they had found sustenance. Adrian and Will pored over the guidebook and suggested a visit to Bom Jesus, a religious pilgrimage site after lunch. Matthew and Tanya agreed, despite neither having any religious proclivities.

After a few minutes, Leon arrived, hot and irritable. He muttered something about unhelpful locals and a lack of flexibility. "You'd think they'd realise how much the tourist trade is worth in a backwater like this."

Matthew tried to cheer him up. "It was awfully good of you to go in search of something for us. We didn't even think this joint was open. The owner is friendly, you know, and has offered us his house special. Seemed a bit off to refuse. Would you like one of these?" He offered the bowl of *tremoços*.

"Thanks, I won't. Just some still water, cold if possible. I think once we've eaten, I'd like to head back to the villa. Catch a nap and perhaps..."

"Your lunch, ladies and gentlemen!" The little man in the powder blue suit carried three plates and the waiter followed with more. "Hello, Mister!" he said to Leon. "One of these is for you. Enjoy, a Portuguese speciality!"

Leon stared at the yellow lump in front of him and Adrian burst out laughing.

"It's a sandwich, Leon, not an alien life form."

"Try a bite, you might like it," said Will.

Leon did cut off a corner of the impressive slab, but made a show of forcing it down and shook his head. "Not for me, I'm afraid. I prefer something light at lunch. Could I get a green salad?"

The owner shrugged his shoulders and turned down the corners of his mouth in a 'what can you do?' pout and returned to the kitchen while the rest of the party moaned and groaned in delight.

"We were planning a trip to the religious pilgrimage site this afternoon. It's supposed to be spectacular in itself with amazing views," Tanya said.

"According to the guidebook, pilgrims used to climb the stone steps on their knees as a show of penitence," added Will.

Marianne looked at Leon, who was taking a long draught from a glass of water. "That could be interesting, don't you think?"

Leon swallowed, wiped his mouth and said, "We'll see."

After the food had been attacked with intent but not quite finished off, the group drank coffees and chatted about nothing in particular. Tanya told Adrian all about her business idea for outdoor summer schools, to educate children about the value of nature. Matthew and Will played I-Spy with Luke while Leon and Marianne spoke in low voices on a topic Adrian couldn't catch.

The owner emerged with the bill, which Matthew insisted on paying. The man asked several times for their opinions on his *francesinhas* and then asked where they were staying. When Will told him the name, his face lit up with recognition.

"Beautiful place. And only a few kilometres from the best fish restaurant in Northern Portugal. The *Marisqueira do Miguel*. My cousin's father-in-law owns it and it has a fantastic reputation. You must go! Here, I write down the name." He scribbled on the back of one of the paper napkins. "Tell him Pedro Pereira sent you and you will get five-star service. Try the *Bacalhau a Zé do Pipo*. Paradise!"

They thanked him and he shook everyone's hands, even Luke's, as they said goodbye. The amenable atmosphere left Adrian with a very good feeling about Braga. Back at the cars, Marianne announced she and Leon would prefer to miss Bom Jesus and head back for a rest by the pool.

"Can we go back to the pool too, Mum?" asked Luke.

"Don't you want to come and see this church with us?" Tanya's question was addressed to Luke, but Adrian sensed there was a broader target.

Luke shook his head with great conviction.

"If you like, we'll take him back with us, Tan," offered Marianne. We can keep an eye on him while he's in the pool. And I won't forget sunscreen and hats and all that."

Luke cheered. "Do you want to come too, Will?"

"No thanks. You practise your shark-wrestling techniques and I'll test you when I get back. Why don't you guys take the Panda and we'll take the Peugeot? We'll see you back at the ranch later this afternoon. Tanya, do you want to drive?"

Adrian and Will sat in the back, Adrian reading out some of the titbits from the guidebook. "Eighteenth century sanctuary, commissioned by the Archbishop, Baroque stairway with Stations of the Cross, sculptures on each landing depicting Christ's Via Crucis, some alarmingly graphic, 300 feet up, journey of purification... it sounds fabulously gothic. I can't wait!"

A full afternoon of gothic religious architecture was certainly intimidating, and the climb to the church in the late afternoon heat wore Adrian out. In the car on the way back, he tried to keep awake to talk to Will while Matthew dozed off in the passenger seat. Shortly afterwards, Tanya's head dropped onto his shoulder and his own eyelids grew heavy. Next thing he knew, Will was parking outside the villa. He glanced at his watch. It was half past six.

A figure appeared in the doorway, holding a glass aloft.

"Beatrice!" exclaimed Will, waking his sleepy passengers. He was out of the Peugeot and across the drive before Adrian had even gathered his belongings. He roused Tanya and Matthew then hurried to join in the greeting hugs.

"Finally! So pleased to see you!" he exclaimed.

"I'm so pleased to see all of you! Sorry to take so long. What a glorious spot you chose, Professor Bailey! This is the perfect retreat from it all. Hello Tanya, you look tanned and relaxed already."

"Just woke up, that's why. Great to see you, Beatrice. When did you arrive? Have you seen the others?"

Beatrice kissed Matthew and clutched his arm. "Yes, I have. Well, Marianne and Leon for a few minutes, before they retired for a nap. Luke was already in bed when I got here. Bit too much sun this afternoon, I believe. How was Braga?"

A frown of concern flashed across Tanya's face. "I'll go check on him."

Matthew squeezed Beatrice to his side. "Braga was quite out of the ordinary. An experience I would not want you to miss. If you get time, Old Thing..."

"I'd love to see it, if I can get away from this whole sorry business. I'm not going to bore you with the details, but I hope you'll understand this week will be more work than play. A dustman's holiday, unfortunately. But at least we're all here together at last." She indicated her drink. "I thought you'd understand if I started without you all. It is cocktail hour, after all. Can I make anyone else a martini?"

Will stroked the back of Adrian's neck. "I'd love one. Can I have an olive in mine? I'll just grab a quick shower and start cooking. We'd planned stuffed squid tonight."

"Yes please to the martini and the olive," said Adrian. "We'll freshen up and then get into the kitchen. It really is great to see you, Beatrice. I hope the work situation... well... works out. Back in ten." He followed Will upstairs, admiring the view and calculating how much could be achieved in ten minutes.

Sounds of splashing, gargling and brushing came from the bathroom as Adrian billowed the sheet, wafting a gust of air over his damp body. The cool cotton settled on his skin and he released a contented sigh. Five minutes lie-down and then get dressed to say hello properly to Beatrice. He wished she could be there tomorrow for their day at the beach. She always managed to act as a dynamic force of perspective. He would miss her terribly when she finally moved to Devon.

Will came out of the bathroom and leapt onto the bed, bouncing Adrian three inches off the mattress.

"The boy who never grew up," murmured Adrian.

"The old fart who grew up too soon," said Will, wrapping himself around Adrian's body.

They lay in silence, temperatures adjusting.

"Seaside tomorrow," Will whispered. "Can't wait."

"Don't know who's more excited, you or the five-year old child."

"Me, of course. No contest. As for the child, I'll mind him."

Adrian rolled over to face Will. "We'll all mind him. You might be the strongest swimmer, but everyone looks out for Luke."

Will didn't answer.

"What?"

Still no reply.

"William Quinn, if you have something to say, spit it out."

"I have nothing to say. Yet. But the thing is, you don't watch like I do. Beatrice got here at six o'clock and Luke was already in bed. Why? His mother told us yesterday his bedtime is seven o'clock, even on a school night. Did you notice the tension between Tanya and Marianne at lunchtime? Why were none of the pool towels even damp when we got home?"

Adrian laughed, his eyes closed. "Stop it. You are on holiday and are forbidden to see suspicious signs, clues or footprints till we get back to Boot Street. There is nothing to investigate here, DI Quinn. Although, on closer inspection..."

Adrian caught Will's hand and pulled it under the sheet.

Chapter 11

Beatrice enjoyed dinner enormously. It was a lively affair as she did her best to make up for her absence by catching up with everything at once. She avoided any mention of the sudden death of her colleague, but engaged and teased and entertained throughout. It wasn't easy to get a handle on the new addition to the family, as Leon and Marianne conversed quietly together, whispering sweet nothings as new lovers tend to do. The stuffed squid was perfection, and Adrian assured everyone he now understood the quirks of the cooker. The Gerês hotel might boast five stars but Adrian's culinary skills were of an equal standard. Beatrice sighed happily and tucked in.

Luke flatly refused to even try the squid, claiming it looked like an alien. He'd been crotchety and irritable since he woke up, so Tanya made him beans on toast and took him off to bed once he'd finished. He wouldn't say goodnight to anyone, burying his face in his cuddly dolphin.

When Tanya returned, Beatrice voiced her concern. "Is he all right, Tanya? He seems a bit upset about something."

"Don't think so. Just overtired and probably not that hungry after that mahoosive lunch. You should have seen it, Beatrice. A sandwich the size of a pillow containing an entire farmyard's worth of meat. I am going to put on at least a stone this week."

"No you won't," said Will. "Tomorrow we're at the beach, so we can swim it all off."

A pang of envy pierced Beatrice. She loved the seaside. "Stop it. I've got to attend dull seminars with stiff suits in air-conditioned rooms. I only manage to stay awake because the chairs are too hard." She waved her empty wine glass at Matthew, who duly filled it.

"Don't you have a pool at the hotel, Old Thing? I can lend you a shower cap if you're worried about your hair."

Beatrice pulled an expression of outrage as everyone burst into laughter.

Matthew had been on top form the whole evening, cracking jokes and including everyone in his merriment. Holidays obviously suited him. The room rang with laughter, so much so Beatrice wondered if they might wake Luke.

Just before dessert, Tanya brought in two champagne bottles in ice buckets, distributed glasses and popped both corks.

"We're toasting our local hero. Adrian won't tell you himself, but when we were at Heathrow Airport, his quick thinking saved a child from getting mashed into an escalator. The parents were in tears, other passengers wanted to shake his hand and I was so proud, I could burst. Raise your glasses, ladies and gents, to Adrian Harvey, aka Superman!"

Glasses chinked, Tanya told her version of the story with bells and whistles, Adrian delivered a downbeat, modest version and everyone applauded both. The intensity of Will's expression delighted Beatrice. She herself was puffed up with pride for her friend but recognised the look in Will's eyes as much more than that.

The clock struck eleven. Tanya drained her bubbles and announced it was her bedtime. Leon and Marianne went shortly afterwards, wandering across the garden path along a trail of solar-powered lights. Once the newcomer had departed, conversation naturally turned to opinions on his character.

"Polite, well mannered, if a bit fussy about food," pronounced Beatrice. "And looks-wise, I'd give him an eight if he tidied his hair up a bit."

There was a moment of silence until Will, Adrian and Matthew caught each other's eyes and burst into an explosion of laughter. Beatrice, feeling the pink in her cheeks, joined in with a knowing grin.

She was curious how the first two days had played out in her absence. It was one thing to talk about what had happened on the surface, but it was the subtext that interested her.

Matthew rubbed his face, still smiling. "He's all right. A bit prickly, which I can understand. He's in enemy territory and an obvious outsider being judged by a tight-knit pack. I have a feeling he'll settle down. Thing is, he needs to do it on his own. While Marianne insists on acting as his spokesperson, he can't realistically engage with us on his own terms." He paused. "Did that sound a bit esoteric?"

"Yes, it did," said Beatrice. "But enough of Pater's fence-sitting. Will, you're a pretty good judge of character. What do you think?"

Will looked into his champagne flute. "Jury's out. He's tender and sweet with Marianne, which is what counts, I guess. But a good guide for me is how people behave with animals, kids and waiting staff. So far, I'm not impressed. All I can see is an almighty ego."

"Will!" Adrian sounded truly shocked. "Is this all over the who-gets-to-drive issue? Because you, Tanya and Leon were all waving your petrol-head credentials about this morning. It's unfair to pick on him for that."

Will lifted a shoulder in a half-shrug, which could have meant anything.

Beatrice fixed her eyes on Adrian. "We haven't heard from you yet."

"He's insecure, probably a bit defensive as he's in the lion's den. He has an ego but let's just look around this table. We all have reasons to be proud of ourselves and not one of us can claim to be self-effacing. Imagine what he's heard about each of us. Wouldn't you come out sabre-rattling in such company? And aside from all of our irrelevant opinions, Marianne loves him. For that reason alone, we should give him a chance."

His speech seemed to chasten the party and conversation turned to safer waters, such as how many visits to castles and waterfalls could be fitted into one day.

Chapter 12

The post-prandial sensation of well-being and familial contentment was punctured as soon as Beatrice checked her emails
before bed. Gilchrist had called a breakfast briefing for all senior
officers at eight in the morning and would she please confirm
attendance on receipt.

Three things about this put Beatrice in a furious temper.

First, she had to get up at six in the morning in order to make
the journey back to the hotel in time. It was already quarter to
midnight.

Second, breakfast was a time for re-engaging with the world,
adjusting to other people and most importantly, eating.

Third, Xavier, Roman and André were not deemed suffi-
ciently senior to merit an invitation.

She sent a curt reply in the affirmative then picked up her
phone, pressed a number and launched into a whirlwind of
ranting as she applied moisturiser to her face. When her annoy-
ance had blown itself out, Xavier's calm voice at the end of the
phone soothed her.

"No, listen. This actually works in our favour. Roman and
I have two paths to pursue and need some time to do so. I'll
explain tomorrow. The briefing means we can disappear for a
few hours in all innocence, come back with our findings and
share all our news over lunch. Don't raise any objections on our
behalf, B. We can use the time."

She softened at the use of her initial. "OK. I suppose that makes sense. See you at lunch for a general catch-up. Sorry for disturbing you."

"I planned to call you actually. We need to keep in touch, even if we have to be quiet about it. By the way, André is back. We had dinner together tonight. He's a very useful source of information. Sleep well and see you in the morning."

She wished him the same and got into bed beside Matthew, who was reading some tome about explorers.

"I've got to get up at six, I'm afraid. A bloody nuisance I know, but the boss wants all senior personnel in early for a briefing. I'm sorry."

He placed the book on the table. "So we should get some sleep. And yes, you are a bloody nuisance but I'm awfully glad you're here. By the way, I bought you a present."

He rustled in his bedside cabinet and handed over something heavy wrapped in tissue paper.

She tore away the wrapping to reveal a six-inch highly coloured metal cockerel with bright red comb and yellow feet. It looked both sharp-eyed and cheerful; a ferocious defender of happiness.

"It's lovely, thank you!"

"Very local and somehow, it reminded me of you."

"And I'm supposed to take that as a compliment, am I?" She smiled and kissed him goodnight, and placed her cockerel beside her phone before she turned out the light.

Six hours later, the sunrise was a bonus. Foul-tempered and dry-mouthed, she couldn't even doze in the taxi, as the driver's choice of radio station played endless howling laments. Instead, she observed the dawn scenery as the sun emerged over black silhouetted trees. As the not-yet-brilliant ball of fire ascended, a rush of wonder and awe filled her, erasing all her negativity. Even the music seemed to fit.

She made a promise to herself. She would pull every trick

in the book to solve this case. If that meant spending less time with Matthew, Adrian and the gang, then so be it. Some things were more important. With a deep intake of breath she prepared herself for a heavy week ahead. In her pocket, she ran her fingers over the little cockerel, another harbinger of dawn.

Within the first minute of his speech, Gilchrist took the wind out of her sails. The murder of Samuel Silva was being treated as a botched robbery. The man's wallet had been emptied, the watch removed from his wrist, and the murder weapon, also missing, was his own revolver. The likely scenario was that someone had been in his room when he returned. Silva disturbed the burglar who panicked and used the psychologist's own gun against him. There were no fingerprints, but the window had been forced from the outside. Local police were following several leads and were optimistic the perpetrator would be found in the next twenty-four to forty-eight hours. The conference would go ahead with some minor changes, but Gilchrist exhorted everyone to focus on the task in hand. A memorial book would be available at reception for colleagues and friends to leave their thoughts. At the end of the week, it would be sent to his widow.

He finished with a warning. "The press already know there has been a homicide and are desperate to get more on the story. From their perspective, a murder at a convention of police detectives is great entertainment. In order for the local force to do their job and for us to maintain our collective reputations, I must ask you not to speak to anyone on the issue, either formally or informally, and refrain from discussing the incident in front of the hotel employees."

Beatrice looked around at the empty salvers in the serving area where a buffet breakfast would normally have been waiting for them, with staff on hand to refill the salvers, coffee dispensers and bread baskets. Her stomach rumbled.

"Please continue to share pictures and videos of our EPIC event but on no other social media platform than BluLite, which is the only one we can be sure is secure. I'm sorry this tragic event has happened and I am as shocked as the rest of you. However, we are professionals and must continue in our duty out of respect for our colleague, one of the most honourable men I have ever known. Ladies and gents, would you get to your feet for a minute's silence to remember a great detective, teacher, friend, colleague, husband and father. Samuel Silva."

They rose, bowed their heads and remained perfectly still for sixty seconds, united in the subject of their thoughts. Beatrice recalled the last funeral she had attended, that of Superintendent Hamilton. The silence as his friends, family and colleagues paid their respects contained such a range of emotions and feelings towards the suddenly departed. Not just his choice of exit – a clinic in Switzerland – but how much of his manner had aroused resentment and animosity. As if he had made enemies to save himself the trouble of being liked.

Somehow, here in this room, there was more harmonious warmth towards the man they had lost. After the minute was up, Gilchrist thanked them and invited them to eat. The doors opened and the staff hurried in with stainless steel trays of eggs, bacon, sausages, hash browns, tomatoes, toast, beans, pancakes and warm plates. Junior officers, who had been waiting outside, swarmed in after them.

Beatrice was out of her seat immediately, barrelling directly towards the buffet with ruthless intent. She heaped her plate with all the elements of a full English, added two slices of brown toast and turned victoriously towards her seat when André hailed her from across the room.

"Beatrice! Join us!"

He and Cher occupied a table near the door. She changed direction and set her tray on the table next to Cher's.

"Whoa, Beatrice! You got some appetite!"

Beatrice looked at Cher's bowl of fruit and yoghurt with some disdain and gave André's American-style selection a nod of approval.

"I have been up since six this morning so I deserve every mouthful. If I ate nothing more than a bunch of berries, I'd faint by eleven o'clock. Hello André, good to see you again. I'm truly sorry about the loss of your...colleague."

She chose not to mention the personal information Samuel Silva had shared. André met her eyes and gave her a brief nod of understanding and a warm smile.

"Thank you, Beatrice. Everyone in our Lisbon office is shocked and saddened more than we can express. He was one helluva guy, not just to me, but the entire force." He reached over to the coffee pot and poured them both a cup before filling his own. "For such an incredible life to end this way is incomprehensible. I just don't get it. On any level."

Beatrice added milk. "A tragedy, for all concerned. I must add my own comments in the book of remembrance."

"There'll be a whole bunch more now," said Cher. "Yesterday's new arrivals."

Beatrice looked around. "Yes, I saw a few unfamiliar faces this morning. How was dinner last night?"

Cher cupped her hands around her coffee mug. "Nothing special. Only one topic of conversation at every table. To be expected, I guess, but so much speculation is just so much speculation, know what I mean? How was your evening?"

"Good fun. Some of my favourite people all in one lovely place. And a stuffed squid dish I will never forget. Did you see Xavier this morning?"

"I saw him." André cut into a pancake, added a slice of bacon and dipped it into some maple syrup. "He and Roman left in a taxi. Must have been around six-thirty? I was just warming up for my morning run. Xavier said they were going to watch the sunrise at a local tourist spot. Those guys. I think it's very romantic." He forked his creation into his mouth.

"Romantic?" Cher twisted her body towards the young man. "You don't think...?"

André swallowed and nodded. "Come on. Two good-looking

men, obviously attracted to each other, spend every minute together and get up early to watch the sunrise?" He pulled down his lower eyelid in a gesture of 'you don't fool me'. He drained his coffee and looked back at them. "And why not? This is the twenty-first century. My philosophy? Your happiness is no one else's business. I wish them nothing but the best."

Cher hadn't touched her breakfast. "I thought Xavier was married."

"He might be," said André. "But this morning when I met those two, their eyes were alive, excited and full of joy. I might be kinda green and naïve in some ways, but I can recognise two people in love. This pot is empty, I need to order more coffee."

Beatrice said "Good idea."

While he attracted the attention of the nearest waitress, Beatrice nudged Cher's elbow and shook her head. She gave a pointed look at the neglected berries and Cher picked up her spoon.

"So André," Beatrice chirped, "what sessions are on your agenda today?"

Two hours of 'Culture and Connections', a short coffee break during which Beatrice wrote in the memorial book, followed by ninety minutes on human trafficking initiatives made for a long morning. The prospect of lunch loomed large – and not just for the opportunity for much-needed nourishment. She was eager to hear what Xavier and Roman had discovered and wanted the chance to talk as well as listen.

Her session finished on time so she waited for Cher in reception. The plan was to grab a couple of salads and eat on the terrace. But when she switched on her phone, a message was waiting.

INVITATION: Stubbs, Davenport, Racine. Lunch with Björnsson. 13.00, Room 1126. Room service ordered for 4 guests.

When Cher eventually rolled into the foyer, she flashed her phone to show Beatrice she'd got the message. Avoiding an over-familiar ex-colleague and two seasoned researchers who wanted to discuss 'functioning dysfunctionals', Beatrice excused herself and followed Cher away from the restaurant to the lifts. She hoped Roman had checked the room for bugs.

Xavier opened the door. "Here you are! Finally!"

Beatrice raised her eyebrows.

Xavier understood. "The room is clear."

"We only just got your message," said Beatrice as she helped manoeuvre Cher's wheelchair over the threshold. "It's been a long morning."

"Come in, Roman's in the bathroom, but we have food, drink and news."

Cher took over the steering and parked herself at the dining table, where she began lifting lids. "Let's do it in that order. We only have an hour and I gotta eat."

"I wouldn't like to say I told you so, but that's what happens when you only have a handful of berries for breakfast." Beatrice flung her bag on the bed and sat at the table. "Xavier, do you already know what Gilchrist said in his speech or do you want the condensed version?"

"We heard. But what we learnt this morning doesn't quite fit."

The bathroom door opened and Roman emerged with a towel around his waist. His chest, muscular and lean, was decorated with a tattoo across his left shoulder. His long hair was wet and his feet left damp prints on the carpet as he padded across the room. "Aha! Our guests have arrived. So, who's ready for a debrief?"

Beatrice bit her lip and examined her fingernails, not daring to look at Cher.

Happily, at least in terms of Beatrice's concentration, Roman put on a hotel robe before joining them at the small table. Xavier took his plate to the armchair to give them some space and relayed their morning's discoveries. They'd made contact with the police and hotel management on an informal basis.

The robbery was the only line of enquiry and the police already had a list of suspects. Xavier had spoken to two different officers off the record, both of whom were willing to chat and share experiences with a fellow detective. Silva had been shot twice at close range in the back of the head whilst he was at his computer. So much for surprising a thief. The second detective had referred to it as 'execution-style'. The window had indeed been forced, but contrary to Gilchrist's assertion, several finger-prints had been found. The window pane had a recent set of prints which did not match those of Silva.

Apart from the hotel's closed floors, the conference had booked all available rooms, and more than a dozen casual workers had been taken on as gardeners, cleaners, drivers and kitchen staff. Work on the upper stories had been stopped for the duration of the conference so as not to disturb the participants, so at least they didn't have to check out dozens more workmen and suppliers. Of the casual staff, four had no alibi and two could not be located. It was simply a matter of time until they were found, fingerprinted and a suspect arrested. And time was crucial as the pressure was on, both externally and within.

"And you?" asked Roman, wiping his mouth on a napkin. "What's the news on the grapevine?"

"Not much more than you know," said Beatrice. "Gilchrist made his speech, we attended our seminars like good girls and kept our ears to the grindstone. Everyone's talking, but nobody's saying anything of note."

"Apart from André," said Cher, with a light flush.

"Oh yes. André saw you two leave this morning and assumes you've become lovers. We didn't argue."

Roman yanked the fruit bowl towards him and pulled a grape from the bunch. He popped it in his mouth and chewed, his gaze distant. Finally he swallowed and turned his glacial gaze to Xavier. "That could be a very useful cover."

Xavier's eyes widened and a slow smile began to spread. "I would never have thought of it, but you're right. A hint here, an absence there, don't ask, don't tell, but let the rumours do the work. And no need to hide the fact that we are always together at mealtimes, or in each other's rooms."

Roman clapped his hands together and laughed. "Perfect. We'll have to pretend to be hiding our affair, but everyone knows. I love it. We couldn't have designed it better ourselves. But how do we explain these two?" He jerked a chin at Beatrice and Cher.

"Fag hags?" suggested Beatrice.

Roman and Cher burst into laughter, but Xavier held up a hand.

"Leave it up to them. No explanations. People will create their own story. B, you and Cher can drop lots of hints about the side-benefits of inter-force co-operation, without stating facts, which should create enough of a distraction for us to follow up on the case."

Cher frowned. "Wait up. The case is over, right? In a couple days, they're going to make an arrest. You said so yourself. What more can we do?"

Xavier shook his head with some impatience. "Yes, they'll make an arrest. But all of us who call ourselves detectives can see this case is far from over."

"He's right." Roman reached behind his head and wound his long blond hair into a man bun. "Someone took Silva out. It wasn't a casual thief, it was a planned hit. I want to know where the internal pressure is coming from and why it's so vital for the local police to wrap this up. My guess is they will pin this on someone and file the paperwork while the real killer walks away."

Beatrice frowned. "So whoever owns those fingerprints is as much of a victim as Silva himself."

"Exactly." Xavier pointed his pen at her. "I'd like to take this to someone high up in Interpol, but we need more than second-hand circumstantial evidence. We have work to do. First, throw doubt on whoever has been set up as the suspect. Second, investigate who really engineered this killing, bearing in mind it could be one of our colleagues. What concerns me is how much we can achieve in the limited time available. We could use some help. André Monteiro seems the obvious choice, but can we trust any of our colleagues outside this room?"

A pensive silence descended. Beatrice understood. The question in everyone's mind was could they trust everyone *inside* the room? They knew so little about each other and a true sociopath would be very skilled at making others like them.

She looked into each face and made a decision. "If we suspect a police officer could be involved, perhaps we'd be wise not to confide in anyone else at the conference. I like André, but he was more than a police colleague to Samuel. He was also his godson. Without any more background information on the relationship, we can't eliminate him as a suspect. My view is we should use someone outside law enforcement. And I think I know just the person."

Chapter 13

Inside *Casa das Noivas*, Lisbon's premier bridal shop, no one was happy. The bride thought the neckline of her dress was too high, her mother thought it too low. Two of the bridesmaids were bickering over a pair of heels, the assistants' patience was running low and the maid of honour was bored out of her mind.

Ana Luisa Herrero rested her elbow on her knee and her chin on her hand, gazing past all the chiffon, gauze and satin, out at bright morning sunshine in the cobbled street. Workers hurried out of the Saldanha metro stop, tourists dawdled to window shop and ladies with designer handbags sat outside cafés enjoying a coffee, a *nata* and a gossip.

Ana wondered if she could sneak across the road for a *tosta mista*. She wasn't really hungry; she'd do anything just to get out of this air-conditioned dressing-up box. She looked over at the group in the changing area, but her aunt, famous for eyes-in-the-back-of-her-head, was one step ahead of her.

"Ana! Please show some enthusiasm. As *madrinha*, you are supposed to be the bride's constant support. Your cousin's not sure about the alterations on the dress. I think..."

Gisela interrupted. "I know what you think. But I'm the one getting married and I think it's all wrong. I look like a doll."

The other bridesmaids whose names Ana couldn't remember stopped their circular debate on kitten heels and rushed to the bride's side.

"No, not a doll! You look perfect!"

"Definitely not a doll. It's very glamorous but without being too obvious."

"The cleavage is too low, in my opinion."

"I WANT to show some skin."

"Skin maybe, but half your breasts?"

Ana hauled herself out of the chair. "Gisela, come here."

Her cousin shuffled over, pouting. Ana got it. Neither of them wanted to be in this position. Gisela wanted one of her best friends as *madrinha*. Ana would have been fine with that. Playing chief bridesmaid for her self-absorbed cousin ranked lower than an extended session with the dental hygienist. However, Aunt Candida believed family came first. So Ana must be Gisela's best woman, despite the fact that they barely tolerated each other.

"Show some skin but be subtle. Channel Brigitte Bardot. Pull the dress just off the shoulders like this. There. Beautiful neckline and it lifts the front to suggest at the cleavage. Sexy but sweet."

Gisela looked at her reflection and her eyes softened. Aunt Candida clasped her hands together and nodded. The brides-maids applauded, the shop assistants sighed with relief and Ana's phone rang.

"I'll take this outside in case it's urgent." No one was even listening.

She shoved her way out the door and across the road to the café, while checking her screen. She widened her eyes at the name of the caller.

"Beatrice Stubbs? No way! Is this really you?"

"Ana, hello! It's great to hear your voice. How are you? Is this a good time?"

"It's a bloody brilliant time. I'm so happy to hear from you. Is everything OK at your end?"

Beatrice paused. "Personally, yes. Professionally, I might need some help. I'm in need of a Portuguese-speaking mine of information with an intelligence network, who's also trustworthy and discreet."

Ana leaned on the bar and beckoned a waiter, mouthed *uma bica* and indicated a sparkling water. She continued speaking into her phone with a huge grin.

"I know just the girl. I have to warn you she's half-Irish and curses like a trooper. "

"Sounds just what I'm looking for. Are you still in the Basque Country?"

"No. After that whole wine fraud story, I got offered a job back home in Lisbon. I've been here almost a year now. Is that a problem?" Ana took her drinks outside and sat at an empty corner table, turning her back to other patrons and donning her sunglasses.

"Not in the slightest. Your physical location is immaterial. I know you can dig out all kinds of information from anywhere with your phone, laptop and charm. And for this case, Lisbon is a very good place to be."

"Is it now? Come on then, what do you need?"

"Well, if I could give you an exclusive story only to be reported once this case is over, would you do a little subtle investigation for me? It's about a crime in Portugal. Obviously, off the..."

"...record. No need to ask. You're in Portugal? Where?"

"In the north. Gerês. Half-holiday, half-work. Are you terribly busy at the paper?" Beatrice's voice sounded tense.

"Not a paper, I'm on the telly now, don't you know. But it's too damn hot to work and shag-all happens in the summer. I'm officially on holiday for the rest of this month anyway because my cousin is getting married. I'm the *madrinha*, sort of chief bridesmaid. So come on then, tell me what you want me to do."

"Do you have time? I imagine you've got your hands full with bridesmaid duties." Ana could hear the smile in her voice.

"Yeah, you can just imagine how much fun I'm having. Flowers, dresses, decorations... Beatrice, I am bored out of my mind. Rescue me. Give me a job and a story and I'll name my first-born after you."

"Deal! But I'll let you off if it's a boy. I need you to find out all you can about a Portuguese psychologist called Samuel Ramiro Silva of the LIU. You'll have to be very hush-hush and I'll send you an email with the details. I'm particularly interested in any tensions between him and his colleagues in international law enforcement."

"Silva?" Ana sat up straight and dropped her voice to a fierce whisper. "Shit! He's all over the news! Of course! Sometimes I'm so slow I could kick myself. OK, so if we're talking about that situation, hush-hush won't be necessary – just a bit of discretion. Everyone is scrabbling for information. Send me everything you've got and I'll do whatever I can to help. Can you really get me an exclusive on this?"

"Yes, I can. Thank you, Ana. You're one of the few people I can trust. I don't suppose you could bring me your findings in person? Matthew and I are renting a villa near here with Tanya and Luke. And Adrian's here too. We have a spare room. Or am I being too demanding?"

Ana slugged her coffee in one. "You're all there? I'd love to see Adrian and the Prof again! And I've not seen Tanya since we were exchange students! All this and a shit-hot story? It must be my birthday or something. Count me in. Thanks, Beatrice, you've saved me. This week was rammed with duties, but now I have a get-out clause. I'll start digging today and if the schedule works, I'll get on a budget flight to Porto tomorrow. I can't wait!"

Ana paid the waiter, declined to give him her number and took a second to compose a suitably sad face before returning to Casa das Noivas to break the news. Tragically, she would be unable to fulfil her duties as *madrinha* due to an urgent work commitment. A great deal of feigned sadness and regret later, five women left the shop vastly happier than when they'd gone in. Ana was making calls before she even got on the tram. Work versus wedding? No contest.

Chapter 14

All things considered, Adrian was quite pleased with the way things had worked out. The only missing element was Beatrice. Breakfast was long and haphazard, as everyone rose at different hours. Adrian, always a light sleeper, had woken on hearing the sounds of Beatrice's departure. He slipped out of bed, sat on the terrace and read the news on his phone until Matthew came down. They discussed international politics over coffee until Luke arrived, at which point the conversation turned to Coco Pops.

When Will came down, Matthew began frying some bacon and Adrian brewed fresh coffee. The smells woke Tanya, who emerged barefoot in her shortie pyjamas and the early part of the morning passed in comfortable banter. Finally, Marianne and Leon joined them for coffee. Marianne announced their intention of travelling across the border to Vigo and Pontevedra in Spain. Would anyone mind if they took the smaller car?

There was a puzzled silence. Tanya was the first to speak.

"If you like. You don't fancy coming with us to the beach, then?"

Leon shook his head, his expression regretful. "I'm afraid I get bored sitting in the sun. Marianne and I are well matched that way. Neither of us is a beach person. We'd far rather go exploring."

Tanya's eyebrows lifted. "Yeah, right. I remember how much

she hated Lanzarote. Sun, sea, sand... she said it was her idea of hell."

Marianne gave her sister a dry look. "Tastes change. OK, so if no one objects, we'll see you back here for dinner. Leon and I are cooking tonight. Chicken piri-piri with wild rice."

"Piri-piri? That's chilli, right? I'd better make something else for Luke," said Tanya.

"Yeah, it's pretty spicy. And we plan to eat about eight, so it would be too late for him anyway," Leon replied.

"I like chicken pirry!" said Luke.

Leon shook his head again. "I don't think so. Is Beatrice joining us? Just to know if I should buy enough chicken for seven."

"Buy enough for eight, if you don't mind," Tanya said, her voice tight. "Beatrice said she'd be here and Luke likes to eat with us. I'll do a lighter version for him and he can sleep late tomorrow."

"Sure. No problemo. Will, where can I find the car keys?"

Packing for the beach was almost as much fun as being there. They borrowed beach umbrellas and windbreaks from the villa's cabana and crammed them into the Peugeot's boot along with sun creams, insect repellent, football, bucket, spades and naturally, the picnic. Adrian and Tanya organised the latter, leaving everything else to three excited males of varying ages.

Tanya was soothing company. She worked with cool capability, achieving six dishes to Adrian's one, although his was a truly sublime tortilla. She hummed and sang random tunes and didn't seem to expect a constant flow of small talk. The hamper gradually filled with three different salads, sardines for grilling, a batch of mini fishcakes and a flask of chocolate ice-cream.

"So all we need now is water, wine and fresh bread, which we can buy in Viana do Castelo. Are we ready?"

Adrian wrapped his tortilla in foil. "Yes! I'll just add the icepacks to the cool bag and we're good to go. Do you think we have enough?"

"There's only five of us, remember. Well, four and a half. Luke stuffed himself at breakfast so he won't eat much. You know what? I'm pleased it's just us today."

This was a tricky moment. *Tread softly*, he advised himself. He wasn't family, and a careless comment could still give offence years later.

"Me too. I like Leon, I really do, but I feel we're on best behaviour when we're all together. I feel much more relaxed when it's just you and Luke and Matthew."

Tanya wrinkled her nose. "That's as much her fault as his. She's watching us all, marking our reactions to Mister Wonderful on some kind of score sheet. Do you really like him?"

Adrian zipped up the hamper. "He's pleasant, polite and makes Marianne happy. He might be a bit defensive, but how do you think he feels, under such scrutiny? I think we should all give him a break and get on with our holiday. Come on, let's go to the beach, sunbathe, swim, build sandcastles, grill fish and indulge ourselves. I intend to pursue my latest hobby, which is finding you the perfect man."

Tanya sniffed. "I'm off men. Present company excepted."

"The perfect woman, in that case. Can you manage that cool bag if I carry the hamper? Come on then, tell me the top five characteristics you want in your ideal partner."

Viana do Castelo was not exactly the dream beach Adrian had envisaged, but it was certainly the perfect location for a family day out. On this Monday afternoon, the sand was sparsely populated, the sea calm and the sun brilliant. The heat drummed down relentlessly and Adrian decided to be judicious with his tanning. Burning would be an amateur error and red skin was dreadfully gauche.

Luke, impatient to get to the sea, harassed and chivvied each of them in turn as they unloaded the car and set up camp under two large sun umbrellas. He squirmed and wriggled under sufferance as Tanya smeared him with Factor 50, then raced Will into the surf, shrieking all the way. Matthew drew his fedora lower and donned aviator shades to watch his grandson splashing and laughing in the shallows.

Tanya peeled off her sundress and headed off to join them. Reminded of his mission, Adrian scanned the beach for any gazes following her shapely form across the sand. He counted at least four.

"I'm glad you and Will are here," said Matthew.

Adrian lifted his sunglasses to look at him. Matthew's attention was directed at the sea, where Tanya was running into the water, chased by Luke and Will.

"We're glad to be here. And at least we get our Beatrice fix once a day. I have to say, you're taking her absence very well."

"Par for the course. We never get enough time together. Always wringing out the moments until we part. Our relationship thus far has been built on missing each other; either savouring the last time or looking forward to the next. So this is no surprise. The real shock will come when we have all the time in the world."

Six teenagers ran past in baggy swim shorts, their skins the colour of toffee.

"You're as nervous as she is, aren't you?"

Matthew dragged his gaze from the shore to Adrian's face. "If you'd spent twenty years trying to persuade her to move in, wouldn't you be nervous? The funny thing is, you are part of it. You and Will represent her London life, something she feels she'll lose when she retires. That's another reason I'm glad you're here. You are more than a neighbour."

"I should damn well hope so! She's nearly got me killed twice so far. She'll be fine, Matthew. You'll both be fine. I wish you wouldn't worry." He lathered sun cream onto his skin, wincing as he touched the bruise on his shin. It had developed into an ugly inky smudge, toned down by his tan but still sensitive. If only heroism could be achieved without personal injury.

"Worrying is an integral part of having a relationship with

Beatrice Stubbs. That and the 'nearly killed' thing. Anyway, I rather think I might chance a paddle. Would you keep an eye on our things?"

"Of course. I'm busy working on my tan anyway. Paddle away and bring me back any nice shells you find. I'm amassing a collection."

Adrian lay back and stared up at the impossible blue of the sky, recalling times when he'd sneered at a future with one person for the rest of his life. How things change. Now he found himself envying Matthew and Beatrice their future contentment, their pretty Devon cottage and their kitchen garden filled with sweet peas and courgettes. If Will got a transfer to the countryside, Adrian could sell up in London and open a wine emporium somewhere on the coast. Less violent crime, more romantic sunsets, endless relaxing weekends and maybe a dog to walk on the beach...

He sat up with a gasp of shock as cold wet droplets spattered his skin. Will stood over him, shaking his wet hair and laughing. "Come on. Matthew's got his knees wet and is coming back to start the grill. Time for a serious swim before lunch."

"You play hell with my tanning routine," Adrian said, accepting Will's hand and hauling himself to his feet. Hot sand forced him to run towards the sea, and exhilaration overcame his self-consciousness as he plunged into the waves, gasping as the cool water made contact with sun-warmed skin. He struck out towards the horizon in a powerful crawl, trusting Will would overtake him in seconds.

He was right. Adrian slowed and rolled onto his back, kicking lazily and scanning the beach for their friends. He spotted the two red polka-dot umbrellas and a wisp of smoke. So Matthew had managed to light the barbecue. He was about to raise his arms in a wave when a sudden tug on his shorts dragged him underwater. He swallowed a mouthful of sea and coughed, his vision blurred. He surfaced to see Will a safe distance away, grinning like a dolphin.

Adrian pulled his shorts back up, took in a deep breath and allowed himself to sink under the next wave. Then he took off beneath the surface with a deadly purpose. No one debags Adrian underwater.

By the time the two men finished fooling around and made their way back up the beach, the picnic was all prepared. Matthew was using his fedora to fan the coals under the sardines while Tanya had opened all the salads and distributed plates, cutlery and glasses around the mat-tablecloth. Luke, huddled under a towel, was gnawing on a slice of tortilla.

"This looks amazing! Thanks, Tanya and hats off to Matthew. Luke, how's the tortilla? You may answer using any of the following words: divine, fabulous, absolutely," Adrian said, sitting cross-legged in the sand.

Luke giggled. "I like it. It's got cheese and potato and egg. Cheese and potato and egg are my favourite foods. As well as sausage and tomato sandwiches."

Will pulled a beer from the cool box and offered it to Adrian.

"I'll stick with wine, thanks. Luke, you should go to Spain. They make a tortilla just like this but with tomatoes and a special Spanish sausage called chorizo. All your favourite foods in one dish."

Luke's eyes widened. "Marianne's in Spain now! We could call her and ask her to bring some back!"

Matthew ladled sardines onto everyone's plates, crisp, slightly blackened and with a hint of smoke. Adrian was salivating.

"That's not a bad idea," Matthew agreed. "They're going to a supermarket anyway so I could put in a request for chorizo. Tanya, would you give her a call or send her an app, however you people communicate these days."

"Yeah, OK. I'll text her after lunch. Adrian, do you want vinho verde or this white Rioja?" she asked.

Adrian glanced briefly at Matthew and shared a knowing look while tearing off hunks of bread.

"Vinho verde, I think. Let's go local. Did you two have a good swim?"

Luke nodded with enthusiasm, reaching for some bread. Tanya poured three glasses of white wine, her face relaxed and glowing.

"Yeah, it's brilliant. Can't believe the beach is so quiet and the water is gorgeous. I'm going back in when I've digested all this."

"And me!" said Luke.

They ate in silence for a few moments, savouring the pungent sardines and sampling Tanya's salads.

"What to have next, Small Fry?" asked Matthew. "I rather fancy something eggy and cheesy, and if it had potatoes or onions, that would be a bonus."

"Tor-*tee*-ya!" yelled Luke.

"Me too ya!" yelled Will, sending Luke into a fit of giggles, his towel dropping from his shoulders.

Matthew sliced a portion each for everyone, including a second piece for Luke, and conversation became nothing more than appreciative murmurs.

Will reached across to squeeze Adrian's knee. "It's delicious. You are a domestic god." Then his attention was caught by something else. "Luke, what happened to your arm?"

Adrian followed his gaze and saw four small bruises on the boy's upper left arm. Luke glanced down and shrugged.

"Oops, did we get a bit too rough in the water just now?" asked Matthew.

"Bruises don't develop that fast," said Tanya. "How did you get those, Luke?"

Luke shook his head. "Dunno."

"Probably all the rough and tumble in the pool on the first day," Adrian suggested. "You need to be more careful, Will."

"Will didn't do it," muttered Luke, scooping the towel back over his shoulders. Adrian understood the signal. *Stop staring!*

"Can you imagine what it must have been like?" asked Matthew, his eyes on the horizon. "Six hundred years ago, to step off the only land you've ever known and set sail with nothing more than optimism, courage and hope? Knowing nothing of what might be out there, yet risking your life in the name of discovery? Could you board a wooden ship and sally forth into the open sea, with only the vaguest idea of where you were going and no idea if or when you might return? The people of this country did. The Portuguese took off from these shores in fragile crafts and mapped the world. We owe these explorers more than we realise."

Despite Tanya's sigh as she spooned out the ice-cream, the entire party was enthralled, including the five-year old.

"Think about it. Here we stand, a family of fisherfolk in the fifteenth, sixteenth century, unsure of what's out there or what mythical monsters lurk beneath the roiling waves. We wave goodbye to our courageous sailors, our hearts full of fear and dread. What terrors will they endure, what strange lands will they encounter?

"Many will never return, but those who do shall be forever heroes. Henry the Navigator, da Gama, Magellan, Dias and Cabral were the astronauts of their time, going bravely where no man had gone before. We owe these extraordinary intrepid adventurers a profound debt. They connected the atlas and discovered the world we know today."

They applauded his monologue, turning heads from other parties on the beach. For the first time, Adrian understood why Matthew was such a valued professor. He loved his subject and made it human.

Will tilted his head backwards to catch the sun on his face. "This is what holidays should be like. Sunshine, seaside, lovely food, beautiful views, good company and a great storyteller. But nothing puts the cherry on the cake as much as beach volleyball!"

Luke leapt up so fast his plate went flying. "Beach volleyball! Three against two! Come on Granddad!"

"Granddad doesn't want to play beach volleyball," said Will. "He wants to doze with the crossword. Listen, you and I will play against your mum and Adrian. Why don't we let them clear up while you and I go set up the pitch? We also need to warm up and talk tactics."

Matthew's expression was one of relief and Tanya gave Will a grateful smile, so Adrian overlooked the number of assumptions made in that comment and resolved to discuss it later. Matthew retired to his deckchair as Adrian and Tanya cleared up the picnic. They both gazed down the beach to watch the mismatched pair playing Head, Shoulders, Knees and Toes. Then with a handshake, Tanya and Adrian stepped out into the sunshine to meet their opponents.

By the time they got back to the villa, sandy and sun-pinked, the Panda was parked outside. Will lifted a sleeping Luke from the back seat up and took him upstairs to finish his nap, with Tanya yawning in his wake. After unpacking the remains of the picnic, Adrian wandered outside to the pool. Marianne and Leon lay in the shade, him face down, her reading a gossip magazine.

"Hi! How was Vigo?"

Marianne looked up. "Hi there. It was OK. Nothing to write home about. What about the beach?"

"Perfect. Loads of space, hot, sunny and Matthew grilled some sublime sardines. But after beach volleyball and swimming in the sea, I think we're all fit for a nap. Luke was asleep before we left Viana do Castelo."

Leon rolled over, shielding his eyes with his hand. "Sounds like a fun day. What time should we plan dinner?"

Adrian looked at his watch. "It's half past five now and Beatrice won't get here for another hour and a half. So shall we say aperitifs at seven, and dinner at eight?

"Ideal. The chicken is already marinating so we'll start the roasting at seven."

"Oh, one thing about the oven. The temperature dial is a bit dodgy so you need to watch whatever's cooking."

"Don't worry, Adrian, it's all under control. Can we leave you in charge of the cocktails?"

"Cocktails are my speciality. See you later."

Leon put on his sunglasses. "So I hear. See you at seven."

Marianne snickered.

The sun reflecting off the pool and the scent of rosemary made Adrian dozy. With a salute to the reclining couple, he returned indoors, wondering what Marianne found so funny.

They overslept. Will kissed his shoulder, told him it was quarter past seven and dragged on some clothes. Laughter from the poolside rippled through the window and Adrian recalled his promise to be barman. He threw on linen trousers and T-shirt, checked his hair and followed Will downstairs. Leon was adding the finishing touches to the dining-table, which looked spectacular, with orange napkins, sparkling glasses and a centrepiece of dramatic red flowers to match the sunset. Marianne was in the kitchen, rinsing rice. Everyone else was poolside, nibbling on nuts, olives and breadsticks while Will made martinis.

Adrian spotted Beatrice and opened his arms. "Are you coping?"

She leaned into his hug. "I am. Are you?"

"Actually, we're having fun. Have you got a cocktail?"

"I have an Old-Fashioned, made by that handsome barman over there. If I were you, I'd get his number."

As if he'd heard her, Will looked up from his preparations and grinned.

"Hmm, you might be right. He looks the sort to go for a golden tan, which you have not yet noticed." Adrian pulled up the arm of his T-shirt and Beatrice responded exactly as she ought.

"Adrian! You look so sun-kissed! Have you been on holiday at all?"

Luke wandered over with a closed hand. "Guess what? Do you know which way is north?"

Beatrice looked to the sky. "My guess is that way." She pointed east.

Adrian shook his head. "I'm afraid you're wrong about that, Beatrice. I think you'll find north is that way." He pointed south.

"Wrong!" Luke opened his hand to reveal a tiny compass, the sort one might get in a Christmas cracker. "North is up there," he whispered, his eyes wide with drama. "Beatrice, is your working place in the north?"

"No, a little bit south. But the weather is the same. My only problem is we have no beach. Can you believe it? One week in Portugal, a country full of beaches and what do I get? A big pond!"

Luke laughed and started to tell Beatrice about the picnic when the smell of burning and the sound of swearing drifted from the villa. Matthew broke off his conversation with Tanya and went indoors.

The group drew together near Will's makeshift bar and took turns to reply to Luke's knock-knock jokes. Adrian winked at the barman and got himself a second martini. He was just requesting an olive when Matthew emerged from the French windows and clapped his hands.

"Folks, change of plan. The oven malfunctioned and burnt the chicken. So I suggest we head down the hill to the fish restaurant tonight. Apparently we get five-star service if we mention our friend from Braga. Anybody sober enough to drive?"

Twenty minutes later, Will parked the Panda next to the Peugeot beside a very dark, closed restaurant. Adrian's spirits sank. If it were only Will and himself, they'd laugh and go exploring elsewhere. But tonight there were seven adults and a hungry child to accommodate.

"You didn't think to book a table?" asked Leon.

Matthew shook his head. "No, not at such short notice. I'm sorry, I thought we could just walk in on a Monday. Do you suppose all restaurants close on Mondays? Like hairdressers?"

Beatrice walked to the door. "Ah. The notice is in five languages. 'Closed for two weeks for the annual family holiday.'

What a shame, I love that little pier and the boathouse on the lake. Too pretty. Still, there's no food on offer here and time's getting on. Back to the ranch for omelettes or a local café for a toasted sandwich?"

Will rested his chin on Adrian's shoulder. "I'd chance the local, but happy to fall in with what everyone else wants to do. What do you say, Luke, omelette or toastie?"

Luke didn't answer. Adrian looked around the car park, but there was no sign of him.

"Luke!" Tanya called. "Luke, where are you?"

After calling his name a few times, Will gave the party instructions. "Split up. He's probably hiding from us. Leon and Marianne, look round the back of the restaurant, Tanya, you check the terrace. Beatrice and Matthew, search in and under both cars. Adrian and I will cover the pier and the boathouse."

They spread out, calling Luke's name with a false cheerfulness. Adrian tiptoed along the short pier, squinting into the black water, his mind playing out all kinds of nightmarish scenarios when a voice rang out.

"He's here!"

Will guided Luke out of the boathouse onto the wooden boards of the pier, his hand on the boy's shoulder.

Tanya rushed down the steps. "Luke, where have you been? Don't you ever do that again! Wandering off in the dark! You scared me half to death. You always stay with the family, understand?"

"I only wanted to have a look." It was clear from Luke's expression he had no idea what all the fuss was about.

"Well, don't! If you want to go somewhere, you only ever go with one of us," said Tanya. She turned back to the others. "Look, can we just get back to the villa and eat whatever we've got in the fridge? I'm kind of done with today."

Leon and Marianne shared a look and stalked back to the car. The drive back was cold and awkward, unlike the villa, which smelt of burnt food. Everyone congregated in the kitchen for omelettes and toasties, but despite Matthew's best efforts at inclusion, Marianne and Leon would not be mollified and retired to the garden flat.

Adrian was not sorry to see them go.

Chapter 15

One advantage of getting your face on TV most evenings is that people tend to know your name. This can open a whole lot of doors.

Yesterday Ana had sent out a dozen emails to colleagues, relatives and contacts of Silva's hoping for at least one bite. She got four. One of whom refused her enquiry in the bluntest possible language. Two offered some personal platitudes and information on Silva but neither added much to what she already knew from her research. The fourth, however, made all Ana's efforts worthwhile. Silva's sister, Olivia, was willing to talk. Even better, face to face.

Ana stood at the faded wooden door on Rua Mirabilis, took a deep breath and rang the bell. She tilted her head towards the fish-eye lens so her face could be seen and pulled out her press pass. A tinny voice came through the intercom.

"Ms Herrero?"

"That's me. Here's my ID." She held the card up to the camera.

"That's not necessary, I recognise you from *Telejornal*. Come in. Directly across the courtyard and I'm on the second floor."

A buzzer released the door and Ana pushed it open. The gloomy hallway gave way to a beautiful interior courtyard with trailing plants and tubs of flowers. Parakeets chattered and squawked from a cage on a balcony above and a cat lay in a patch of sun, watching her with indifference.

When she reached the second floor, an apartment door opened and Olivia Tavares appeared, a silhouette against the sunlight. Ana moved towards her, hand outstretched and was met by a study of grief. Not just the black clothes, wan complexion and puffy eyes, but a palpable feeling, like a musty smell. It was a salutary reminder that loss could be unexpectedly violent, attacking when you are least prepared. The two women shook hands and Olivia made a valiant effort to return Ana's smile.

"Come in."

Ana did as she was asked and stepped into a large room in which every surface held a plant. The profusion of greenery against blue walls gave the impression of an aquarium.

"You are alone?" asked Olivia.

Ana nodded, puzzled by the question.

"I'm glad. I'm not ready to face a camera crew today. Please, have a seat. You'll take a coffee?"

Ana recalled the fictitious commission she had invented. The Life of Samuel Silva, a profile of the man and his achievements. Not entirely a lie, she argued with her conscience. If she found enough material, she could try to get the green light for some in-depth reportage. In return, her conscience gave her an arch look.

"Just water, thank you. No, it will be some time before we start filming. I have a lot of research to do before then. That is why I'm so grateful for your help. To be able to start with the family is exactly what I wanted. Thank you for meeting me, especially at such a difficult time." She sat at the dining-table and took out her notebook.

Olivia poured a bottle of Salgados into two glasses. "Of course I will help. To be honest, I want to talk about him."

"I can understand that. My aim is to profile the man as a whole, not just the professional. Can you tell me a little about your family? I know there are three children and Samuel was the eldest."

"That's right." She sat opposite Ana, her face partly shadowed by an overgrown spider plant that hung from the ceiling, filtering the light. "Samuel, then me and Salvatore is the youngest. There are two years between each child. Our parents were good planners. We grew up in Sintra, on a beautiful *quinta*, with vineyards. My father inherited money and my mother had land. A wealthy, respectable family and three children destined for great things."

"Were you three kids close?"

Olivia's face crumpled and she pulled a tissue from her sleeve to press to her eyes. She held up a shaky hand as if to ask for patience. She took several uneven breaths and started to speak.

"We used to be. Samuel was the oldest and we both adored him. He was clever and kind and very protective of his siblings. He defended us against my father. Papa was an authoritarian, very old-fashioned with a quick temper. Samuel was always smart. He went to university and studied psychology, even though our father wanted him to be a doctor. Our mother was so proud of him and displayed all his certificates on our living-room wall.

"The trouble started when Mama died. She was the calming influence, a force for balance. Without her, my father became more conservative, less tolerant." She heaved an enormous sigh.

"He was obsessed with class and education. He wanted Salvatore to study like Samuel, to become an engineer, but Salvatore trained as a mechanic and now works for the railway. As for me, his only ambition was to find me a good husband. I refused to cooperate and trained as a teacher. When I got married, it was for love, not for status. Our choices were a constant source of conflict between us, and family occasions became a source of stress, not comfort. But until our father's death, the three of us were a unit, a team who looked after each other.

"Papa died four years ago and left his estate to Samuel as the eldest male. It was profoundly shocking. Of course Samuel was ready to be generous and share his good fortune, but Salvatore disputed the will in court. That put a terrible strain on the family. After the verdict, which was to uphold the will, Samuel and Salvatore no longer spoke. I hoped that one day they would reconcile, but now..."

Her voice cracked and Ana handed her a clean tissue.

"Take your time. There's no rush," Ana lied. To catch the 11.25 flight to Porto, she would need to leave within the hour and that was looking unlikely.

Olivia gulped some water. "It's heartbreaking. My father and his money have made us angry and unforgiving. Even from beyond the grave he still divides us."

"You too? Because you had to side with either Samuel or Salvatore?"

A grimace crossed Olivia's face. "It was horrible. I tried to stay neutral but when I heard the terms of Papa's will, I had to support Salvatore. You see, the will states that in the event of Samuel's death, Salvatore inherits our father's estate, bypassing me and ignoring Samuel's own family. My father intended to ignore Samuel's wife. It was an injustice I could not bear."

"You can't have been too happy yourself."

Olivia shook her head, a quick, impatient gesture. "I don't want it. That place holds nothing but bad memories and ghosts. What made me so angry was the unfairness of his final gesture. Papa wanted to keep stirring trouble long after his death and by writing such a bequest, he made sure he succeeded. When Samuel met Elisabete, a successful, independent doctor who had no need of financial support, my father called her a gold-digger. Grace be to God he died before they adopted Marcia. An orphan from Romania as his grandchild? He would rather have me inherit his estate. Me, a woman!"

The venom in her tone surprised Ana, but gave her cause for optimism. Anger has all the energy grief lacks. She drank some water and checked her watch. Forty minutes to mine this seam. It could be done.

"You said Samuel and Salvatore weren't on speaking terms. What about you?"

"I talked to both my brothers. I love them and that will never change. Family is everything to me. After the court case, I tried to build bridges. Samuel and Elisabete embraced me immediately. Salvatore did not judge me for being in the middle, but refused to listen to any attempts at reconciliation. He just switched off whenever I mentioned Samuel's name."

Ana calculated. So the younger brother certainly had a motive. One of the oldest in the book. But why wait four years and take revenge at a conference of police detectives?

"Is Salvatore married?" she asked.

"Yes. He has a wife and two lovely boys. When Samuel and Elisabete adopted Marcia, I thought the children might provide some common ground." She shook her head sadly. "Salvatore did seem to be softening, but when he heard about the court case, he shut down again."

"The court case? For adoption?"

"No, this was a claim against the adoption agency. Those terrible people! They delayed the process, inventing red tape and administrative fees to extort more and more money from Samuel. Marcia's case was so badly handled that when Samuel finally got custody, he sued the agency for emotional distress and damages.

"The judge found in their favour, but the agency declared itself bankrupt. Samuel didn't mind about the money. He said he was happy no one else would suffer the way they had done. Then the whole situation got very ugly. The boss of this disgusting company, who made children's and prospective parents' lives a misery, threatened to take his revenge. He targeted Samuel in particular. It cast a dark cloud over the joy of bringing Marcia home."

Ana stopped writing and stared at Olivia. "He threatened to hurt Samuel? When was this?"

"Almost three months ago. He threatened to do more than hurt him. He said he would take Marcia away and he promised to kill my brother." She covered her face with her hands.

"Olivia, have you shared this with the police?"

She wiped away tears and met Ana's gaze. "Nobody asked me. Do you think I should?"

"Listen, I need the name of this guy, the adoption agency and anything you can tell me about the court case. If you can give me everything you know in the next twenty minutes, I'll make my flight. I'm heading north, to Gerês. I know someone who can help us both."

Half an hour later, Ana dashed through Portela Airport and arrived at the check-in to find her flight had been delayed by ninety minutes. She checked in, sent Beatrice a message and found a quiet seat facing a wall. She opened her laptop and inserted earphones which weren't connected to anything, but would ward off chatty fellow passengers. She had work to do and there was no such thing as wasted time.

Chapter 16

Beatrice knew from experience that in any investigation, the urge to get a result is like acid, eroding principles and burning its way through assumptions of moral superiority. When four upstanding officers of the law combine forces, no matter how informally, a code of conduct will be required. This is why investigative ethics are so important

But at Tuesday morning's coffee break, while Roman charmed hotel security, Xavier bought the local police coffee and Cher spent every spare minute with André Monteiro, Beatrice looked the other way. After all, she would be fraternising with a journalist in a couple of hours, so who was she to judge? Instead, she walked the grounds, called Matthew in anticipation of their dinner party that evening and spent the time on a logical assessment of the circumstances. It didn't help much.

She returned to the hotel for all the EPIC events of the day, her mind turning over each piece of evidence, even while attending a seminar on Big Data – Finding Needles in the Haystack. Her problem was the opposite. She and her impromptu team were searching for clues based on almost zero data. She cocked her head in a simulacrum of attentiveness and went over the facts again.

Clumsy window entry and fingerprints on the pane pointed to either an amateur burglary or a professional set-up. Every element of an interrupted burglary offered the local police an easy resolution.

Beatrice worked both theories. Two shots to the back of the head indicated a planned hit, not a disturbed burglar. This person gained access either via the window, a key or as a welcome guest. In the former two scenarios, someone had entered, waited and struck. In the latter, turning one's back on a visitor seemed an unnatural thing to do.

So the Bond-style assassin theory gained the upper hand, but a huge gap of logic remained.

Motive.

Then there was the rumour. Ranga's comments echoed in her mind. *Word is, there's a book ... due to expose, embarrass and possibly even indict senior officers across the continent.* If Silva was connected, the international police convention could have been the opportunity to silence him, the book and its revelations.

If Silva *was* connected with the book at all. His work was professional research, not a vengeful memoir. He didn't seem the type, based on Beatrice's limited knowledge of the man, but she had only conversed with him for a few short hours.

A police detective would know every foolproof method of avoiding detection and how to throw enough circumstantial evidence to implicate someone else. Who would have known he would be in his room at that time? If Xavier had made his lunch invitation to the professor in public, any one of the seminar goers might have overheard. Then whoever it was could have preceded him before the doting family man made it back to his room to phone his wife.

When lunchtime rolled around, Beatrice ducked out of the seminar in full awareness she'd learned nothing about Big Data and it was all her own fault. Hurrying up the stairs to Xavier's room for their previously agreed meeting, she checked her messages and cursed. She had hoped Ana would arrive in time to join them, but according to the latest message – 'Sodding plane delayed. ETA circa 14.00.' – the girl had just touched down in Porto.

Xavier opened the door and welcomed her in. Cher was

sitting at the table, waiting. A deliciously fishy scent emanated from the silver cloches at each place setting.

"That smells heavenly!" Beatrice tossed her bag on the bed and joined Cher at the table. "Ana's flight was delayed, so I'll skip the first session of the afternoon and hang around to meet her. Where's Roman?"

"Just gone back to his room for a shower," said Xavier, pouring water into her glass.

"The man is obsessed!" exclaimed Beatrice. "How many times a day does he perform his ablutions?"

Cher laughed. "I'm pretty sure it's only once. He overslept again this morning. He'd better hurry because I want to eat."

"Let's give him a minute before we start," said Xavier. He picked up a basket covered in a napkin. "These rolls are still warm. Anyone?"

Beatrice and Cher both took one and Beatrice started buttering.

"How did you get on with André Monteiro?" she asked Cher.

"Smart kid. Like us, he thinks something about all this stinks. I agreed but didn't say too much. He knew Samuel his whole life and talks about him with real affection. But he has a little chip on his shoulder. His father and ..."

The doorbell rang and Xavier admitted Roman. The Icelander squeezed both Beatrice's and Cher's shoulders before flinging his long body into a seat and lifting the silver cloche.

"Right, let's get down to business. We need to talk."

By the time the plates were empty, everyone had shared their information and thoughts. Xavier summarised them above the buzzing clatter of the coffee machine, where Roman was making each of them an espresso.

"Key information is this. Cher discovered a potential motive in jealousy. Samuel is André Monteiro's godfather and best friend to Nelson Monteiro. Nelson and Samuel are peers, but Samuel is the one who got promoted and received all the accolades for the work he and Nelson have done. André feels some injustice on his father's behalf.

"For my part, my police sergeant contact told me there is CCTV footage of the first floor corridor at the time Samuel Silva was killed. I did not see it, but he tells me no one enters Samuel's room but Samuel himself. Then André Monteiro knocks on the door, receives no reply and leaves.

"Roman's conversations with the staff show that only reception and housekeeping have access to master keys. The Do Not Disturb sign was on the door and the key log confirms the video footage. The only person to go in and out was Samuel Silva.

"Access from the window would be difficult. The room is on the first floor so you would need a ladder to climb onto his balcony. During lunchtime, when people are milling around the grounds, it would be unmissable."

The room fell silent and everyone sipped their coffees.

Beatrice looked at each face in turn. "Thank you Xavier, but this is all hearsay. We are not in control, we cannot see the footage for ourselves, we can't interview the staff as police officers, we can't take official statements. We're basing an entire investigation on gossip and we don't know any of it is true. Some of these suppositions sound plausible but could be inverted by testing the hypotheses. Come on, let's think like detectives, not nervous house guests."

Roman rolled his shoulders, arched back his neck and fixed his gaze on Beatrice. "You have a point. Based on reading people as opposed to forensic evidence, these are the facts as we know them. I have faith in professional detectives' opinions but you're right, we need to challenge our assumptions. What might we be reading wrong?"

Cher raised a finger. "Access to Samuel's room. If someone in uniform was up a ladder, I wouldn't think twice. I'd guess the guy was doing his job. There's all sorts of renovation work on the upper stories. I know it's been suspended for the week, but there are still ladders and equipment lying about."

"True," said Beatrice. "And there's a balcony outside. If it's anything like mine, you could hop over onto next door's as easily as getting out of the bath. Which means it could have been anyone who has a room on the first floor."

Xavier stirred his coffee. "All of this is true. We need more facts. But the one thing we must find..."

"... is a motive," Roman interrupted, placing a bowl of sugar on the table.

Xavier inclined his head. "My thoughts exactly."

"Oh you two," Beatrice laughed. "Finishing each other's sentences? You should get married."

Roman rested his chin on Xavier's head, his blond locks framing both their faces. Beatrice smiled while Cher took a picture. She turned the phone to show them.

"We would have made such a beautiful couple." Xavier exaggerated a sigh.

"Listen, we have ten minutes before the afternoon sessions start," said Beatrice. "This is how I suggest we proceed. Xavier, you need to get the details about the fingerprints in Silva's room. Were there any others? Where were those deemed to be the suspect's? Any other relevant information on the room? Roman, we need to know who's on the first floor, especially the rooms either side. Can you also try and get a look at that footage of Saturday lunchtime? As for you, Cher, try to get close to André Monteiro, earn his confidence, ask more about the relationship with his godfather, you know what to do. Listen very carefully to what he doesn't say. I'll meet Ana and hope to high heaven she's found something for us."

Xavier slapped his thighs and got to his feet. "OK, let's meet up at afternoon coffee break at the end of the terrace. Hopefully Beatrice's friend will be here by then. Let's keep digging."

Beatrice hid in her room, studying the list of delegates until two o'clock, and then descended to the gardens. She wandered aimlessly behind some shrubs with half an eye on the drive, trying to appear interested in horticulture. While she walked, she added up all she knew and reached a different conclusion every time.

"Oi!" A long-legged figure waved at her from the terrace, a rucksack dangling from one shoulder.

"Ana!" Beatrice waved back and hurried up the slope to greet her guest, already elated by the sight of the girl.

Ana dropped her rucksack and bent to embrace Beatrice in a crushing hug. Her long hair was the silvery-brown of melted chocolate, the same colour as her Fiat 500, carelessly parked on the forecourt. A delightful smile illuminated her lovely face.

"You look more beautiful than ever! I am *so* pleased to see you," Beatrice said, holding Ana's shoulders.

"You look shitloads better than the last time I saw you. Thanks so much for giving me this tip. This story is the dog's bollocks and getting to see you, Tanya, the Prof and Adrian is the custard on my plums. Come here to me, I've got some intel and a ton of questions for you."

"I thought you might. Let's drop your bag in my room and I'll order room service so we can get up to speed in private."

Ana scribbled notes in shorthand and interrupted frequently.

"Do we know which publishing company is handling the book?"

"I'll get the names of everyone who had rooms on that corridor."

"How do you spell Gilchrist?"

"Have you a minibar? I could murder... sorry. I mean I'd love a beer."

Beatrice's fetched Ana a bottle of Super Bock. "Your turn," she said.

Ana swigged at her beer then flipped open her tablet. "First thing I can tell you is there's plenty of motive. I spoke to his sister."

Beatrice stared at her. "His sister!"

"Don't worry. This wasn't a pushy journo intruding on grief.

I dropped her a note saying I'd been commissioned to do a reportage on his life."

"Have you any such commission?"

"Not yet. But I will get one. Beatrice, you're going to have to trust me on methodology, OK?"

Beatrice nodded, aware she'd asked Ana to get information off the record. "OK. I just don't want to..."

"Neither do I. His sister is a lovely person. She adored her brother. Silva's wife is a doctor and they recently adopted a child from Romania."

"Marcia."

"You knew about her? So you heard all about the adoption agency hassles?"

"No, just the child's name and where she came from."

Ana rotated her laptop so Beatrice could see the screen and navigated to the website.

"Cloverfield – Creating Happy Families. Or more accurately, ripping off well-heeled couples and making kids miserable until they squeeze out every last cent. Silva sued them for emotional damage to the kid, himself and his wife. Their lawyer accused Cloverfield of 'naked profiteering from the vulnerable' which by all accounts was a pretty generous description. These guys were traffickers in all but name. Judge found for Silva, Cloverfield went bankrupt and the disgraced manager made a death threat. Motive One."

"Where is the manager based?" asked Beatrice.

"Bucharest. I've looked him up and it seems he was at a wedding on Saturday, but this guy has connections. He could easily have called in a favour."

"Go on."

Ana slugged her Super Bock. "There's another possible motive tucked away in family history. Samuel Silva fell out with his brother after their father died four years ago. Pops left his estate to Samuel as the eldest male. We're talking a valuable property. Unless you flog it, you can't exactly divide it by three. Little brother Salvatore disputed the will and the two fell out. The real kicker is that Pops was typical old-school. The will states that on Samuel's death, Salvatore inherits his estate, leaving second-born Olivia and Samuel's wife – and, as of then, hypothetical kids – out of the picture. So we've got money as Motive Two. Here's a picture of Salvatore. Geeky, right?"

Beatrice studied the bespectacled image, a screenshot from his employee page on CP Railways. He looked harmless and rather sad. Yet the same could be said of many of the world's worst serial killers.

"Then there's Motive Three – Jealousy. We both reached the same conclusions about Nelson Monteiro. He and Silva were colleagues and friends, working on the same subject. But only Silva was offered a contract to publish his findings in a book..."

Beatrice snapped her head up.

"Wait, I'm not sure it's *the* book. Silva was working with a ghostwriter to produce something called *Lone Wolf*. It's not fiction, more a sociological or psychological study on individual terrorists. Don't give me that look, I'm using the term terrorist correctly. Not random violence but driven by a mission to change the status quo. And before you start, no, I've not attended a seminar on politically correct phrasing, but I do my homework."

Beatrice nodded as she scooped the froth off her coffee. "Fair enough. I assume you know the name of the ghostwriter? Then we can find the publisher."

"Not yet. I called Olivia from the airport and she'd never heard of the book. I asked her to find out what she could from Silva's widow. I took the opportunity to mention Monteiro and she dismissed the jealousy motive out of hand. As you said, the two men were godfathers to each other's kids and Monteiro even testified as a witness for Silva in the court case. She insists Nelson Monteiro and Samuel Silva have always been like brothers."

"In which case, two of Samuel Silva's 'brothers' are under suspicion," Beatrice muttered.

"True. As I see it, we have three leads. Revenge, family money and professional rivalry. Which one do you want me to work first?"

"I'd like to put that question to the rest of the team. We're due to meet on the terrace in ten minutes. I suggest you use this room as a makeshift office while I attend the last sessions of the day. As soon as I'm done, which will be five or near as dammit, we leave for the villa."

"Sounds like a plan. Can I use the loo?"

Over many years of managing teams, Beatrice had learnt that regardless of how well you balance skills, cultural compatibility, gender and experience, there is one factor that can wreck the most harmonious and focused of groups.

Sex.

Introducing the undeniably attractive Ana to a new, loosely formed team was a risk. Especially if Beatrice's instincts were right, and the accidental team already contained a level of sexual tension. Not to mention the fact Gilchrist had issued an explicit order, asking them not to discuss the case with anyone external. All of this had flammable potential.

So as they strode across the terrace to meet the Swiss, American and Icelander, all Beatrice's senses were on high alert. She noted the curiosity in Xavier's eyes, the appreciative interest in Roman's expression as he stood to meet them and Cher's brief assessment of this naturally lovely creature as they shook hands. The one thing she'd not considered was Ana's forceful personality and direct expression.

"Good to meet you all. I want to say that I'm willing to chuck everything I've got into helping you solve this. For me, the story comes second. You can count on my discretion. Beatrice called me for a favour because she trusts me to keep my trap shut. You don't know me from Adam, but I hope you will all give me the benefit of the doubt. What I do best is find information. It's up to you what you do with it."

A silence lingered for several seconds then Cher's eyes bulged.

"Beatrice, Gilchrist is heading our way. What is our story? Who is Ana and why is she here?"

"An old friend. Exchange student from years back. All true."

"And what innocuous job does she hold?" Cher hissed.

"Good evening!" called Gilchrist, as he took in the group of five. "New face on the block if I'm not mistaken." He flashed a dazzling smile at Ana.

Beatrice stepped up. "Commander Gilchrist, this is Ana Herrero, an old friend who lives in Portugal. As mentioned, I'm combining work and leisure, so invited Ana here to meet me today."

"Delighted to meet you, Ms Herrero. Do you live in the region?"

"Porto. It's just over an hour away. I'm a tour guide of the port wine caves. Like a bat, I spend a lot of the time in the dark."

Everyone at the table laughed just a touch too heartily.

Gilchrist grinned. "How fascinating! Are you staying the night? I'd love to hear more about your insights."

"No, much as it looks a grand place, I can't. As Beatrice said, I'm a friend of the family. Tonight, we're all having dinner together. A reunion I'm looking forward to more than I can say."

"Oh well, perhaps I'll be able to visit the caves before I return home. Do you have a card?" Gilchrist bestowed another charming smile.

"If I worked for a single company, I would. As a freelancer, I'm not tied to a particular house, so I don't know which one will hire me from week to week. Vila Nova da Gaia isn't that big, though, so you'll probably find me coming up for a few minutes of sunlight. How do you all like Gêres?"

Cher spoke first. "We only saw a little but it is incredibly beautiful. I want to come back here for a holiday. I think Beatrice organised this work-life balance perfectly. I envy you, Ana."

"Ah yes, you can count on Stubbs for European cooperation," said Gilchrist. "Well, nice to meet you and enjoy your reunion. Good evening, all."

Cher looked from the retreating Commander's back at Ana and spoke in a low voice. "You are one class act. Even I believed you. I think you're going to work out just fine." She raised a clenched hand and Ana returned the fist bump while Beatrice exhaled a guttural sigh of relief.

But she knew that from now on, Gilchrist would be watching.

Chapter 17

Porto's art installation, the steep cobbled backstreets, the blue-tiled station, the cathedral, the bridge, the port wine-caves and all the little squares, statues and parks were each uniquely absorbing. Adrian could have spent hours meandering around any one of them. Hours were not an option with Will, who urged him from one sight to the next, cramming as much as possible into their day.

The heat grew so oppressive that by midday even Action Man began to flag. They walked back across the Dom Luis bridge and sought a restaurant on the Ribeira to sit, rest, eat and people watch in the shade. Will ordered two beers and scrutinised the menu, while Adrian sat back and relaxed. Children chased each other along the quay, oriental-looking boats bobbed in the river and cats prowled the walls in an attempt to charm tourists in the same way their ancestors must have beguiled fishermen.

"That guy in Braga recommended something with *bacalhau*, or salted cod, didn't he? Do you remember the name of it? They've got several *bacalhau* dishes on the menu here and I'd like to try it at least once."

"No idea. I gave the note to Matthew. Let me have a look and see if anything jogs my memory."

Will handed over the menu. "Then after lunch, what about taking the tram up the river to the beach? Spend a while exploring Foz before we head back to the car."

"As long as it involves sitting down, I'm ready for anything. This one looks possible. All I can recall of what that bloke said is it sounded like peephole." Adrian pointed to a dish described as *Bacalhau a Zé do Pipo*.

The waiter placed two beers on the table and Will asked him to describe the cod dish. Adrian tuned out, his curiosity piqued by three vociferous old women on the quay, all dressed in black, yelling and gesticulating at each other as if about to throw a punch. Then the most grizzled of the three burst into wheezy laughter and the only punches thrown were gentle bunts on the shoulder.

"It sounds delicious so I ordered it for both of us and a half bottle of white," said Will. "I have to drive later, so you can finish it. Are you listening?"

Adrian reached across to squeeze Will's thigh. "I wasn't, but I am now. So we're having Peephole Cod? Good. Which wine did you choose?"

"Vinho verde. I wish we had time for a cruise up the Douro. I'd love to see the vineyards at sunset."

"We can always come back. Anyway, we hate cruises. Far too many other people. Look at that kitten! It's actually squaring up to a Jack Russell!"

Will looked and laughed. "The dog's backing off. It may only be a ball of fluff, but it's fluff with attitude."

"Too cute. If only we could pop it in a pocket and take it home. A little kitty-kat around the flat until we have space for a... what's the matter?" He followed Will's sightline.

Leon and Marianne, arm in arm, strolled along the quay laughing at something on Marianne's phone. Adrian's spirits sank. That morning, when discussing plans, Will had announced their plan of visiting Porto. Leon and Marianne said they wanted to explore the national park of Gerês. Matthew, Tanya and Luke were happy to stay by the pool, so the party set off in different directions. Now, it appeared, all four were in the same place. He knew Will would chalk this up as another instance of Leon's bad character. Adrian didn't want any embarrassing drama or fuss.

"Well, well, well. A long way from the park, aren't they?" Will's tone was snide and Adrian sensed a tension, an urge to challenge.

"Leave them. They don't want to be with us and we don't want to be with them. So they told a little porkie? What of it?"

Will took a long draught of his beer and got to his feet. "I want evidence of this. I won't talk to them or make a scene; I just want proof that he's a liar. Stay there, I'll be back before the food arrives."

"Will!" Adrian protested, but DS William Quinn had already joined the slipstream of tourists thronging the promenade, camera at the ready. Adrian shook his head, irritated by his boyfriend's obsessive behaviour but still appreciative of how good he looked in a pair of shorts.

Lunch was tense and awkward. Will, fired up by what he'd seen, wanted to discuss the other couple's behaviour. Adrian did not want to hear anything about Leon or Marianne or listen to Will's theories. They ate in silence, both pretending it was companionable. The coolness persisted even as they boarded the rickety wooden tram to Foz. It trundled along the riverside, affording the occupants a variety of views; fishermen drying nets, boys playing football in bare feet, two older women smoking in a doorway. Anger subsided and Adrian pressed his shoulder against Will.

"You should get a shot of that," he said, pointing to a line of washing, quite literally all the colours of the rainbow, fluttering across an alleyway.

Will obliged and replaced his camera in his bag. "Sulk over?"

"I wasn't sulking. I was angry with you. But I've said my piece and we moved on. All I want is a peaceful, friendly holiday and I'm prepared to compromise. Your contribution is a promise not to stir the shit. Can we please just enjoy ourselves?"

Will gave a slow, guilty smile and draped an arm around Adrian's shoulder.

"I love you," he whispered.

"I love you too. Especially when you're off duty."

They rumbled along, the silence more harmonious. A woman in a flowery pinafore boarded the tram carrying a bag of salt cod. The smell pervaded the whole carriage and Adrian turned his face to the open window.

Above the noise of the tram, Will spoke into his ear. "The thing is, Adrian, I'm never off duty. Can you live with that? A detective who never stops using his eyes and ears? Or is that going to be a deal-breaker? I'd like to know sooner rather than later."

Adrian turned back and shook his head. "Don't be so Inspector Morse. I already live with it, from you and from Beatrice. All I want is a nice peaceful holiday without inventing theories and spying on our companions. Look! There's the sea! Portugal is so beautiful. I really think I could live here."

The camera snapped and Adrian saw Will had photographed him rather than the sea. "Me too. In fact, I could live anywhere with you."

"You're changing the subject," he said, but moved closer till their legs touched on the creaking wooden bench.

Chapter 18

As the Fiat 500 pulled up outside the villa, slightly later than expected due to Beatrice's inexact navigation, Tanya careened across the drive, arms spread wide with a grin to match. Ana leapt out of the driver's seat and rushed into her embrace. The gasps and laughs echoed across the courtyard and Beatrice found herself beaming as she heaved the bags from the boot.

"Talk about a rabbit out of a hat!" Tanya said, her arm around Ana's shoulders. "What is it, twenty years? I'd never have thought of finding you. Yet again, DCI Stubbs, you're full of surprises."

"Frankly, both of you need a kick up the rear," said Beatrice. "When you find a friend, someone you connect with, regardless of what personal dramas you have in your lives, keep in touch. There. That's your lecture for today and I'm ready for an aperitif."

The welcoming committee had prepared canapés and chilled white port by the poolside. Beatrice stood back to allow the party to reunite. While Ana had first met Tanya as an exchange student under the charge of herself and Matthew, her familiarity with Adrian was relatively new. Yet for all the effusive hugs and squeals, it looked to Beatrice as if they'd known each other for ever.

"You look fabulous!"

"So do you! Look at the colour of you!"

"I take tanning seriously. I'm so happy you're here!"

"Me too! Where's this gorgeous man of yours?"

"Will, come meet Ana."

While introductions were made, Beatrice sat down with a thump on a sun bed. Matthew joined her and placing his hand on her back, asked in a low voice, "How was today?"

"Useful. I'd go so far as to say we have a lead or two. Yours?"

"Very relaxing. We explored the valley and found hundreds of lizards. Luke will show you photos of every last one. However, storm clouds have gathered over the sisters. Couple of tiffs and a bit of tension. Hopefully, the lovely Ana will defuse all that. It really is a pleasure to see her again."

"Nice for Tanya too, having a friend her own age. So, what's for dinner? I'm ravishing."

A small voice came from behind her. "So am I."

Beatrice half turned and saw Luke's steady blue eyes flick between her and Matthew. She got to her feet. "In that case, let us demand to be fed. After all, we've both had a hard day."

"Have you been swimming too?" Luke asked, slipping his hand into hers.

"Yes, but not in the water. Did you go back to the beach?" she asked, as they made their way indoors.

"No. Grandad, me and Mum stayed here all day. Will and Adrian went to Porto and brought me a hammer. I'll show you." He rushed back outside and returned with a large squeaky plastic hammer which he bounced lightly off Beatrice's head.

"The perfect present! Mind you don't mess up my hair. What about Marianne and Leon? What did they do today?"

The smile left Luke's face and he shrugged. "Dunno. Are you staying here now? With that lady?"

"For tonight, but we have to get back to work tomorrow. It's a shame because I really wanted to explore this park. Apparently there are a lot of lizards. I wish I could have seen some."

Luke's cheeks rose into apples. "Wait there! I've got something to show you!"

He pelted up the stairs and Beatrice wandered into the kitchen. Tea towels lay across a variety of dishes, actively encouraging curiosity. Salads, breads, cold meats and several colourful dishes rested beneath and a tray of potato wedges glistened in the oven. Beatrice stole a slice of bread and a glance at the door.

Will leaned on the door jamb, a reproachful look on his face.

"It's a fair cop, guv," said Beatrice, with her mouth full.

"Hard day?"

"Yes, but Ana made it easier. How was yours?"

Will frowned. "I'm a bit concerned and wouldn't mind picking your brains. If we could find five minutes for a chat sometime this..."

The sound of small feet thundering down the stairs made them both turn.

Beatrice swallowed her bread. "Course we can. But first I need to look at some lizards."

The meal went perfectly until dessert. Ana had a wealth of stories to tell and made an instant connection with Will. Adrian's food and wine choices were sublime, as expected, and almost everyone ate heartily. Having her own friend seemed to release Tanya's sparkle, so the table rang with laughter and memories. Beatrice was surprised how much the girls could remember from the exchange trip nineteen years previously. In her own mind, it was all a bit soft-focus and vague. So much energy and congeniality filled the room; it was almost possible to ignore the near-silent couple at the end of the table.

Matthew made several attempts to offer them more ham or peppers or wine, which were consistently refused. Marianne ate a small portion of potatoes and a few fried whitebait, but Leon merely shoved a few pieces of meat around his plate and left a single bread roll untouched. He drank only water and made no eye contact with anyone. Passive-aggressive attention-seeking infuriated Beatrice into active aggression, so she chose to completely ignore him.

Just after nine, Luke said his goodnights and Tanya took him off to bed, while Beatrice helped Adrian clear the table. The second time she came out of the kitchen, she sensed something had changed.

Will was speaking. "We thought Porto was beautiful. So atmospheric, and the architecture is a constant surprise. Even the train station deserved a photograph. As for the riverside, it's a people watcher's dream. Did you and Marianne like it?"

"Sorry?" asked Leon, his expression so contemptuous it was close to a sneer.

"I asked if you liked Porto. We saw you there this afternoon. Obviously we were a bit surprised. When we announced we were going to Porto today, I could have sworn you told us you were going to tour the national park. Had we known, we could have taken the one car and left Matthew with the Panda."

Adrian brought out a large plate with oranges and meringues and set it on the table. Only then did he notice the atmosphere. "What?"

Marianne rested her hand on Leon's arm. "Easy to make a mistake in a bunch of tourists. I imagine there are a lot of couples who look like us."

"I'm a detective, Marianne. I don't make assumptions. To be honest, I don't need to when you walk right past our table. I even took a picture, want to see?"

An unpleasant silence hung over the table and Beatrice saw Adrian throw a thunderous glare at Will.

Marianne began. "Look, the thing is..."

Leon pulled his arm away from Marianne and stood up. "I can speak for myself, thank you. Yes, we were in Porto. We chose to tell a white lie and go alone because the truth is I don't want to spend every single second in the family pocket. I respect the fact that you want to organise your lives around the whims of a child but I don't. This is my holiday too and I want to do what I enjoy and spend some time with my partner. And I am not going to apologise for that. Thanks for dinner. Goodnight."

He threw down his napkin, reached for Marianne's hand and they left the room, to the sound of Marianne's sniffs.

"Will!" Adrian put his hands on his hips and faced his partner. "Why do you insist on winding him up? I thought we agreed not to mention seeing them!"

Tanya came back into the room with a big grin and a bottle. "He's crashed out. Now who's for a vinho do Porto? What's the matter?"

Matthew patted the chair next to him. "Sit down, my dear one. It seems Will and Adrian saw Marianne and Leon in Porto today, despite their apparent intention of going to tour the park. Will just challenged them in the deception and Leon took offence."

"Which was completely unnecessary and ruined the evening," said Adrian. "If they want to sneak off, it's up to them. What is your problem with him?"

Will revolved the stem of his glass between his fingers. "My problem with him is his attitude to Luke. Didn't you just hear what he said? *I respect the fact that you want to organise your lives around the whims of a child but I don't.* Look, I've been watching his behaviour and I'm sorry, but really, really don't like the way he treats Luke."

"He said what?" gasped Tanya.

"That's enough." Matthew didn't shout, but the gravitas in his tone stilled the room. "Ana, I apologise for such a scene in front of a most welcome guest. I think the best thing would be to retire for the evening and consider our respective behaviours. Beatrice and I will adjourn to our room. I appreciate you have things to say, Will, but we can discuss any issues in the cold light of morning. Tanya, I expect you and Ana might enjoy a glass of port on the terrace. Just be aware that sound carries. Thank you all for dinner and I'll be up for breakfast at seven. Beatrice, do you want to bring your dessert upstairs?"

Beatrice hesitated. "Yes, good idea. But before all this blew up, I had planned to talk shop with Will. If you don't mind, Adrian, I'd just like to borrow him for a few minutes."

Adrian shook his head, his face set and stony. "I don't mind."

Ana put her hand on Adrian's shoulder. "Come and have a glass of port with us. I want to try a bit of your Orange Eton Mess or whatever it is."

"It's called a Good Luck Charm cake. Perhaps we could have done with it a bit earlier before *someone* decided to wreck the atmosphere. Yes, let's leave these two to their police gossip and enjoy our pud outside."

Beatrice left them to their desserts and followed Will out the back door towards the pool. They walked to the garden chairs at the far end, the furthest they could get from the house. The evening air, still warm and fragrant, had a soothing effect as they sat and gazed at the underwater lights.

"I assume it's Leon you wanted to discuss?" Beatrice said.

Will nodded twice. "Adrian thinks it's an ego thing between us, but I'm afraid it's worse than that. He forgets that I trained in behavioural psychology. Beatrice, I really believe Leon has a worrying number of signs to indicate Narcissistic Personality Disorder. Did you know Marianne gave her cat away because of him?"

"Gave it away? Why?"

"He told her he's allergic and said he wouldn't move in with her if the cat remained. So she gave it to Matthew. Now, when we saw them today, we were having a beer and they walked right past our table. I left Adrian people-watching and followed them. I was determined to get a photograph. They stopped at a restaurant on the Ribeira, not far from us, and ordered food. I got several shots of their faces with the river and the bridge in the background. Then I noticed movement on the wall behind them. Cats. Lots of them. Sunbathing, scratching or washing themselves, right behind the man with an allergy. And Leon was smiling, chatting and completely fine."

"That's odd, but hardly enough to classify as NPD."

Will hunched forward and dropped his voice. "Narcissists have to be the centre of attention. They dislike anything that takes attention away from them. Luke has bruises on his upper arm in the shape of a handprint. Someone has treated him pretty harshly. Remember how fractious Luke was the evening after Marianne and Leon brought him back to the villa? Often, especially with new partners, narcissists push away the partner's family, friends, children or pets and insist on a hundred percent devotion."

"If you think he hurt Luke, we need confirmation of that. Otherwise I'd class his behaviour as just a bit too possessive," Beatrice replied. "It's quite common, especially with a couple who've found each other later in life. They've both been single a long time."

"Well, that's what he told her. He said he couldn't find anyone who matched up to his ideals. Another narcissistic indicator, incidentally. But I did a little bit of research on social media and found some direct contradictions to what we know. His Facebook profile is squeaky clean, but by befriending a few of his contacts under a false profile, I found a lot of photographs and conversations which at the very least catch him out in blatant deception."

"Everyone exaggerates on Facebook," said Beatrice.

"There's exaggeration and outright lies. Six months ago he had an engagement party with his Polish girlfriend, Iwona, after a 'whirlwind romance'. Shortly before that, a girl called Nicky blogged about Love Rat Leon, who broke her heart. The photos are clearly of him, the most recent dated a year ago.

"It's not just Facebook. He describes himself as a business consultant. The reality is that he works as a salesman for an amusements company, flogging gambling machines to pubs and arcades."

Beatrice placed her hand on Will's forearm. "Why are you doing this?"

He didn't answer right away. He rubbed at his stubble and stared into the pool, his eyes reflecting the turquoise ripples.

"He's a fraud, Beatrice. I have an instinct for people like him. He's going to damage your family and I can't stand back and watch that happen."

They sat in silence for a few seconds, listening to a faint burst of laughter and some subsequent shushing from the other side of the house.

Beatrice sighed. "Marianne is an adult. We have to let her make her own choices, or mistakes."

Will shook his head emphatically. "I don't think she is, emotionally. Even so, Luke is a child. Having such a toxic person around makes him vulnerable."

A light went on above their heads and Matthew's silhouette filled the window frame. He looked down for a moment and Beatrice waved. He turned away.

"Leave it with me. Don't provoke any more confrontations with Leon or Marianne. Don't inflame Tanya with your concerns, but make sure Luke is never left alone with him. I'll arrange some background checks and see if we have legitimate cause to alert the others. Where Adrian and Matthew are concerned, my feeling is to play it down. How do you see it, DS Quinn?"

"Fair enough, Ma'am."

Beatrice stood up and bent to kiss Will's cheek. He reached up an arm to embrace her and she squeezed his shoulder.

"I'm very glad you care, Will. Tell Adrian I said that. Night night."

"G'night and thanks for listening."

Matthew was in bed, reading. Or at least pretending to. Beatrice brushed her teeth, moisturised and sent two rapid emails. One to Dawn Whittaker, with a request for background information on Leon Charles. One to her own counsellor, James, asking for advice on Narcissistic Personality Disorder.

She put the laptop back in her bag, donned her pyjamas and got under the duvet. Matthew accepted her kiss goodnight but said nothing. She lay back on the pillow, unable to resist replaying Will's observations.

Matthew turned out the light. "Stop it."

"Stop what?"

"Thinking. Go to sleep and save it for tomorrow. Otherwise you'll fidget-arse all night and keep us both awake."

"Fair enough. I'll try."

He turned his back to her, pummelled his pillow and let out a deep sigh. "Matthew?"

"What?"

"I never had my dessert."

He didn't reply, but his silent laughter shook the mattress.

Chapter 19

By the time Adrian showered, dressed and descended at half-past eight, the only person up and about was Matthew. In his cargo shorts and blue shirt, he looked like a dishevelled David Attenborough, making coffee after a long night of observing gorillas.

"Good morning! I suppose Beatrice and Ana are long gone?"

Matthew looked up with a vague smile. "Good morning, Adrian. Yes, they left over an hour ago and even then they were running late. How did you sleep?"

Adrian sat at the table and reached for some juice. "When we finally got to sleep, which must have been after two, I slept well. Obviously we had a few things to hash out. Will's in the shower now and before anything else, he's going over to apologise to Leon for last night."

Matthew switched the kettle on and spooned coffee grounds into the cafetière. He selected three cups and poured milk into a jug.

"I'm pleased to hear that. Beatrice and I had a serious discussion this morning. Will's heart is in the right place and we both appreciate his concerns. I feel we should be nice yet watchful."

"So do I. But I hate atmospheres. First thing, I'll go over and get Marianne to come out on some pretext or other, leaving the coast clear for Will and Leon to talk man to man. Then we can all have breakfast like civilised human beings."

An expression of relief smoothed Matthew's features. "That sounds very grown up to me. As to breakfast, I'm toying with the idea of scrambled eggs with bacon. Could I tempt you?"

Adrian slugged more grapefruit juice, relishing the acidity on his palate. "Oh yes, you most definitely could. Have we got any salmon? Because Will..."

"Oh God!" Tanya wandered into the room in shortie pyjamas and fluffy socks, with bed hair and traces of last night's make-up. "I need caffeine and I need it now. Whose idea was port wine and cigars? My mouth feels like a pub carpet."

"Port and cigars?" Matthew poured boiling water into the cafetière and replaced the lid. "Were you founding your own gentleman's club?"

Tanya slumped into the chair beside Adrian and made feeble clutching motions at the table. "Juice! Juice! I blame that wicked Portuguese-Irish female. She always has led me astray. Oh thank you so much."

She wrapped both hands round the glass Adrian gave her and drank deeply, making noises like a suckling calf. Matthew rummaged around in the fridge, pulling out eggs, bacon, milk, salmon, butter and cream, humming something by Vivaldi.

"Is Luke still in the Land of Nod?"

Tanya put down her empty glass. "Yep, flat out when I just looked in. Don't wait for him. Sometimes he'll sleep through till ten if he's had a late night. Feed me and feed me now. Adrian, your cake last night was to die for. Confession time. After you went to bed, I had seconds. Where's the coffee, Dad?"

"Good morning everyone, how are we all today?" Will entered, freshly showered and shaved, smelling divine. Adrian watched him with a mixture of admiration, love and lust.

He met Adrian's eyes as if he could read his thoughts and jerked his head in the direction of the garden flat. "I'm ready when you are."

Adrian checked his watch. "They rarely emerge before nine. Shall we have a coffee first?"

Tanya glanced between them. "Don't tell me you're going to apologise. Will had every right to say what he did and I for one..."

"Tanya?" Matthew interrupted. "Do you want bacon or salmon with your scrambled eggs?"

"Both. But first I need some coffee. Anyway, Will, I really don't think...."

"It wasn't Will's decision, Tanya, it was mine," said Adrian. "I want us to have a nice holiday with no tensions. If Will says sorry, we can get back to enjoying ourselves and perhaps give each other a bit more space. For all our sakes, I think it's best."

Matthew had his back to them, slicing bread, but his silence acted as tacit approval.

Tanya groaned. "Oh God, everyone is dancing attendance on him as if he's a VIP. Well, I'll tell you one thing, when we get back, he can forget the kid gloves and stop being so precious. Because I don't need another attention-seeking child in my life. Luke is five. He's allowed to try it on. Leon is an adult and needs to bloody well grow up. Right, if no one else is making the coffee, I'll do it myself."

Will looked away, towards the open doorway. "They're up. Marianne's sitting on their terrace in a robe. Let's get it over with."

"OK." Adrian drained his glass and got to his feet.

An agonised scream shattered the peace of the kitchen. Glass, metal and liquid hit the tiled floor. Adrian whirled round to see Tanya's shocked face, the smashed cafetière and coffee grounds all over her left arm and down both her bare legs.

"Oh my God!" Matthew exclaimed. "What have you done?"

Will pushed past Adrian and put his hand on Tanya's back. "Cold running water on it, as soon as possible. Quick, let's use the pool shower. Watch your feet."

White-faced and trembling, she allowed him to guide her outside.

Adrian waved a hand at Matthew. "You go and see if she's OK. I'll clear up in here."

He'd just finished mopping the floor and wrapping the broken glass in newspaper when Matthew returned.

"Adrian, the burns look rather nasty. Will's going to drive her to the nearest hospital to get a professional assessment. He says we should cover the scalded areas with cling film. Do we have any? And where are the car keys?"

"Keys on the windowsill and the cling film is in this drawer. Here. Are you going with them? I can hold the fort here, make Luke's breakfast and so on."

Matthew hesitated. "If you're sure you don't mind? She's still my little girl, even if she does drink port and smoke cigars."

"Come on. Let's get her wrapped up and into the car."

When they got outside, Tanya's trembles under the cold water had become teeth-chattering shivers. Will's forehead creased with concern.

"Adrian, could you fetch a bottle of water and a blanket? And in my sponge bag, there are some painkillers."

"It doesn't hurt," said Tanya, her voice wobbling.

"Not as long as it has cold water on it. But we have a bit of a drive ahead, so you should take some now."

By the time Adrian had gathered pills, tissues, blanket, water and a handful of energy bars, the party were already in the car, Tanya half-wrapped in plastic.

Matthew sat in the back seat beside her and draped the blanket around her shoulders. "Adrian, look after Luke, would you?"

"Of course. Don't worry about us and call me as soon as you know anything," he said and kissed Will goodbye. The Peugeot crawled across the bumpy track to the road then picked up speed once on tarmac. Adrian watched till it turned the corner and disappeared.

Back in the kitchen, he dug around in the cupboards until he found an old aluminium Moka coffeepot and started the essential process of getting his morning fix of caffeine. It would help him think straight. He was just smiling to himself at the pun when the door opened. Marianne walked in without looking at him, went straight over to the windowsill and picked up the second set of keys.

"Seeing as someone's already taken the Peugeot without even discussing it, I hope you won't mind if Leon and I use the Panda?" she said, heading for the door.

Adrian's mouth fell open in disbelief. "Will took the Peugeot to drive Tanya to hospital. You weren't consulted because serious burns take priority over petty squabbling about cars."

Marianne's sour expression turned to one of confusion. "What are you talking about?"

"Tanya spilt the contents of the cafetière over herself. Will thought the burns were serious enough to need medical attention, so he and Matthew have gone to the local A&E to get her checked out."

"Oh shit. Is she all right?"

"No. She's badly scalded. And for your information, before that happened, Will was coming over to see you this morning to apologise. We don't want any tensions to spoil this holiday, so it would be really helpful if you could drop the attitude so that we can all behave like adults."

"Yes. Sorry. We were both upset, that all." She sat down, her voice quiet. "We thought some space would be best."

"I disagree. I think clearing the air with an apology and accepting your wishes to do whatever you want would be best. Especially for Matthew and Luke."

Marianne's eyes flicked to his face. "Where is Luke?"

"Still in bed. I offered to stay and look after him. Tanya said he..."

"Problem?" Leon stood in the open doorway, addressing Marianne.

Marianne's expression was a mixture of guilt and concern. "No...well, yes. Tanya scalded herself with coffee this morning, so Will and Dad took her to hospital."

"Sorry to hear that."

The coffeepot began to gurgle.

Adrian took a deep breath. "Good morning, Leon. As I just told Marianne, Will and I were about to come over and apologise this morning when Tanya had her accident. We don't want an atmosphere between us. Would you like some coffee?"

Leon kept his eyes on Marianne. "No thanks, I think we should go."

Adrian continued as if he hadn't spoken. "And Marianne agreed it's better if we all behave like grown-ups and enjoy the holiday." He poured coffee into three cups. "As far as Tanya will be able to enjoy herself after this morning. Boiling water burns are very painful. I just hope she won't end up with any scars." He placed the cups on the table. "Help yourself to milk and sugar. I'll just pop upstairs and check on Luke."

He bounded up the tiled staircase, releasing some of the pent-up anger triggered by Leon's petulant expression. He sulked more than a five-year-old, which was a frankly unattractive trait in a grown man. Adrian pushed open the door and looked in on the sleeping figure of Luke in his Spiderman pyjamas. His duvet had been kicked to one side, but even so his fringe seemed damp with sweat. Adrian tentatively pressed the back of his hand against Luke's cheek to gauge his temperature. Warm, but not feverish. Good job. He had no idea what to do with children when they were healthy, let alone when they were sick.

He crossed the hall to his own room, for no other reason than to give the couple downstairs time to review their stropping policy. While he was there, he went into the bathroom to check his hair and wash his face. Voices floated up from the terrace, through the open window. Despite himself, Adrian crept closer to listen. He knew eavesdroppers rarely hear good of themselves, but they often hear worse of others.

Marianne and Leon were leaning on the terrace railing.

"Because I don't want to!" hissed Leon.

Adrian noted he was carrying a coffee cup. One point to Adrian.

Marianne's voice was harder to hear, her tone low and her face directed out over the valley. A few words floated up. "...can't just leave him here... surely?"

"I'm not staying here. I want some space. I thought you understood that."

Marianne stayed silent. *Go on. Tell him to piss off,* Adrian willed her.

She turned to Leon with an imploring look and Adrian could hear her more clearly. "How about we take him with us?"

Leon's head retracted, affecting mock disbelief, as if he were an affronted turtle. "Take him with us? How does that give me space? I can't believe how my needs are always at the bottom of the list. Everyone treats that bloody child like some kind of princeling, as if his welfare trumps all. So his dad left. Happens to half the population. He's nothing special. If you want to stay here, you're welcome. I'll go on my own."

Marianne's pitch rose. "No, darling, I don't want that. But you know why I can't leave Luke here, alone with Adrian. You must understand that."

Leon placed his empty cup on the terrace table. "Let me ask you this. Who is more important to you? Your sister's kid or the man you say you love? Think carefully, Marianne. I'm leaving in five minutes, with or without you."

Adrian stepped away from the window and rested his head on the shower stall, trying to block the echo of her words. *I can't leave Luke here, alone with Adrian. Alone with Adrian. With Adrian.*

When he heard the car drive away, Adrian washed his face again and went downstairs. As expected, the kitchen was empty. Their coffee cups, still wet, rested on the draining board. He made a fresh pot of coffee and sat down to read the online news till Luke awoke. He checked his mobile every few minutes but it showed no messages. At quarter to nine, he heard a toilet flush upstairs. He closed his laptop and waited.

"Where's Mum?" Luke was dressed in an Ice Age t-shirt, shorts and trainers. He carried a mini iPad.

"Popped out for a bit. She'll be back soon. What do you want for breakfast, or should I say brunch? I can do scrambled eggs with bacon or salmon."

"Bacon, please. Salmon pongs. What's brunch?"

"What do you call the first meal of the day?"

Luke sat on a chair and put down his iPad. "Breakfast."

"Correct! Do you want juice?"

Luke nodded.

Adrian poured half a glass and asked, "And what do you call the meal in the middle of the day?"

"Lunch."

"Correct once again. You may have extra bacon. Now, what happens if you combine breakfast and lunch?"

"Brunch! Oh."

"What?"

"Does that mean I can't have any lunch if I have both together?"

"It depends. Some people don't want lunch as well as brunch. Brown or white?"

"White, please."

"Others, who run about a lot, swim, dive and expend a lot of energy, get hungry at lunchtime. Those people definitely deserve lunch. Shall we see how you feel when your mum gets back?"

"Yes. Because I think I probably am going to be hungry at lunchtime. And Will is definitely going to want lunch. He runs about a lot and swims and things."

"I think you might be right. We'd better make an extra huge lunch for them when they get back. Luke, does your mum let you have ketchup?"

"Yes, but only on burgers. With fish fingers we have tarty sauce."

"Right. Scrambled eggs aren't really either so I'll just leave it on the table and you can have some if you want. Here you go. We can make more toast if that's not enough."

Luke tucked in and Adrian searched for a topic of conversation before realising it was unnecessary. He ate his eggs, read his news and kept half an eye on his young charge in case he overdid the ketchup.

"Where's Grandpa?"

"He went with them."

"Why?"

"Luke, your mum had a little accident this morning. She spilt some hot water on herself. Don't worry, she'll be fine. When she gets home, she might have a few bandages and we'll have to take good care of her."

Luke's long-lashed blue eyes fixed on him. "OK. I had a bandage one time when I fell off my bike. All up here was covered in blood." He indicated his shoulder.

"Really? I would have fainted. Did you faint?"

"No. I cried though."

"Of course you cried. It must have hurt. I always cry when things hurt. Somehow that makes things better. But blood makes me faint."

Luke patted a pile of egg onto his toast and dabbed it in some ketchup. "My friend Ben says only girls cry." He stuffed the toast into his mouth.

Adrian curled his lip. "Then your friend Ben needs to grow up and develop a little emotional intelligence. More toast?"

"Yes please. Are you and Will going to have kids?"

Adrian popped two slices in the toaster which gave him time to frame his response.

"It's not something we've discussed. Even if we wanted children, it would be complicated. Biologically, men can't have babies, as I'm sure you know. We could adopt or use a surrogate, I suppose, if we really wanted a family."

Luke squirted a blob of ketchup onto his plate. "You totally should. You'd be great dads. I wish Mum would marry both of you. That'd be so cool!"

"Enough of the ketchup now. Here's your toast." Adrian started the washing-up so Luke couldn't see his face.

"Good morning, Flukey Lukey! That looks yummy!"

Adrian turned to see Marianne enter the kitchen, a bright smile on her face despite her puffy, reddened eyes. He watched her stroke Luke's hair, keeping her face averted from Adrian's gaze.

"It is! There was bacon too but I ate that already."

"Would you like some, Marianne? There's salmon if you prefer," Adrian offered, with an olive branch smile.

She shook her head. "Thanks, but Leon and I already had breakfast. Any news from the hospital?"

Luke looked up at her. "Who's in hospital?"

Adrian shot Marianne a glance and her complexion flushed salmon-pink.

"Oh, no one you know, darling. Just a friend of mine," she smiled down at him.

"Is it Mum? Adrian said she had an accident."

Marianne glared over Luke's head. "Mummy will be fine. In fact, I expect she'll be back any minute. Why don't you go outside and see if there's any sign of the car?"

"OK." Luke picked up the last bit of toast, hopped off the chair and ran out through the kitchen door.

With her scowl and folded arms, Marianne epitomised judgement. "You had no business telling him that. You'll only worry him."

Adrian struggled to keep his voice calm and his temper in check. "He came downstairs to find his mother and grandfather weren't here. What was I supposed to tell him? I told him the truth but played it down. Tanya doesn't wrap him in cotton wool. As she left him in my care, I followed her example."

"Yes, well, thanks for making him breakfast but I'll take over from here. He'll feel more comfortable around family."

Adrian stared at her. She lifted her chin and gave him a defiant look in return, then turned on her heel and left the kitchen.

"Any sign of that car yet, Lukey?"

Adrian finished the washing-up, tidied the kitchen and went

upstairs to change into his trunks. Thirty lengths of front crawl should take the edge of his rage.

When he finished his swim, he showered and rested in the shade until his pulse returned to normal. Neither Marianne nor Luke had made an appearance. He returned indoors to find his phone and saw a message from Will.

Tanya OK, but dr wants her to stay overnight. M & I leaving soon – back around midday. PS: Hungry!

Adrian checked his watch. Ten past eleven. He ran upstairs to change into a shirt and shorts before starting on lunch. He had his head in the fridge when a splash from outside caught his attention. Luke's head bobbed up in the middle of the pool, his water wings bright red against the turquoise water. He shouted something and Adrian followed his line of focus. Marianne reclined on a sun lounger, wearing oversized sunglasses and a floppy hat. She waved at Luke and went back to her laptop. An intense heat spread up Adrian's neck. She had waited till he left the pool before letting Luke go for a swim, as if Adrian represented some kind of danger.

His hands shook as he chopped onions for the fish chowder and he told himself that was the reason his eyes were watering. He followed the recipe and won a magnificent argument in his head.

Melt butter and fry garlic, leeks and onion.

Marianne, can I just pick up on something you said? 'He'll feel more comfortable around family'. You're aware that the vast majority of paedophiles are members of the victim's own family?

Stir in potatoes and season. Cook for three minutes.

And you should know that gay men are interested in other consensual gay men, rather than anything with a pulse and a penis.

Add the stock, wine, herbs and fish. Simmer for five minutes.

Child abuse is less about sex or sexuality and more about power, so why would you think a happy, healthy gay man in a loving relationship cannot be trusted with a child?

Strain liquid and reduce by boiling.

And one last thing, regarding Luke's welfare, I'd like to tell you what he said this morning. Out of nowhere, he told me he wished Tanya could marry Will and I because we'd be great dads.

Blow nose, wipe eyes, put bread in oven to warm.

He was adding cream and parsley to the chowder when he heard the car pull up outside. He threw the tea-towel over his shoulder and went to meet them.

Matthew's tired, grey face lifted into a smile as he saw Adrian in the doorway. "All well. She needs to stay in overnight, but due to instant expert treatment from Will, she's likely to escape without a scar. Please hang onto this man, Adrian. He is a true asset."

Arms full of stuff from the back seat, Will gave Matthew a friendly shove with his shoulder. "Of course he'll hang onto me. Good looks, fast car and first aid, what's not to love? His side of the bargain is good food and wine. So what's for lunch?"

"Fish chowder. Is she in much pain?"

Matthew shook his head. "Morphine. No more sunbathing for her, I know that much. Where's Luke?"

"In the pool. I'll give them a call and we can eat."

He gave the chowder a quick stir and made his way to the back garden. The pool area was empty. There were splashes and wet footprints all over the tiles, but no sign of life. He hadn't heard them go upstairs so Marianne must have taken Luke back to the garden flat. She really wasn't taking any chances.

In the kitchen, Will lifted the lid and inhaled. "I could eat all of this on my own. Are those scallops?"

"Yes. Don't touch. Matthew, do you want to choose a wine? Something light, I recommend."

Matthew opened the fridge. "I concur. Perhaps something suited to a spritzer. If I drink a glass of something strong on an empty stomach, I will collapse."

Will replaced the lid and took his seat. "Five places? You, me, Matthew, Luke and...?"

The kitchen door opened and Marianne burst in, wild-eyed and tearful. "I need the keys. Please, I need the keys to the car. Leon's gone!"

Adrian was the first to recover. "He went hours ago. What's the emergency?"

"I mean gone permanently! He sent a text." She waved her phone at them. "Said this holiday wasn't working and he had to leave. I need to get to the airport. I have to talk to him and he won't answer his phone. Keys, Will!"

Matthew closed the fridge door. "Marianne, sit down."

"Dad, I don't have time! I have to catch him before he gets on a plane."

"I said, sit down. You are in no fit state to drive. I want an explanation first. But before anything else, where is Luke?"

Marianne looked out of the window. "Still in the pool, I expect. When I got the message, I went back to the flat to see if Leon had taken his stuff. I left Luke here with Adrian."

Matthew looked at Adrian, blinking just once.

"He's not in the pool. I thought he was with Marianne. He must be upstairs. Will, can you..."

Will was out of the room before Adrian could finish. Matthew picked up the car keys and put them in his pocket, without looking at anyone. He opened the back door and called, "Luke! It's lunchtime! Luke? Are you hungry? We've got a surprise for you!"

Cicadas chittered and a magpie rattled from a nearby tree. Other than that, silence. Will's footsteps thudded downstairs.

"He's not there. Floor dry, no swimming trunks, nothing. Marianne, go back and check your flat. Adrian, search the house. Everywhere a kid might hide. Matthew and I will comb the gardens."

Marianne let out a short sob. "The thing is, I..."

Will rounded on her. "Sorry, this is no longer about you."

Chapter 20

When Ana and Beatrice had arrived at Gerês College of Hospitality earlier that morning, Roman, Cher and Xavier were waiting on the terrace to tell them a suspect had been arrested in the Silva murder case.

"His name is Marco Cordeiro and he's a casual labourer. He works for the hotel every summer as a gardener," said Xavier. "His prints match those on the window and they found Samuel's watch in his bike pannier."

Cher chimed in. "We don't have much information. My gut says we need to get to that police station and find out more, but today it's going to be pretty much impossible. Some of us are giving seminars and the rest of us need to show our faces."

"Ana doesn't." Roman looked at her. "What were your plans today?"

"To hide out in Beatrice's room and make some calls. But if you like, I'll see what I can find at the station first. I'm guessing he was taken to PSP in Viana do Castelo?"

"I guess. They didn't give out that information," said Cher.

Beatrice spotted Gilchrist talking to another man just inside the foyer. "OK, let's make a big show of saying goodbye and I'll call you during our lunch break."

Ana got to her feet and shook hands with each member of the party, ending with a hug for Beatrice. She walked off to her car, waving and waggling her fingers as if to remind Beatrice to email.

"Beautiful girl," said Cher.

"Stunning," agreed Roman.

"Very useful ally too," said Xavier.

"Yes, yes. Have I missed breakfast?" asked Beatrice.

The bitter truth was that she had. Nothing more than coffee carried her through the dull-as-ditchwater Compliance and Governance workshop, but the Unconscious Bias session was a revelation. Especially as she looked around the room and saw the lack of diversity amongst her colleagues.

When lunchtime finally arrived, she scurried out of the seminar and shot across to the canteen. She added black pepper and Parmesan to a large plate of Spaghetti Puttanesca and went to find a seat outside. She chose a table away from the general hubbub, hoping for some privacy to check her emails and call Ana. But after one mouthful, a voice said, "May I join you?" and she looked up. Commander Gilchrist beamed at her, the sun behind his head creating a Christ-like corona, giving the impression of a divine visitation.

Beatrice swallowed. "I would be honoured, sir."

She removed her handbag for him to place his tray beside hers. Beatrice noted the abundance of 'superfoods' on his plate, the majority of which she couldn't even pronounce. He wore a pale grey suit with a pink shirt and lilac tie. Up close, he was undeniably handsome, in a slightly over-groomed sort of way.

"How was your morning?" he asked, placing his napkin on his knees.

"Extremely beneficial. Dr Ruishalme's presentation on implicit bias was a real eye-opener. I plan to repeat the exact same session for my colleagues."

"Ah yes. Ruishalme knows her stuff. Scientific minds fascinate me. I'm more of a people person, bumbling along on instinct."

"Likewise. But you've done rather well without the science, sir."

"Allow me to return the compliment. In fact, I have heard

certain stripes say you could go still further." He smiled his TV-friendly smile and bit into a broccoli floret.

"As I'm sure you know, sir, my plans are to retire at the end of the year. I've had a good run and intend to quit before fulfilling the Peter Principle."

"Ah yes. Promotion due to competence till you reach a level at which you are incompetent? Does that ever happen in international law enforcement, do you think?" He widened his eyes in mock surprise, his smile still broad.

There was something in his manner that bordered on camp, as if he were playing to the gallery.

"It most certainly would if I were promoted any further. I'm already feeling a total fraud. A feeling which is exacerbated by having such a consummate professional and all-round nice guy as my boss."

Over Gilchrist's shoulder, she saw Cher, Roman and Xavier sitting at a nearby table, throwing concerned glances in her direction. She twisted strands of pasta around her fork.

"Of course," he said. "Rangarajan Jalan, known as The Incorruptible. A rare breed indeed," said the Commander.

Beatrice didn't like his tone. "Do you think so? In my experience, admittedly vastly inferior to your own, I have found my British and European colleagues to have the highest integrity, often in extraordinarily challenging circumstances. There might be the odd one whose motives are penal, but on the whole, I'd say I'm proud to be amongst our number."

Gilchrist had finished his measly portion of salad and dabbed at his lips with his napkin. "A noble sentiment I wish I could echo. My experience in the higher echelons is a different story, one of politics, intrigue and backstabbing. You know, the tales I could tell are downright Shakespearean. I suspect if one were to dig deeply, even the saintly Jalan has a skeleton in his closet."

At her feet, Beatrice's mobile vibrated silently through her handbag.

"I'm sure many senior executives in the business world

would say the same, sir. Sharks, piranhas and jellyfish swim in every corporate sea. Still, I can honestly say I have never heard a bad word against our Super, at any level."

"You're very loyal, Stubbs, and I admire that. As for the worlds of business and politics, do you know why our television screens are dominated with crime series, police dramas and detective stories? I'll tell you. Because we are the front line. We are the ultimate good guys. Politicians and businessmen face the same kind of power struggles, but those worlds can never deliver the thrills of police work. The reality is that we have the sexiest job in the world!" He laughed loudly and heads turned at other tables. Beatrice laughed too, hoping she didn't have basil stuck in her teeth.

"On which note, I will leave you now as I must catch up with Fisher," he said. "We're doing a repeat session on media briefing in the morning, streamed live on BluLite. You should try to catch it. Do you know Fisher? Our man from Interpol?"

Beatrice resisted the urge to curl her lip. "The name rings a bell. I'm sure our paths must have crossed somewhere," she lied. "Well, thank you for your company today."

"My pleasure. Oh, one more thing. Your friend I met yesterday? The young woman who works in the port wine industry. I'm rather a hobbyist wine buff, so thought I might pick her brains while I'm in Porto this weekend. How might I contact her?"

"If it's alright with you, sir, I'll give her your number. I follow police policy and never give out anyone's number or email without their permission. Even to those I trust."

Just the tiniest tightening of the jaw before the smile came again.

"Very wise. Yes, here's my card. Feel free to pass it on. Thank you. Must dash and see you later."

She checked her mobile. A voicemail from Ana.

"Call me when you get this. Someone here you should meet."

The taxi dropped her and Xavier outside the Café Camões at half past one. Ana was sitting in the window with another woman. She raised a hand in greeting as she saw them arrive.

"Beatrice, Xavier, this is Sandra Cordeiro, the mother of the suspect. *Sandra, posso apresentar a minha amiga Beatrice e o seu colego Xavier. O Xavier fala muito bem portugûes.*"

Sandra stood, shook their hands with a firm grip and said "*Muito prazer.*"

Xavier repeated the words so Beatrice attempted the same.

"I just explained that I'll need to translate for you, Beatrice. When I got to the police station, Sandra was there, pleading with them to let her see her son. They told her she should come back later, so I caught up with her as she was leaving. She is adamant her son did not kill Silva. I know, I know, what mother would say otherwise? But Sandra has some important details the local police dismissed as irrelevant, and I think someone ought to hear this."

Ana gestured for the woman to speak.

Sandra's demeanour impressed Beatrice. She seemed calm and dignified, with steady brown eyes in a careworn face. She spoke slowly and with emphasis, addressing Beatrice and Xavier in turn. Without understanding a word, Beatrice was already convinced by her sincerity.

Ana waited for her to take a pause then rattled off a translation.

"Marco is a migrant worker. He goes wherever he can to make money. He gets repeat employment because he's reliable and he's strong. In winter, he works in Andorra at a ski resort. In spring and autumn he usually gets employment on a farm, but can spend the summer at home with his family because of the hotel. He started there as a teenager and is well liked by the management. They find something for him every summer, gardening, driving, painting, anything that doesn't involve dealing with the public. He's not good with people.

"He works five days a week and Saturday mornings. On the day Silva died, Marco went to work as usual and came home for his lunch. Sandra says she shouted at him for leaving bits of grass all over the floor and the green stains on his trainers. He said he'd been mowing the hotel lawns. After lunch, he played football with the village team and came home for dinner because it was his sister's birthday."

Xavier made a note and Ana opened a palm to Sandra. She spoke in a rush, a mellifluous waterfall of whispery sounds, intense and emotional, almost like a song. Finally, Beatrice saw the tears build and her eyes redden, but she did not cry. She stopped, inhaled deep breaths and waited for Ana to catch up.

"Her son is well-mannered, respectful and very kind. He is always bringing home stray dogs, cats, injured birds and won't even let her use mousetraps. He might be big and he's certainly strong, but his soul is gentle. He lives by the motto 'Do No Harm.' There is nothing that will convince Sandra her son could shoot a man. As for something as material as a watch and some money? Never. That is not her son."

Beatrice nodded and tried to look reassuring but Sandra was speaking rapidly and with some agitation, this time directly to Ana.

"He's not a good communicator. Being under interrogation will make him stressed and he will panic. She wants to get him out, but if that's not possible, she needs to be with him. She can't bear to leave him on his own."

The tears escaped, but with great dignity, Sandra Cordeiro pulled a tissue from her sleeve and patted them away.

Beatrice took a deep breath and turned to Xavier. "None of us has any authority here. All we can do is talk to the local police and ask for a sympathetic hearing."

"Could we get any of the senior officers at EPIC to use their influence?" he asked.

"Gilchrist is the obvious choice," said Beatrice. "He handed them this case and asked all of us to keep out. The thing is, if we go to him for support, how do we explain how we found Sandra and why we were digging in the first place?"

"Me," said Ana. "Tell him the partial truth. I'm a journo and I've sniffed out a story. When I find me old mate Beatrice is involved, I probe her for intel. A total pro, she gives nothing away, so I go snooping alone. When I meet Sandra, I take the info back to Beatrice, my professional police connection, and ask her advice. She does the responsible thing and passes it upwards."

Sandra's focus switched from one face to another as they cogitated.

"Gilchrist won't swallow that. He's already fishing for info on you," said Beatrice.

"So confess. I don't work in port wine caves, I'm a hack. You deflected all my enquiries but when I came back with a story, you felt it incumbent upon yourself to fill him in. You regret telling half-truths but ethics are more important than face-saving."

"He won't believe me."

Ana folded her arms, a challenge in her eyes. "He will if you play it right."

Chapter 21

By the time Beatrice left Gilchrist's office, it was four o'clock. Her hands were shaking and her knees were weak, but her fists were clenched in triumph. She hurried back to her room and tapped on the door. It opened in seconds and Xavier ushered her in, his eyes bright with curiosity.

Inside, Ana sat at the table, one ankle resting on her knee, a pen in her mouth and a large piece of paper in front of her. On the floor, Roman sat cross-legged with Cher in his lap, her legs flopped out in front of her, a computer on her knees. The windows were open and the pungent scent of honeysuckle wafted in on the breeze. Beatrice had an overwhelming feeling of coming home.

She threw her bag on the bed, looked into each face and made a theatrical eye-sweep of the room. Roman, Cher and Xavier all understood the question and gave the thumbs-up. Beatrice relaxed. If these professionals had found no bugs, there were none.

"So you're all skipping class this afternoon? Disgraceful."

"No classes to skip," said Xavier. "Instead there's a Wednesday afternoon excursion around the national park. We sneaked off."

Beatrice turned her attention to the couple on the carpet. "Have you two got an announcement to make?"

Cher laughed. "My butt got a little numb after all morning in the chair. Roman offered an alternative and threw in a free massage. No complaints from the FBI."

Xavier took his seat opposite Ana. "We've been waiting for you, B. What happened with Gilchrist?"

"He'll recommend bail. He had a whole barrage of questions and was less than happy, but yes, he'll advise letting Marco Cordeiro out this afternoon. Ana, he wants to talk to you tomorrow."

"He can. I've got my story straight. I can give him the family background and there's even a development on one of my leads. Pretty much public on the wire, but backs up my story as a journo on the trail."

"Of interest to us?" Beatrice sat at the desk, quashing another twinge of guilt regarding Matthew, Will and the gang. Tonight would have been her turn to cook.

"Could be. More info on the Monteiro angle." Ana flipped over the pages of her notebook. "Nelson Monteiro has been overlooked for promotion in favour of Samuel Silva no fewer than five times. The guy is a friend and supporter in public, but it's no secret that if Silva were removed, Monteiro's career would take off. We're talking a fifty-year-old man who's not got that much longer to climb the ladder."

Xavier threw Ana a disapproving frown.

"Chill out, Xavier, I've not offended Beatrice. She's leaving at the end of the year anyway. This fella is a career cop and getting to the stage where he's gonna need to skip a few rungs. Saying that, they're old pals and he's godfather to the little girl, so I can't really see him in the frame."

Cher sat up. "I'd have to second that. I spent a lot of time with André and he's totally determined to bring Silva's work to light. He respected and liked the guy and I don't feel any kind of insincerity there at all."

"Right," Beatrice wanted to remind them all to stick to facts, but she was not their boss. The only way was to lead by example. "Ana, what did you find out about the death threat from the adoption agency?"

"Dead end. The man's a chancer with a big mouth. He's practically bankrupt and has more enemies than friends. His own alibi is solid and the fella has a record of making wild threats. One even landed him in court. I'd say he's just a bad loser."

"It was a long shot," agreed Beatrice. "Silva's brother?"

"That was more of a challenge. He was away on a boys' weekend and neither his wife or sister knew exactly where. I started to get excited till he called me and confessed to a gambling weekend in Cascais. A whole list of folk who'll corroborate his story and credit card details at the casino match what he says. Incidentally, when I explained I was eliminating suspects, he mentioned more than one woman scorned. Samuel had quite a reputation, according to Salvatore. I've had a dig around but as yet, no info on any vengeful ex-girlfriends."

Roman reached into his jacket pocket, easing Cher forwards for a moment. "I got a list of all occupants on the first floor. My room is 1126, so I tested your theory, Beatrice. By sliding over the dividing rail, I managed to enter my neighbour's room, Silva's and Gilchrist's office. It wasn't difficult. The windows are simple to open from the outside."

"You went into other guests' rooms?" asked Xavier.

Roman reached up to pass Beatrice the papers. "Yeah. The BluLite app is very useful if you want to know where someone is at any precise moment. I waited till Gilchrist began filming himself as a panel guest and slipped into his office from the balcony. Nothing much to see, but I noticed a couple of strange things. It's a suite, but he's using another room for his private quarters, so you'd expect very few personal items in the suite. But in the wardrobe there's a full SOCO outfit. Shoe covers, gloves, the standard white non-contamination suit but none of the usual equipment. In the bathroom, there's a bottle of isopropanol, nail varnish remover and hand sanitiser. There's a hallway between his office and the corridor which is empty apart from a small table with a Bose speaker."

Xavier shook his head with a frown, his eyes flickering back and forth across the carpet as if seeking an explanation. "Maybe the SOCO suit is a demonstration sample. The liquids you mention sound like someone obsessive about hygiene. He shakes a lot of hands."

Roman gave a brief nod, but seemed unconvinced. "Maybe. What about you and the fingerprints?"

Xavier placed a scanned document on the table. "The fingerprints were poor quality, as if they were made earlier than Saturday. There's only one set, outside the French windows. The police found none of the same prints in the room."

Cher, reclining in Roman's arms, took a deep breath. "Guys, this is a wild card, but what if we're talking about a different sort of jealousy? We all know Silva was writing a book, to be published on the internet. It's a collection of all his teachings, kinda non-fiction research on sociopathic tendencies. Then there's this other book, a novel on similar themes, which might cause a few red faces. It's supposed to be hush-hush, but pretty much everyone at this conference heard the same jungle drums."

Roman's forehead wrinkled. "A literary rival? No way. That really is something out of a TV series. It could only be more clichéd if he'd been poisoned. You don't really think someone would shoot him over a book?"

Cher hunched her shoulders. "Just throwing it out there."

Beatrice sat on the end of the bed. "But the book in question is apparently an exposé of some of the most senior figures in international policing, disguised as fiction. I can't see why Silva publishing his work would clash."

Cher shook her head. "Nope, me neither. But I keep circling back to the idea that there's something more to this. Call it a hunch."

"A hunch?" Roman laughed. "Have you been reading crime fiction?"

"Never dismiss a hunch," said Beatrice. "Ana, this is a lead we need to work. Can you locate that ghostwriter, sniff around publishers, legal firms and recent deals? The rest of us should test the waters internally and find out which kind of ego would risk his or her career for a story."

Roman exhaled in derision, blowing Cher's hair over her face. "Ninety percent of the people in this hotel, for a start. I think we need to prepare a strategy, split up and start asking the right questions. Ana, it might be better if you stay out of sight. You're a little too memorable."

Ana shrugged. "Not a problem. I need to get to work on all this, so I'll stay here and see you all later."

Xavier looked at Beatrice with an expression of concern. "Do you have to leave or can you join us this evening?"

"I'll stay. I won't be popular but it's absurd to rush off now." Beatrice pressed the bridge of her nose. "Especially with Ana here to help."

"Right. Beatrice, Xavier, Cher and I can work the room between us." Roman looked down at Cher. "Now we should get back to our lines of enquiry. Ready?"

"Aww, I was just getting comfy."

Xavier cleared the table of papers and laptop. "Good idea. Enjoy your evening, Ana. See you in the morning. Breakfast at eight?"

Roman scooped Cher up, placed her gently back into her chair and the three of them left with the minimum of fuss and noise. As Beatrice closed the door, she had a thought.

"If I'm staying here tonight, I'd better organise a room for you. I'm far too long in the hoof to share a bed. I'll nip down to reception and sort it out now."

Ana looked up from her screen. "Oh thanks, but no need. Xavier already gave me his room key. He's sleeping in Roman's room."

Beatrice stared but Ana's attention was back on her laptop. "Well, I must say they're taking this gay couple cover very seriously. All credit to them."

"What? Oh right. Yeah, that's part of it, but the real reason is that Roman spends all his time in Cher's room. Those two are getting it on. You didn't miss that, surely to God?" She snorted. "Call yourself a detective?"

While Ana tapped away at her keyboard, Beatrice fetched a bottle of water from the mini-bar and wondered exactly when the world had started moving so fast, and why sometimes it seemed to be leaving her behind.

Room 1106 hummed with activity. Ana spent her time alternating between calls to various contacts and rattling off emails. It didn't disturb Beatrice. Firstly, all Ana's conversations were in Portuguese and secondly, it reminded her of the office back in Scotland Yard. Noise, work, action, progress, it was all rather comforting.

Beatrice was scanning the profiles of every conference attendee to find personal or professional connections to Silva when Ana's mobile trilled.

Ana answered, stating her name. Whoever was on the other end had a remarkable effect on Ana's hunched, screen-facing posture. She sat up and stared at Beatrice with wide eyes as she replied.

"*Si, estou aqui, Senhora Doutora. Obrigada para a chamada.*"

She reached across to a hotel notepad and scrawled the words *Silva's wife!* before returning her attention to the call.

Beatrice watched her body language and listened to the conversation as far as she could, but could only detect an empathetic intonation and one word in fifty. She couldn't even read Ana's notes, typed directly onto her screen in some kind of shorthand. After Ana opened several other tabs and ran searches, Beatrice realised she was wasting time trying to second guess her. Patience and persistence would be the best way to proceed.

She continued her cross-checking of the delegate database and created a grid. Of the fifty people on the course, eight had previously worked with Samuel Silva—all of them men, including Xavier Racine. That came as no surprise; Beatrice knew her Swiss friend was a fan of the professor's work.

Of the eight, two had enjoyed a closer friendship, one of whom was Gilchrist. Close friends for some time, attending football matches together, they seemed to have drifted apart of late. The other was Portuguese detective sergeant André Monteiro, godson and colleague. She trawled BluLite for any interaction between them to reinforce her findings but found precious little. She was making notes on her file when Ana ended her call.

"How on earth did you manage to get his wife to call you?" asked Beatrice.

Ana shook her head in disbelief. "The way I always try. Contact them or close relatives, explain I want to share their story, emphasise that I want to help bring justice to the victims. Two people advised her to talk to me. Samuel's sister, Olivia, and remember I mentioned Nelson Monteiro?"

"Good Lord, I was just digging for info on André Monteiro online. Why would his father advise a grieving widow to talk to a journalist?"

"André thinks there's something wrong and his dad agrees. Bear in mind what I said, though. Nelson has good professional reasons to wish Silva out of the way. And his son is right here with easy access. Wait now, I'm getting sidetracked." Ana glugged a third of a bottle of water and checked her phone.

She took a deep breath. "His widow is wrecked. New kid, start of the rest of their lives, coasting on their successes and now he's dead." Ana ran a hand over her face. "The poor creature."

"I'm amazed she could even talk to you," said Beatrice.

"Me too. But she wants us to find who did this and she's not buying the casual worker chancing his arm either. She thinks it's either politics or jealousy. We'd be wise to keep an open mind on that one. Mind, according to her Nelson Monteiro could never be in the frame. She swears André's dad has wings growing out of his shoulder blades but we'll be the judge of that."

"Of course we will. So who's jealous, if not Monteiro?" asked Beatrice.

"The ghostwriter. We know Silva was writing a book. He has no time to do it himself so he hired a ghostwriter. He sends her a set of notes for every chapter and she turns it into something readable. They'd been working on this for eighteen months, then it suddenly stopped. Silva never told his wife why, just said it wasn't working out. After his death, she heard some rumours. Seems there'd been a brief affair or possibly one sexual encounter. Hard to tell. But apparently this ghostwriter woman was obsessed, convinced they were destined to be together and threatened to tell his wife, wreck the adoption and basically ruin him."

Beatrice considered the idea. "Motive for him to kill her rather than the other way around."

"That's what I thought. The interesting thing is there is no record of any dialogue with a ghostwriter on Silva's computer. Either he deleted it all, or used an email address she doesn't know anything about. Now, Nelson Monteiro calls bullshit. He says Silva dropped the ghostwriter due to a conflict of interests. Apparently, a colleague in international policing was using the same ghostwriter for his own book. Monteiro Senior says either Silva didn't know or wouldn't say who it was.

"One thing I don't get is why there's a conflict of interests. Like you said, Silva was more or less publishing his teachings as a manual. We only have rumours about the other book. But to all intents and purposes, it's a very different beast. Fact disguised as fiction, designed to embarrass a shitload of head honchos. Bottom line, Beatrice, I need to talk to this ghostwriter."

"I know! But we don't know who or where she is."

"Sure we do. Elisabete Silva told me why her husband chose this particular woman. She used to work in the Communications Department at Europol. The only other details she knew were the woman's first name and two other books she's written. She's in the acknowledgements of both, so it took me five minutes to find her details. She's based in Paris and her name is Georgina Bow."

Beatrice gave her a gleeful grin. "Ha! I knew you were the right one to find this level of detail. Is there a phone number?"

"Yeah, but I think I've a better chance of getting her to talk if I go there in person. I could probably get a flight out tonight."

"Right, let's do it. Check she's home, and if she is book the first available flight. I'll reimburse you. This woman is the answer to several questions and we need to act fast."

Ana snapped her laptop shut and grabbed her bag. "On it! I'll go back to Xavier's room and collect my stuff. Good luck with pack hunting tonight and I'll keep you informed every step of the way."

Once she'd gone, Beatrice decided to bite the bullet and call Matthew to offer an explanation for another night's absence. As she composed her speech, she brushed her hair. She was interrupted by her mobile ringing and winced when she saw Matthew's name on Caller ID.

"Matthew, hello. Bad news I'm afraid."

"You too? What's wrong?"

"Nothing serious. Just need to spend another night here. Is there a problem at your end?"

"Not too sure yet. We had a mishap this morning when Tanya spilt hot coffee all over herself, but she's all patched up and staying overnight in hospital."

"Good heavens! Is she badly hurt?"

"She has some burns on her arm and leg, complicated by the fact her skin was already overexposed to the sun. The doctor says she'll be fine and back home tomorrow. What's bothering me now is we can't find Luke."

"What do you mean? He's missing?"

"We're still looking. Adrian and Marianne were supposed to be watching him while we were at the hospital, but each thought the other was responsible. It's all rather complicated, but the point is, no one has seen Luke since around two o'clock this afternoon. Will, Adrian and Marianne are still out searching but before it gets dark, I wondered if I should call the police. Hence seeking your advice, Old Thing."

Without even wondering why, Beatrice asked "Where's Leon?"

"Ah yes. Another complication. He left this morning, by all accounts, in a bit of a huff. It's a very awkward situation but my concern is that my five-year-old grandson is somewhere out there and I am closer to panic than I can ever remember."

Beatrice squeezed her eyes shut. "Right. You stay home and check the entire house, cupboards, attics, under beds, every possible hiding-place. Get the others to check all the outbuildings and the nearby area. I'll alert the police and explain the situation. I'll call in an hour and if there's no news, we'll decide how to proceed."

"Thank you. I'm sorry to ask, but truth be told, I'm at my wits' end."

"I understand. He's most likely somewhere close by, hiding or asleep. But let's take all reasonable precautions. Now I'm going to hang up and phone Will directly. Easier to discuss procedures with a fellow copper. Try not to worry. If you've not found him in the next hour, I'll come back. Everything else can wait."

If the afternoon had been buzzing, the next hour was frantic. Beatrice spoke to Will and got the number plate of the Fiat Panda, then called the Viana do Castelo police force and alerted them to a missing child. Meanwhile, the sun began to sink towards the horizon. Beatrice scoured her hard drive for images of Luke to share with the search team and spoke to border control regarding the possibility of an abduction.

She phoned Matthew exactly one hour after his previous call. He confirmed there was no sign of the boy, but the police had arrived and begun a search using dogs.

"In that case, I'll order a taxi and join you as soon as possible. I doubt I can be of use, but at least I can be there for moral support."

"I'd be most grateful if you would."

Beatrice repacked her suitcase, her mind on Luke and any reasons he might have to run off. Just as she was ready to leave the room, a knock came at the door.

Gilchrist stood in the corridor, his expression grave.

"Good evening, Commander. What can I do for you?"

"I'm the bearer of bad tidings, I'm afraid. I relayed your information regarding Marco Cordeiro to the local Inspector as soon as you left my office. As a result, the detectives released him on bail. A few minutes ago, I received word of a street brawl involving the Cordeiro boy. It seems he suffered a serious stab wound. He's currently in ICU."

"A street brawl? He didn't seem the type."

"One can never tell, especially when the only account of his character came from his mother. Anyway, you know these Latinos. Hot-headed and ready to defend their honour. His family is with him as we speak but the detective I spoke to was less than optimistic. Sorry to put a dampener on your evening. However, I thought perhaps you and your friend could join me for dinner?"

"I can't tonight, Commander, much as I appreciate the gesture. I'm heading north to be with the family. Thanks for letting me know and see you in the morning."

"Ah." Gilchrist shook his head. "I'm afraid I must ask you to stay put for the time being. Your connection to the injured party means you need to help the local police with their enquiries first thing tomorrow. Same goes for your colleague. It would be preferable if you would both remain in the hotel. Just until we clear this up. I would like to be civilised about it. So, dinner at my table?"

Beatrice opened her mouth to explain about Luke but stared past the plastic smile into his cold eyes instead. Appealing to his human side wasn't going to work. She could make a fuss and leave anyway, but something told her to feign obedience.

"I see. Dinner is fine. If you'll allow me to shower and change, I'll join you downstairs in an hour."

"And your journalist friend?"

"Ana's already gone back to Porto, I'm afraid. She'll be back sometime tomorrow." It was not a lie, just an omission of certain truths.

"The police would like to speak to her first thing in the morning. She needs to be here at eight o'clock for an informal interview."

"I'll let her know. See you shortly."

She gave him a tight smile, closed the door and looked through the peephole. Gilchrist stood there for a few seconds, apparently checking his phone. The second he'd gone, Beatrice hurried into the bathroom and switched on the shower. Then she dialled Ana's mobile, hoping she had already left the hotel, if not the country.

The girl answered on the first ring. "Beatrice? What's the story?"

"Where are you?"

"About half an hour from Porto. I've booked the ten to seven flight and made an appointment with Georgina Bow for nine o'clock tonight. She thinks I'm a potential client."

"Ana, listen. Gilchrist has grounded us both as witnesses. I'm not allowed to leave the hotel and he wants you back here for eight in the morning."

"Why? Witnesses to what?"

"It's our connection to Marco Cordeiro. He's just been stabbed in a street fight."

Ana exhaled. "Dead?"

"No, but he's in Intensive Care and Gilchrist says it's not looking good."

"Shitting shit on a shitty stick. If he dies..."

"There is no way he can be proven innocent. Which is convenient for whoever really killed Silva."

"Bastards! Do you think I should come back?"

"No. I think you should stick to Plan A and we'll improvise tomorrow. I really can't see why the police need to talk to both of us. We're certainly not suspects."

"What about you? What do the others say?"

Beatrice bit her lip. "I'm telling Xavier, Cher and Roman nothing yet."

There was a pause at the other end of the line. "Feels a bit weird not to share developments with the team. Is there something I need to know?" Ana's voice, clear, sharp and intelligent, cut right to the heart of the matter.

"Who else knew the Cordeiro boy was about to be released? The five of us and Gilchrist. You and I were together all afternoon, but what about the other three? I suspect we have a mole. If one of our 'team' is party to this, we have a problem. That I can deal with on my own. Go talk to this woman, keep communications open and please be very, very careful."

Ana's voice, when it came, sounded uncertain. "Ooh-kay. Is everything else all right? You sound nervous."

Telling Ana about Luke's disappearance was impossible without admitting her worst fears. She just had to keep working. "Just unsettled, that's all. Talk to you tomorrow. Good luck."

Outside her window, the onset of evening created a spectacular lightshow as the sun sank behind the trees, radiating fiery spotlights like angels' wings. It would be dark in a couple of hours. Tears of frustration, isolation and fear welled up to blur the beauty of the scene. Beatrice shook her head and shucked off her clothes. Shower, dress, call Matthew, dinner, focus. *Concentrate*, she told herself, *you cannot afford to lose it now.*

Chapter 22

Once the police took over the search, there was nothing else for Adrian, Will or Matthew to do but gather in the villa's kitchen, waiting for news or darkness. No one spoke, their faces drawn. Adrian made a pot of tea which went untouched. The news that Beatrice was unable to join them had come as a real blow, adding to the sense of abandonment. As the light leached from the sky, police officers returned sniffer dogs to their vehicles while the detective in charge came up to the house. Marianne materialised from the living room, phone clutched to her chest. Adrian did not acknowledge her, convinced the news she craved was of Leon, not Luke.

Detective Machado seemed unsure as to whether to address Matthew or Will. He chose both.

"As expected, my officers found nothing. The search was only a formality, as the dogs traced the child's scent to the end of the drive, where it disappeared."

Marianne clutched a hand over her mouth to stifle a sob.

"Thank you, Detective. I understand why you are no longer searching the grounds," Matthew's voice was weary and defeated.

Adrian glanced at Will, expecting him to ask more questions, but his gaze was distant, lost in thought.

"When you say his scent 'disappeared', what do you think happened?" asked Adrian.

The detective, who smelt of aftershave and tobacco, blinked

while formulating his reply. "The scent is traceable to the end of the drive. Then there is nothing. We think the boy walked to the main road where he got into a car."

Matthew massaged his forehead. "Luke is only five, so one can never be sure, but he has been drilled never to accept sweets, lifts, presents or anything from strangers. I don't know why he would wander down the drive on his own and I cannot imagine he would get in a car with someone he doesn't know. The boy is shy with people."

"Unless it wasn't a stranger," Will said, his arms folded as he leaned against the worktop. "As I said before, you need to locate that rental Panda."

Marianne shot Will a look of pure venom and stalked out of the room. In a way, her absence was a relief. She added nothing but tears and an endless loop of alternating self-blame or exoneration.

"We will follow every lead, I assure you. As soon as I have any information, I will telephone you. We are doing everything we can. I will return in the morning. Goodnight, everyone."

Matthew, Will and Adrian returned the farewell.

The three men listened to the cars drive away, leaving them in a hollow silence. Moments ticked by. No movement, no sound apart from the cicadas, nothing to say. Finally Will took a deep breath.

"We need to keep our strength up. Matthew, you've eaten nothing since breakfast. Let's eat the fish stew or we'll be useless. Adrian, warm it up and I'll ask Marianne if she wants to eat." He strode out the door towards the garden flat.

Adrian got to his feet and switched on the hob. If he was hungry, how must Luke feel? He stirred the chowder and glanced at Matthew.

"Will's right, we have to eat. I'll slice some bread."

Matthew twisted in his seat to face Adrian. His eyes, shadowed and hollow, bore no warmth. "The last thing I said to you was 'Look after Luke'. I distinctly remember. *Look after Luke.*"

Adrian's mouth opened to protest but found his throat had closed. Matthew dropped his forehead into his hands and turned his back. The only sound in the kitchen was the bubbling chowder until Will returned.

"Can't find her. Come on, let's get this down and leave some in case she's hungry later. Any bread to go with it, Adrian?"

The three men ate steadily but without enthusiasm in a gloomy silence. Matthew emptied his bowl and pushed back his chair. "I'm going to have a lie down. Please call me if there's any news at all."

Will and Adrian cleared up and left a plate for Marianne. For want of something better to do, Adrian made another pot of tea.

Will checked his mobile, shoved it in his pocket and caught Adrian's arm.

"You've got something to say and I want to hear it. What exactly happened this morning? Keep your voice down but tell me the whole story."

In urgent whispers, Adrian told him everything. He explained with as little emotion and as much fact as he could manage, but his voice broke as he relayed Matthew's accusation. Will sat still, intent on his words until Adrian ran out of steam.

"I just don't know what happened. I wasn't there. I know I should have been. I should have ignored her and watched out for Luke, regardless of her opinion. This is my ego getting in the way. I got offended and stomped off, leaving Luke in the care of..."

"His aunt." Will hissed. "His aunt, for God's sake. You've no chance against someone pulling the family card. Adrian, this is Marianne's fault and I won't allow you to take any blame for it. Leon has taken Luke to make a point and hurt Marianne."

"Well, I don't work for Scotland Yard, but I'd worked that much out for myself." Adrian pressed his own cold palms to his face. "The question is, what's Leon going to do with him now?"

Will rested his chin on his fists and gazed out at the night.

"Will? What do you think Leon is planning?"

"I don't know. I honestly don't know."

Chapter 23

Entering the bar for pre-dinner drinks, Beatrice scanned the scene and noted several points of interest. Cher having a flirtatious chat with one of the hotel staff. Roman with a group of men in the humidor, laughing at someone's joke. Xavier in earnest discussion with André Monteiro, walking in the direction of the dining-room. Two plain-clothes officers feigning nonchalance by the door, fooling no one. Gilchrist was doing his usual butterfly act, gliding from table to table until he spotted her and excused himself.

"Good evening. Lovely dress. Can I get you a drink?"

Conscious of her mission, Beatrice opted for a lime and soda. While he ordered, she checked her phone.

Message from Adrian: *No news. Everyone tense as hell just waiting.*

Gilchrist guided her in the direction of the dining-room. She passed Cher, who looked up with a friendly acknowledgement. Beatrice returned the smile but pushed on, fearful of what signs even the blandest small-talk might reveal.

The menu offered some cheer. Chicken and cherry tomato skewers with chilli oil, followed by pork with clams and a dessert of chocolate salami. Gilchrist's table was similar to that of a head teacher – elevated above the crowd and occupied on one side only, leaving its occupants exposed. Gilchrist sat on her left, and her neighbour on the right was a pleasant surprise.

Dr Ruishalme, whose workshop on implicit prejudice she had enjoyed, greeted Beatrice with a strong handshake.

The two women dispensed with small talk and fell into intense conversation, ignoring the men either side of them. Beatrice could have happily chatted to her all night. But as the starters were cleared away, Gilchrist slanted his head towards her and tapped her arm.

"Can I suggest a glass of wine to accompany the main course? I know you fancy yourself a connoisseur. Try this one."

Beatrice registered the patronising tone but accepted the glass. As she sniffed, she surveyed the room. Xavier sat beside the Monteiro boy, while Roman seemed to be in the thick of it with the Russians. Cher was nowhere to be seen.

Gilchrist claimed her attention once more. "This is one of my favourite Portuguese reds. Light yet full of flavour. I believe it would complement the pork perfectly."

"Just the one. If I'm to be interrogated tomorrow, I'd like to keep a clear head."

Gilchrist smiled, an attempt at reassurance. "It's not an inter-rogation. Just a clarification of your connection to the victim."

"Commander, I had no connection to Silva whatsoever. I met him for the first time here, on Friday night."

"I was talking about the boy. Marco Cordeiro. You certainly had a connection to him. It was you who brought him to my notice."

Beatrice swivelled in her chair to address Gilchrist face on. His smile had vanished and his expression gave her every reason to feel that he was the predator and she was his prey. A vision of Sandra Cordeiro floated into her mind, a mother fighting back tears as she defended her son.

"Indeed. Due to the diligent work of my friend, we met his mother and found out a few basics about the young man. Any element of which should have been obvious to the police. We did the correct thing and brought the information to you. I fail to see why myself or Ana should be under any kind of suspicion."

"Oh come now, no need for melodrama. The police want you to share what you know, that's all. As do I, to be honest. You may remember I did make a point of asking delegates not to investigate by themselves or involve any external parties, especially journalists."

"I remember and I followed your edict. I had no idea Ana was already on the trail. She reads the newspapers and when she found out I was representing Scotland Yard at the conference, seized her chance. You can hardly blame her. What else would a good journalist do?" Beatrice tasted her wine.

"Her doing her job is one thing. Your compromising the police investigation is another. Nevertheless, I appreciate your confidence and shall say no more about it. I'm assuming no one else apart from the three of us knew the boy was due for release?" Gilchrist looked pointedly across the room to where Xavier sat, fork in his right hand, gesticulating with his left.

The waiter placed two steaming plates in front of them. Beatrice inhaled, giving herself a second to think.

"Thank you. That smells delicious!" she told the waiter.

Returning her attention to Gilchrist, she added, "Not unless my room is bugged. Sorry, I didn't mean to be flip. This is not a Bond movie. *Bon appétit.*"

"*Bon appétit.* No, it's not a Bond movie. Real life is far more dramatic. If the general public knew half of what goes on in our world, they wouldn't believe it."

"If the general public knew half of what goes on in our world, they'd die of boredom. Let's face it, Commander, ninety percent of what we do is dull and dreary paperwork. About as gripping as watching stains dry."

Gilchrist cut his pork into small strips. "Oh I don't know. You've had a few adventures yourself, so I hear. Ever thought of putting your escapades on paper?"

On paper? Beatrice chewed, shaking her head with emphasis, trying to control her amusement. He must have heard the rumour and was doing exactly as she had been instructed to do by Ranga. Sniffing, trying to find out who was writing that book. However, he was rather less than subtle.

The waiter topped up their glasses.

Ranga's words echoed in her mind. *In your shoes, I'd be unimpressed and under awed.* She swallowed and responded to her host's question, consciously casting a lure. *Patience, Beatrice, is the angler's friend.*

"Oh God, no. Sharing some of the situations I've encountered would result in calls for my resignation as a result of gross incompetence. No, I think the old adage holds true. Everyone may well have a book in them, but most of them should stay there. Unless of course it's question of sharing practical knowledge and expertise, like Samuel Silva. His work I would have loved to read. It's a real shame."

"How do you know what he was writing?"

Beatrice dabbed her mouth to hide a smile. *The fish approaches the hook.*

"He told us at dinner on Friday night. That's one of the reasons I switched sessions on Saturday. He was so fascinating on the subject, I had to hear more. It pains me to think he won't be able to finish it. Oh, this is a super combination, don't you think? I'd never have paired pork with seafood, but it works a treat. And you were right about the wine. Perfection!"

Gilchrist nodded with a hum of assent but said nothing. Moments passed as they continued eating and Beatrice was considering throwing out another worm when Gilchrist put down his knife and fork.

"Yes indeed, Portuguese cuisine is underrated. This place was an inspired choice, if I say so myself. As for Silva, I always found him rather dry. Great on science but not much of a one for entertaining stories. My view is whether you're expounding a theory or spinning a yarn, you have to draw the reader in."

Either the man was feigning literary ambition or trying to trip her up. *Reel him in sideways. No sudden movements.*

She took another sip of wine. "I'm sure you're right,

Commander. I know nothing about his writing, but he was one of the best speakers I ever heard. I wonder how far the two skills cross over."

"Depends what you're writing, I suppose. Presenting slides and statistics must be pretty similar to writing a textbook. Creating a full-length narrative based on fact is a wholly different proposition. Have you read Rimington's stuff?"

"The fiction, yes. Very enjoyable. But I'm afraid I abandoned the memoir. Even if the thing hadn't been so heavily censored so far as to make it moth-eaten, it seems impossible to me to write your own life story with any kind of objectivity. It would be a constant clash between facts and ego, surely. Not my sort of thing."

Across the room, she watched as Xavier walked over to whisper something in Roman's ear. She didn't miss Roman's meaningful squeeze of Xavier's hand and the exchange of looks. Neither did Roman's companions, judging by the good-natured nudges and winks around the table.

The waiters cleared the plates and presented something resembling a Yule log. Beatrice accepted a portion but excused herself briefly for two reasons. She wanted Gilchrist to stew and come to the boil. She also needed to check her phone.

Ten emails in her inbox and three messages awaited.

Matthew: *Still no news of Luke. Wish you were here. Mx*

Dawn: *Mr Leon Charles is very interesting. Emailed with detail*

Ana: *Arrived Paris CDG. RU OK?*

She replied to each and took her time getting back to the table, composing herself and packing all these issues into the 'Nothing you can do, worry later' compartment of her brain.

Her chocolate salami was still there, but Gilchrist had gone. She had just picked up her fork and resumed her conversation with Dr Ruishalme when a waiter hovered at her elbow.

"Excuse me? Commander Gilchrist would like to see you in his office. Please will you follow me?"

Beatrice abandoned her dessert and companion with some

reluctance to follow the young man through the dining-room. An uncomfortable sense of threat dogged her and she opted for an insurance policy. As she passed Xavier and young André Monteiro, she stopped.

"Gentlemen, I know I promised to join you for a digestif after dinner. I intend to fulfil my promise but first I have to meet the Commander in his office. I shan't be long. See you in half an hour?"

Xavier's expression showed full understanding. "We'll look forward to it."

Beatrice knew he had decoded her message and would act accordingly. He knew where she was going and if she had not returned in thirty minutes, he would come looking for her. She continued to the first floor and stopped at Room 1101, but the waiter kept walking.

"I think this is it," she called after him.

The waiter stopped, surprised. "No madam, that is the Commander's personal room. He uses a different room as his office, at the other end of the corridor. Suite 1120. This way."

"Really? I assumed he'd have them next to each other," she said with some disingenuity.

"He did two rooms. Unfortunately he found Room 1122 too loud to sleep, so changed his personal accommodation to 1101."

"Oh, I see. How many nights did he spend in Room 1122?"

"Just the one, madam. Here we are."

Gilchrist's temporary office was crowded with police officers. Phones rang, screens glowed and a smell of stale coffee clouded the air. A small balding individual ushered her towards the central desk, where Gilchrist was ending a telephone conversation. His eyes flickered over her and he indicated a seat. Two young men in suits tapping at laptops on a sofa shifted sideways to make room without lifting their eyes from their screens. She spotted the hotel manager standing by the door, his expression concerned.

Gilchrist ended his cryptic conversation and addressed a heavy-set plain clothes detective to his right. How these men could ever call themselves 'plain clothes' was a joke. They were the most obvious plants you could imagine. Their conversation was incomprehensible to her but the effect was immediate. The detective made a hissing noise between his teeth and the uniforms dispersed. The laptop lads clicked their machines shut and followed, leaving Beatrice, the hotel manager and Gilchrist in relative silence.

"Marco Cordeiro died just over an hour ago. Internal bleeding," Gilchrist announced.

"*O meu Deus!*" The hotel manager crossed himself and muttered a prayer. He seemed genuinely distressed at the loss of his casual worker.

"Yes, very sad. My condolences to you and your staff." The manager shook his head in regret, wished them goodnight and left the room. Gilchrist continued, addressing Beatrice. "And in a further development, the murder weapon used to kill Samuel Silva has been found. It was in the compost bin behind the kitchens. A dishwasher-cum-dogsbody emptied the green waste this evening. The local detectives confirmed it matches their records and the case is now closed." He looked rather pleased with the intelligence.

"And the people who killed Cordeiro? I presume the police are on the hunt?" asked Beatrice.

"I am sure they will be. But enthusiasm for finding a knife-happy thug who took out the murderer of a police professional may not be high on their list of priorities. Plus we now have Silva's gun, dumped in a staff area, Cordeiro's prints on the window pane and the watch in the boy's bag. I'd say that's our final loose end tied up. Sorry to abandon you in the middle of dinner. How was dessert?"

"It looked delicious. Why did you need me here, Commander? Seems you have it all under control."

"Courtesy, DCI Stubbs. Given your interest in the case, just thought you'd like to know it is now closed, bar the paperwork. In the morning, I can offer your friend an exclusive quote, if you like."

"In the morning? We're still being interviewed despite the case being closed?"

Gilchrist looked back at his screen. "Not my call, really, but the local lads want to dot the Is and cross the Ts. Formalities, that's all. Nothing to worry about."

"Well, that's good to hear. Thank you for your excellent company at dinner. See you bright and early for the police interview. Goodnight Commander."

She returned to her room and called Matthew. His voice was thick and slow, and he admitted to taking a sleeping tablet. She told him she approved of his getting some rest and called Will instead.

"No news, and there won't be any till tomorrow. Adrian and I are staying awake though, just in case. I know Leon took him, I just don't know why."

Beatrice clenched her fists then remembered her emails. "I agree. I have some intelligence on Leon, for what good it might do. I haven't had a chance to read it all yet, but I'll do so immediately and forward it to you. This is confidential police data, obviously."

"Obviously. Thank you. I have to do something. Sitting here drinking tea is driving me mad."

"As soon as we've done our interviews tomorrow, Ana and I will travel up there and do whatever we can to help."

"Good. We need you. All of us."

Beatrice brushed her teeth and took a mood stabiliser. Her emotions in flux, she sensed an emotional downswing looming. Before she switched off the light, she set her alarm and pictured Luke's serious blue eyes.

Keep him safe, please.

Chapter 24

Parisian traffic. What a pile of crap. The cab crawled along Rue du Renard and Ana looked at her watch. Again. Ten-minute train journey from airport to city, twenty minutes from Châtelet-Les Halles station to Voie Georges Pompidou. She was going to be late. She shouldn't mind; she was the 'client', so it made no difference. But Ana detested lateness in everyone, especially herself. A wave of brake lights ahead coloured the taxi interior with a sordid rouge. Ana checked her watch.

"*Deux minutes, mademoiselle!*" The taxi driver was watching her in his mirror. His expression was probably intended as kindly reassurance but the red uplighting twisted it into a demonic grimace.

"*Merci, monsieur*," she replied, with little enthusiasm.

Ghostwriter Georgina Bow had chosen Chez Julien just off Pont Louis Philippe for their meeting. 'Just around the corner from me and the waiters are divine!'

The cab eventually deposited her outside the restaurant at ten minutes past nine. She hurried in to find that Georgina had not yet arrived. The waiter, who was admittedly damn close to divine, suggested she enjoy the house cocktail until her guest arrived. Ana agreed and made a decision. This was work and therefore a legitimate expense. Cocktails, haute cuisine and fine wine would suit her role perfectly. She repeated her cover as an internal monologue.

Ana Herrero is a Portuguese journalist who needs help with an exposé on wine crime. She heard of Bow via a security officer. Discretion and ethics are essential. Tonight's meeting is simply testing the waters.

The waiter brought her a French 75 and did something subtle with his eyebrows. Ana thanked him and returned the charming smile. *OK, so Parisian traffic may be a bag of shite, but the city has some fine-looking men.*

She sipped her drink and considered her surroundings. St Gervais and Le Marais equals expensive. Ghostwriting as a profession is unreliable. Unless Ana was very much mistaken, the girl she was about to meet would probably be some kind of trustafarian. The minute the door opened, Ana knew she was right.

Georgina Bow wore denim shorts, cowboy boots and a voluminous, ruffled white shirt over a dishcloth-coloured crochet vest. Her blonde-streaked hair was woven into a messy plait and topped with a battered top hat. Around her neck and both wrists were various bits of silver, leather and feathers, all presumably deeply meaningful and highly symbolic.

Ana stood up. "Hi Georgina, I'm Ana Herrero."

Georgina's face broke into a broad smile, a testimonial to her dentist. She took Ana's hand and leaned in for the cheek kisses.

"So pleased to *meet* you!" she breathed, her entire vocal range exercised in a mere five words. She smelt of citrus fruits and rosemary.

"Likewise," said Ana, sitting down again. "One of your divine waiters talked me into a French 75. Would you like one?"

"Oh wow, they are a*maz*ing! Yes, please. Have you been waiting for me long?" She glanced at her watch.

Ana noted the Breguet steampunk timepiece and smiled. *Yes, living the dream on the Bank of Dad.*

"No, not really. Fifteen minutes or so." She hailed a passing waitress who took her order with nothing more than a nod and glance of disapproval at her guest's Glastonbury-style attire.

Georgina rolled her eyes. "The waiters here are to die for, but that waitress? She has *such* an attitude problem. What can you do? Haters gonna hate. French fashion, at least at the bourgeois level, is just *so* conventional. I mean, really? This is *Paris*, for Chrissakes!"

And a spouter of clichés. Please don't say City of Light or I may have to slap you.

"You've lived here a while?" she asked, just to cut her off.

"Oh yeah, it's been over a year now. I *adore* it. London was special, but here in the City of Light, I'm at home. What about you?"

"I live in Lisbon," muttered Ana through gritted teeth. Then she remembered her cover story. "But the book I want to write is set in Spain."

"Right, your book! Sounds intriguing! Let me take some notes." Georgina dug around in something that looked like a black leather designer bin bag as the waitress placed their drinks on the table.

"Oh thank you. And could I get a bottle of sparkling water?"

"*Oui, madame.*"

Ana rubbed her nose to disguise a grin. *'In the City of Light, I'm at home'. Yeah right. So at home you can't even order a bottle of water in French. You may well be able to write, but you are a typical rich kid, living in a bubble, insulated from the real world. Time to wake up and grow up.*

In that instant, Ana made the decision to drop all pretence and go on the attack.

"Georgina, forget the book. It's time I put my cards on the table. I'm not here as a client. I'm here to help you. Very soon, you're going to need professional support and advice. I am a journalist, that much is true, and I'm working on a story at the request of the police. Unfortunately, you are implicated in a murder enquiry. Everything I tell you must be kept confidential, for obvious reasons. But if you can fill in some blanks, we can keep this out of the press and preserve your reputation."

The waitress brought the water but Georgina didn't move, her grey eyes staring at Ana in alarm and mistrust.

"Last week, a Portuguese police psychologist named Samuel Silva was shot twice in the back of the head. There are various lines of enquiry, one of which centres on his book. The one you were ghostwriting."

Georgina pressed her hands to her cheeks. "Oh my *God!*"

"Listen, you can talk to me, off the record. Or I can report back that you were unwilling to help and let the police do their thing. All I want to do is strike this line of enquiry. I have no reason to cause you any trouble; I just want to know what happened with you and Silva. The rumours are..."

"I know what the rumours are!" hissed Georgina. Her face segued from horror to angry frown to mask of misery. She covered her eyes with her hands.

Ana noted the silvery sparkle of her nail varnish. She sipped her cocktail and waited for Georgina to compose herself. The young woman who finally looked back at her seemed suddenly different, the artificial poise and the brash confidence replaced by a serious expression and maybe just a glint of intelligence.

"I didn't ghost his book. I started, but... it didn't work out. I really can't say more than that. I've had no contact with him for months – and as for the rumours, they are as untrue as they are unpleasant. He and his wife were trying to adopt a child. Can you imagine how she must feel, hearing false and hurtful stories about him having an affair with me?" Georgina pointed a painted fingernail at herself. "I met Samuel twice and the only contact we had was a formal handshake. When I read about his death, I cried. He was a lovely, sweet person with the highest code of honour. I'm sorry, I can't help you."

She yanked her ugly bag onto her shoulder and got to her feet.

"Maybe not. But I can help you," said Ana. She leaned back and folded her arms. "I can tell you exactly what the police think and why they believe you are involved. Sit down, Georgina, you've not touched your drink. Talk to me. I'm serious. I really do want to help. Anyway, you can't leave without paying. That waitress would detest you even more than she does now."

Georgina hesitated. "I'm sorry, that's just not possible."

"Sure it is. Now she simply disapproves of you, but I can tell she's capable of hate. Sit down. Let's talk. All I need is for you to fill in the gaps. You might not even need to do the whole statement-to-the-police thing."

Patrons of Chez Julien were openly staring at this mini-drama, so Georgina sat, hugging her lumpen bag to her chest like a comfort blanket.

"What gaps?" she whispered.

Ana leaned forward and clasped her hands under her chin. "The obvious. Why did you stop working on his book?"

"A conflict of interest."

Ana waited for more. Georgina fidgeted with her jewellery and played with her hair. Ana sat stock still and focused.

"Look, discretion is incredibly important in this line of work. I cannot name names but another senior civil servant employed me to write his book. I soon realised some of the fiction in his work was based on Samuel's facts. I told both men I had found a conflict and could not work on both books. I asked if one of them would find another ghost. Samuel agreed immediately and asked me to delete all his notes. Which I did. The other party..."

Ana interrupted. "Man. The other man. You already mentioned his gender. And I know he's also police."

A flush bloomed in Georgina's cheeks. "Yes, I did say a man. But you're making assumptions by saying he's a police officer."

"Why else would there be a conflict of interests?"

If Georgina had possessed a sharper mind, she could have come back with several feasible reasons. But her face gave far too much away.

Ana was winging it, but still flying, so saw no reason to stop. "I'm not making assumptions. I know Silva's case studies provide the essence of the other narrative. I know one is fact and the other is fiction. The other thing I know is that the relationship between these books is the motive for Samuel Silva's murder. This is why the police will be knocking at your door in the next twenty-four hours."

Georgina shook her head. "Dragging me into this is completely unfair! I did the right thing and told them I couldn't do both books."

"Who? I need the other name. You might think I'm going to take your word for it, but how far will you get feeding the police that bollocks? Unless you can give me the name of the other officer, I'll have to report back that my findings were inconclusive and hand this line of enquiry over to Interpol."

Georgina bit at the side of her thumb, her brow arched in concern. "As I said, discretion is incredibly important. I signed a confidentiality contract and I could get into a lot of trouble."

"More trouble than being a witness in a murder trial?"

Seconds ticked by in silence while Georgina played with her crescent-moon necklace and looked down at the table.

"Let me ask you a question," said Ana, changing tack. "You met Samuel Silva twice, right? What did you think of him?"

"Samuel was *so* sweet. Very clever and well-read, but totally a people person, you know? We connected immediately. Actually, I was sorry it was his book I had to stop writing. It was much more cerebral. Samuel was a lovely, warm, intelligent man."

"So I hear. Which is maybe why everyone who met him is pulling out all the stops to try and find his killer. Of all the people who had any contact with him, you're the first one I've met who refuses to help."

"I'm not refusing, honestly I'm not! I just can't divulge names. I mustn't break client confidentiality. As a journalist, wouldn't you protect your sources?"

"Nice try, Georgina. This is not a source. This is not someone sticking their neck out to give me information. This is a client of yours who is implicated in a murder investigation. And to answer your question, I do try to protect my sources unless I can see I'm impeding police work. The basic question? Which is the lesser evil? Protecting your credentials or pursuing justice?"

Her voice had risen and the waitress was watching with a certain curiosity. Ana drained her glass. Sick of playing games with Four Non-Blondes, she decided to call the girl's bluff.

"OK, I can see I'm wasting my time. If you won't help, I'll let the police question you. No doubt they'll get a search warrant and find the information that way." Ana stood up and threw twenty Euros on the table. "That's for the drinks. And here's my card in case you change your mind."

"Wait." Georgina was actually chewing a strand of her hair and looking at Ana from under lowered lashes. The brash character was rising to the surface again. Her style, affectations and entire personality were lifted from a magazine, and not a particularly good one. "I'll tell you as much as I can. Just not here."

Ana picked up her bag but left the money and her card on the table. The waiter hadn't actually asked for her number, but it wouldn't hurt to let him have it, just in case. You never know.

"Come on, let's walk."

Without discussion, they headed towards the Seine, through patches of shadow and lamplight, past bright shop windows and classical architecture, dodging packs of tourists and eager purveyors of tat, ignoring it all. Away from the café, Georgina's assumed persona faded and a more genuine face showed through.

"What you said before, regarding Samuel Silva. There's something you should know. I worked in Communications for Europol, and that's where I met both the clients in question. When I started to make my main income as a ghostwriter, I went part-time. The regular cash is useful because now I'm ghosting more for politicians. They can be a bit unreliable when it comes to payment, so I still keep my hand in with the police. Samuel Silva approached me about two years ago to work on his opus,

Lone Wolf. It was to be a mixture: part theory and part real life cases to demonstrate theory in practice. Terrifically interesting stuff."

"But then you had to stop," prompted Ana.

"Yes," Georgina sighed. "We'd done about a year together when I was contacted by a rather bigger fish. His project was different, more of a fictionalised memoir. Some might call it creative non-fiction. As soon as I started the outline, I realised there was a conflict of interests. Either Samuel Silva had got his facts wrong or the other party intended to appropriate his colleagues' achievements as his own."

"The name, Georgina," Ana demanded.

"Commander Anthony Gilchrist. You've probably seen him on telly."

"Right. Go on. The facts informed the fiction?"

"One incident leapt out at me immediately. A planned act of terrorism was anticipated and defused by exactly the sort of intelligence-gathering Samuel Silva described. The similarities were too close for coincidence, and the key difference lay in style. Silva's facts showed international collaboration, no heroism and the safe apprehension of this particular lone wolf."

Ana gave a dry laugh. "Let me guess. In Anthony Gilchrist's 'novel' the lone wolf is a maverick cop who finds all the data himself and prevents a demented powermonger from releasing nerve gas into the New York subway. And his name is Anthony Bond."

Georgina giggled. "Close! The book is called *Rogue* and the main character's name is Christian Crow."

Ana rolled her eyes.

"Anyway, the real event Silva and his team prevented was due to happen in Porto. There's a big festival in June where tourists, locals, children and old folk gather to celebrate, eat sardines and watch the fireworks. The man had planned to detonate several devices right along the riverside, killing partygoers and probably many more in the ensuing stampede."

"*São João*," Ana muttered, her mind tumbling with images of sardines, music, lanterns, plastic squeaky hammers and revellers. Laughter, dancing and hundreds – if not thousands – of joyous bodies packed into the Ribeira. She squeezed her eyes tight shut, refusing to imagine the carnage. "Sorry, carry on."

"In Anthony's book, the fictional terrorist attack was set in Venice during the Carnevale. Masks and disguises as opposed to sardines and fireworks. But the details were exactly the same. I told Samuel his case was being used in a work of fiction. I mentioned no names and he didn't ask. He immediately cancelled our contract, gave me an excellent recommendation and advised me to get legal advice regarding my own implication. The book might even be libellous, he said, in which case I shouldn't let my name anywhere near it."

They crossed the bridge onto the Ile de France and passed Notre Dame, slowing their pace to a stroll. The warm evening wind brushed Ana's cheek like a caress and she gazed at sparkling lights reflected in the Seine. She took a deep breath. *Paris is like one of those ex-boyfriends you thought you were over. But it turns out you're never immune to classic charm.*

Outside the cathedral, Ana halted to look Georgina in the eye. "Do you think Samuel Silva knew who the other writer was? Is that why he didn't ask?"

"No idea. But I can tell you, Anthony Gilchrist didn't need to ask. He knew it must have been Silva and wanted to know everything about my work with Samuel. He made subtle threats as to my position in the Communications sector unless I was willing to communicate the content of Silva's work."

"Did you comply?" Ana tried to keep judgement out of her voice.

Georgina lifted her chin with a certain pride. "No. I refused and told him I was no longer working with Silva."

Ana was unimpressed. *Ethics are a fine thing if you can afford them.*

"Next thing I know, rumours of an affair are whizzing round

the grapevine. After that, I heard nothing from Gilchrist for months. Then less than a fortnight ago, he suggested he was ready to publish and wanted me to agree to an extra confidentiality clause. He was in a terrific hurry so I signed. That's why I was so worried about talking to you."

They walked in silence along the Ile de la Cité. Ana stopped in the middle of Pont au Change, her nerves jangling. "Georgina, have you an agent? A legal representative? Someone else who knows who you're working with and what you're working on? Has anyone checked these contracts you're signing?"

"Umm… sort of. My brother is in law school and he thinks it's all fair and square. I'm a freelancer so I'm pretty much independent. "

"When and where were you due to meet Anthony Gilchrist next?"

"Sunday afternoon at my apartment. We usually meet in *Les Deux Magots*, but this time he said he'd come to me."

Ana plunged her hands into her hair and stared down at the water beneath her.

"Oh shit."

"What's the matter?"

Ana took a deep breath. "You wouldn't happen to have your passport with you at all?"

Chapter 25

Shortly after eleven o'clock that evening, Xavier, Cher, Roman and Beatrice convened in the hotel gym. They checked the pool for late-night swimmers and decided to retreat into the sauna, which had long since cooled from the afternoon's activities. As Xavier said, the chance of a functioning bug in there was remote, but they performed the usual checks anyway.

Everyone had news. Beatrice waited till last, glad of the opportunity to observe her colleagues. Her radar was alert for any hint of a potential mole. Each face exuded sincerity and enthusiasm, but spies are nothing if not excellent actors. If the motive for Silva's murder sprang from internal politics, it was entirely feasible that someone had been bribed or blackmailed into a hit. Regardless of how much she liked them, any of the people in front of her could be the killer.

Xavier, the self-confessed fan who knew all about Silva and his work. Beatrice knew from their previous dealings that he was well-known as a brilliant shot. She tried to envisage a situation in which this upstanding young man could be turned traitor. But Xavier had joined herself and Cher on the terrace almost immediately after the Saturday morning seminars had ended. He couldn't possibly have had time to follow Samuel Silva, enter his room, kill him and arrive at their table with a plate full of salad. Unless he'd done it *after* lunch.

On the other hand, there was the Viking. He told them he'd

been back to his room for a shower and volunteered the information that his room was just around the corner from that of Silva. His 'romance' with Xavier was perfectly acted to fool most of the delegates. It wouldn't be much of a stretch to employ the same level of deception to the inner circle of investigators. A double double-cross.

As for Cher, she could be the classic innocent. A disabled woman would engender more sympathy than suspicion. She'd been with Beatrice for most of the lunch hour, only leaving briefly to visit the bathroom. How long had she been absent? And this sudden closeness between her and Roman could signify a different kind of collaboration.

She listened to each person's discoveries with a dual filter. One eye on the case, one eye on the messenger.

Xavier began by exonerating André Monteiro. After an unsuccessful experience with a ghostwriter, Samuel Silva had decided against publishing his teachings as a book. Instead he wanted to give his ideas away for free. He had been working together with Monteiro Junior on a website where people could access his case studies and a blog where theories would be up for discussion. Monteiro's web design skills, Silva's material. On the day of the murder, Monteiro received a note from Silva, asking if he would come to his room to discuss the project. He arrived and saw the Do Not Disturb sign. Due to the fact he had an invitation, he rang the bell twice. No reply came but he could hear Gilchrist next door, giving someone a hard time on the phone.

Roman had talked to the Russian intelligence team. None of them believed the violent burglary theory, but they put it down to politics. "Their confusion is around the victim. Silva was an international star in high-level detection methods and universally well-liked. The Russian theories centred on personal vengeance and a professional hit. No weapon, no prints, a simple local lad framed, job done."

Beatrice spoke. "Except the gun was found this evening in a staff only area of the hotel. Confirmed as the murder weapon, property of Samuel Silva. So the professional hit angle gets my vote. Cher, where did you disappear to?"

"I managed to persuade Sergio, the charming hotel concierge, to show me the security system. I told him I was advising an hotelier friend on state-of-the-art systems. While chatting, I asked him about cameras. He told me about the footage of the relevant first floor corridor on Saturday. I said I wish I'd seen it myself. After a little eyelash-batting, he showed me the digital recording. For what it's worth.

"As mentioned, Silva had the Do Not Disturb sign on the door. Just before lunch, Gilchrist goes back to his room. Roman can be seen heading back for his shower. Silva enters and no one else follows. Monteiro comes to the door and rings. No reply and he tries again before leaving. A little while later, maybe ten minutes, Roman walks past, followed by Gilchrist about five minutes after that. Over an hour passes until the concierge knocks on Silva's door. He unlocks it and finds the body."

Xavier nodded his approval. "Cher, that is most impressive! You've now confirmed what we heard from the police."

"You said Gilchrist went to his room?" A chill settled over Beatrice. "Which one?" She already knew the answer. Room 1101 was on the other wing of the building. If the footage Cher had seen was of Silva's corridor, it had to be Gilchrist's office.

"Room 1120," Cher said.

She closed her eyes as a sudden clarity of understanding and a flurry of interlocking images flooded her mind.

When she opened her eyes, all three of her fellow detectives were staring at her. She spoke in a whisper. "You know when the unthinkable becomes thinkable?"

Cher frowned. "Beatrice?"

"Xavier, will you go and fetch André Monteiro? We're going to need all the help we can get."

Fifteen minutes later, Xavier and André entered the tiny sauna and sat on the bench. The wood creaked with a sound like old bones resting.

Beatrice aimed for a friendly smile, aware how shadowy their faces must look, lit by pale blue pool lights.

"André, thank you for joining us. I know a midnight invitation to the sauna must be alarming. But we figured this would be a safe place to talk. We believe, and I think you are of the same mind, that Marco Cordeiro did not kill Samuel Silva. He was framed and murdered so the truth could be buried. We've been investigating and think the perpetrator..." she broke off as her phone trilled.

Her first thought was news of Luke until she saw Ana's name on the display.

"Sorry, I need to take this, it's Ana." She swiped the screen. "Hello?"

"Beatrice, I think we're in trouble."

"I tend to agree. Listen, Ana, I need to put you on speaker. We're all here, including André. We have some more information to share with you but first can you tell us what the ghostwriter said?"

The team listened to Ana, each of them intent and silent. She finished her summary by urging extra caution.

"I've already told Georgina to scram, hide with her folks in the Home Counties until this is over. I think anyone who knows what Gilchrist has written in his book is potentially in danger. Beatrice, that includes you and me."

"Wait, we need to think this through," Roman pressed his palms together. "Who knows we're working as a team?"

Xavier was the first to respond. "Anyone who's watched us over the past few days. Which is pretty much everyone. We're detectives, for God's sake, it's our job. Beatrice hangs out with Cher, you and I are apparently lovers, and Ana and André are implicated by association."

"Which means we gotta act," said Cher. "We need to take this case to the senior officers in charge and get the guy arrested. And I mean right now!"

Ana's voice came from the phone. "I agree with Cher. Don't

wait any longer. We have evidence, witnesses and motive. Take this to the police."

Beatrice considered. "Whistle blowing on one of our own is complex, even in the same country. This situation is a bloody nightmare. We need to get the senior detective here to take us seriously and he or she may take a little convincing. We might want to follow a parallel line by reporting Gilchrist to his own superiors, Europol and Interpol. Then we need to get him home. There's department there that deals with police crime, but I don't expect they can drop everything and fly out here to arrest him at a moment's notice. This is not going to be easy."

She clasped her hands over her face, thinking about how to block every loophole. The room stilled, awaiting her advice.

"Here's what I suggest. First thing in the morning André and Xavier as our Portuguese speakers make a statement at the local police station in Viana do Castelo. At the same time, Cher should contact Buckinghamshire's Assistant Commissioner while Roman seeks out the Interpol rep here, a man by the name of Fisher. Good luck, he's as slimy as frogspawn. We need Gilchrist taken in for questioning at the very minimum, but I would push hard for an arrest."

Roman spoke. "Yes, we should cover all bases. What about you and Ana?"

"This is where the timing comes in. The police are coming here to interview Ana and myself at eight in the morning and Gilchrist wants to be present. I'll make some sort of excuse for Ana, but I can waffle enough to ensure that Gilchrist will be with me until nine. If you can all report to your respective forces at seven, you can get authorisation for an arrest within two hours."

From Beatrice's phone, Ana spoke. "I'm calling in some favours so I might get into Porto on an early flight. If so, I'll head straight to Viana. I'm giving the hotel a wide berth. I'm away to get sorted now but if you need me to do anything, just shout. Goodnight all. And in the immortal words of Beatrice Stubbs, please be bloody careful."

They each responded in kind and sat in silence for several seconds.

André ran a hand over his face. "There are still a couple of things I don't get. When I knocked on Samuel's door, I could hear Gilchrist in the next room, shouting into the phone. How could he be doing that and shooting Samuel at the same time?"

To Beatrice's surprise, Cher asked a question. "Xavier, when you came to my room yesterday afternoon and knocked on the door, did you hear anything from inside the room?"

Xavier thought about the question. "No. It was silent. Why?"

"Because Roman and I were making a helluva lot of noise. You interrupted us in the middle of something. Hey, no need to blush, it's fine. We're the ones who should be embarrassed. But if you really couldn't hear us, how come a loud phone call is audible when the door muffles the sound of uninhibited lovemaking?"

"Good point," agreed Beatrice. "Plus Gilchrist's office room is a suite. There's a hallway between the front door and the room with his telephone."

"So you'd need to amplify your voice, or a recording of it, to play right behind the door at the exact time you expected someone to be passing," said Roman. "For example, via a speaker."

"And the note," said André. "Samuel sends me texts or emails but this was the first note I ever got."

"Lemme guess, it was typed," Cher added.

André gave her a wry smile.

Xavier got to his feet. "We need to prepare our case. It's nearly one in the morning, so I suggest we get a few hours' sleep. I'll order room service breakfast for us at six a.m. in my room, including very strong coffee. Today we'll need to be at our best."

Chapter 26

From: dawnwhit70@btinternet.uk
To: beatrice@beatrice-stubbs.com
Subject: Leon Charles

Hi Beatrice

Thanks for your feedback on the seminar. I thought it went pretty well so I'm glad you agree. Your praise matters more than most.

I would say something trite like 'hope you're having fun', but with a murder on site and background checks required on one of your house guests, I'll just say I hope you're OK.

Leon Charles. I found out plenty from his own profiles then filled the gaps with a few calls. There's a pattern here and you're not going to like it. Our generation would label this sort of man as an egomaniac. Modern psychologists have a variety of terms, mostly involving the word 'narcissism'. You and I would probably just call him a tosser.

Facts: He has been married and divorced twice, and had a string of engagements. Mostly to women from Eastern European countries. I spoke to a Polish woman and a girl from Lithuania, but there are several others. None of these relationships ended amicably.

He meets these women via his job. He's a salesman to pubs, arcades and shopping malls. His company rents and services fruit machines and all their variants – pinball, quizmaster, and one-armed bandit type of thing.

On his police record are two cases of assault (both trying to prevent women from leaving his flat) and one restraining order. The case notes on the latter are worrying. He'd been seeing a nurse for about six months. In her statement, she says she ended the relationship because he was too possessive. After the split, she made him return her house key. But he'd made a copy. She came home to find him waiting for her in bed. She changed the locks. When she left the hospital one night, she found flowers on the windscreen of her car. Then her cat went missing. After she'd spent three days frantically searching for the animal, he turned up, pretending he'd found it. That's when she got the restraining order.

Not Quite Facts: His online profiles are 80% fake. Several pictures of parties in Ibiza, Monaco and Hawaii are stock images. His work history is 90% invention, as are his qualifications. He has a profile on three separate dating sites, each with a slightly different identity and/or age. The one consistent factor is he wants a life partner without children.

Personality: He's possessive to the point of psychosis. He has a compulsive need for attention. Both those women I spoke to told me he often lost his temper if she looked away while he was talking! He is also a fantasist who fabricates tales of heroism. A busy boy, according to his stories – ex-SAS (yawn, who isn't), undercover agent for the drugs squad (!) and Red Cross volunteer/White Helmet.

Bottom line: A man with serious reality issues. Steer well clear.

HTH, love Dawn

Chapter 27

From: james.parker@IGTT.com
To: beatrice@beatrice-stubbs.com

Dear Beatrice

Thanks for your note. I am glad to hear you're well and look forward to our next appointment in September.

I'm happy to share my ideas with you on an informal basis. You didn't say if the person you describe is a friend, colleague or suspect. So here's the usual disclaimer: please remember none of this could be regarded as official psychiatric opinion for the CPS or other legal processes.

To summarise your concerns, your colleague's observations lead you to believe a particular person demonstrates behaviours associated with NPD, such as passive aggression, attention-seeking, self-aggrandisement and possessiveness towards his partner, including rejection of close family.

It's impossible to label a person based on so few examples so all I can do is direct you to further studies on the subject – see attached. You will see there are a whole range of disorders under the Narcissism-related umbrella and often from directly opposite causes; e.g. insufficient nurturing/excessive praise in the developmental phase.

I would add a word of caution – there might also be a range of other reasons for this person's behaviour. NPD is a hot topic in popular culture, with all kinds of blame being laid at the feet of these three letters, and subsequent assumptions made.

However, your question was quite specific. Do you think he might have NPD?

My answer, subject to my caveats above, would be yes, he might. That is precisely the first condition I would suspect, and I'd work towards greater clarification of his attitudes to himself and others before eliminating it as a possibility.

I hope the material attached expands on the above and I look forward to our next meeting. Incidentally, I would like to discuss your ongoing treatment once you leave London at the end of this year. My thinking was monthly check-ins, in person or online. Let's discuss in September.

Best wishes

James

Chapter 28

Hours passed after Will had received Beatrice's emails. He sat in front of his laptop, reading, making notes, checking various websites and emitting the occasional grunt.

Adrian paced the house and garden every twenty minutes, just to keep himself awake and to reassure himself he was still doing something. He made more tea, most of which went undrunk.

Just after midnight, Will got to his feet, opened the fridge and took out the tinfoil-wrapped plate of chowder left for Marianne.

"What are you doing?" Adrian asked.

Will tore off a hunk of bread and laid it on top of the plate. "I'm going to talk to Marianne. Gloves off. I want some answers."

He slipped on his jacket and went out the kitchen door.

Night noises kept Adrian awake. Clicks and creaks from the cooling house, chitters and squawks from outside roused him whenever he fell into a doze. Each time he awoke, he prowled the grounds with a torch, always with a glance at the garden flat. Two silhouettes faintly discernible, no movement. Still talking.

He saw his reflection in the windowpane. White, drawn and with a heavy woollen throw around his shoulders, he looked like a Porto fishwife. He rubbed his face and checked his phone. 05.04. No messages.

It would be light in an hour and they could resume the

search. In two hours, the police station would be open and they could call. Soon they could do something. This endless dark night of horrors, most created by his imagination, would be over. Tomorrow, they'd find him. They would find Luke and he would be fine. Of course he would.

The kitchen door opened. Adrian turned, as he had done for the last six hours, hoping to see a short blond-haired figure. Instead, he saw Will's tall blond-haired figure, his eyes bloodshot.

"No sign of... anyone?" Will asked.

Adrian shook his head. "I've just done another check and Matthew's still upstairs. I doubt he can sleep either, but he'd rather keep his distance from me."

Will threw himself onto a chair and dropped his head on his forearms.

"Should I make tea?" asked Adrian.

His voice, when it came, was muffled. "I'm shit-sick of tea. Can we not have a livener? I need a whisky and Coke. Have one yourself, bar-keep."

Adrian made the drinks, happy to have something to do. When he placed them on the table, Will's head jerked up.

"Good man. I damn well deserve this." He took two enormous swigs and blinked.

Adrian watched him and waited. "I'm feeling a bit under-informed here. You had those emails from Beatrice and a long conversation with Marianne to add to your own observations. So what do you think is going on?"

There was no reply. Will stared into his drink, his face blank.

"Can you at least summarise what Marianne told you? You've been over there for hours."

Will rolled his head from side to side, the muscles in his neck clicking audibly. "Sorry, I was just thinking. What she said, in a nutshell, is that he's special. An introvert who's desperately inse-cure and needs constant proof of her love for him. Also known as a self-obsessed wanker. I apologise, I shouldn't rant at you. It's just that after listening to hours of that bullshit, trying to be diplomatic for half the night, I need to vent a bit."

Adrian squeezed his arm. "For the record, I think he's a wanker too. But what the hell is he doing taking Luke?"

"He's trying to hurt her. He feels undervalued," Will clenched a fist and mimed a backhander. "So he lashes out by taking something precious to Marianne. She doesn't think he'll try to leave the country, although I wouldn't set a lot of store by her opinion of what he may or may not do."

Will swirled his drink around his glass and Adrian waited for him to continue.

"There are medical names for Leon's issues, but in layman's terms, he's basically a dickhead. Interests include he, himself and him. Ego out of control. Only interested in what people can do for him and desperate for attention. An emotional parasite. The damn shame is Marianne is the perfect host. Needy, clingy and willing to make excuses. Luke took up more attention than Leon. So the bigger brat had a tantrum. And he's done it before."

"Leon has taken kids before?" The fishwife shawl fell from Adrian's shoulders as he clasped his hands to his mouth.

"No, I meant he's had a tantrum over Luke before. Marianne used to babysit Luke every Thursday night for Tanya's night out with the girls. She'd cook his tea, put him to bed and watch TV with a glass of wine. When Tanya got home, they'd have another glass and a chat and Marianne would stay over.

"But Leon kept getting tickets for the cinema or booking restaurants for Thursday evenings and when Marianne couldn't make it, he'd throw a hissy-fit. Those weren't her words. She said he got very upset and emotional. In other words, a hissy-fit, a wobbler, a tantrum, call it what you will. When he moved in, he insisted he couldn't spend a night without her by his side, so she had to stop babysitting. Things with her and Tanya have been difficult ever since."

Will took another swig. "You know what else? I think Leon was affected by the fuss we made of you."

"Me? What have I got to do with it?" Adrian gaped.

"The saving-a-kid-at-the-airport story. You were the centre of attention and it pissed him off. Did you notice how quiet he was when Beatrice arrived because she stole the limelight? He has to be the star or he sulks. I reckon he's taken Luke somewhere and will bring him back in a big 'rescue' event tomorrow or the day after. He'll be expecting a hero's welcome. Instead he's going to get a kick in the fucking bollocks." He drained his drink.

Adrian got up to make another, wincing as Will cracked his knuckles. He gazed out at the night, his mind less panicky now his man was back. Then he laughed inwardly, realising that everyone has a touch of Leon in there somewhere. He started thinking about the sequence of events. "Do you think Luke liked him? I mean, would he get in the car with Leon willingly?"

"No." Will was emphatic. "He avoided Leon whenever he could and I'm convinced those bruises on his arm came from that nasty git pushing him around. But if Leon told him they were going to see Tanya or something..." Will tapped a nail against the table. "But where could he take a small child? After a while, Luke would get restless, tearful, and hungry. You couldn't check into a hotel or a B&B with a five-year-old screaming for his mother. He'd have to go somewhere quiet, private."

A chill crept up the back of Adrian's neck and he hunched his shoulders against the panic rising in his chest. "Private? Why? You don't think he'd hurt him?"

Will clenched one hand around his own fist. "It's impossible to guess. If he has Narcissistic Personality Disorder, which I think he does, he will do anything to cover himself with glory. This kind of person, often described as a Lone Wolf, has a distorted world view. In their minds, they have an inflated sense of their own worth and get frustrated when events don't reflect that. A surprising amount of mass shooters have been diagnosed with the condition. Ask Beatrice.

"I don't know Leon very well, but I can see his ego has taken a bashing this week. Marianne's attention is often claimed by her family, and by Luke in particular. We treated Leon as one of us, and didn't put him on some kind of pedestal, which he may feel is his right. No coincidence they made a late entrance, apparently due to Leon's 'promotion'. He resents anything or anyone who draws attention away from himself. He wants the spotlight on him and him alone. Whether he plans to do that by abducting Luke then bringing him back as a generous act, all I can say is that I hope so."

A voice came from the hallway. "I'm afraid you didn't answer the question, Will." Matthew emerged from the shadows, still fully dressed. "Do you think he'd hurt Luke?"

Will pressed his fingers to his eyes. "I can't say either way with any degree of certainty, but I think we should operate on the basis that it's possible."

Moments of silence ticked past. Adrian held his breath.

"Is there anything we can do?" asked Matthew.

Will didn't look up from the table, his head bent over his clasped hands.

The inertia was unacceptable. Adrian smacked his hands together, making everyone jump. "Of course there's something we can do. Marianne and Leon went to particular places each day, so we can trace their routes from here. Realistically, Leon won't have gone too far and will most likely take Luke to a place he knows or has seen before. The last thing he wants to do is get himself lost with Luke. The Panda's not been found so he probably went to ground about an hour, two at the most, after he snatched Luke. Come on, get that laptop open and let's add everything we know to a map of their movements. Where has he been since they got here?"

Will straightened and an optimistic light shone in his weary eyes. Matthew pulled up a chair and the three began to super-impose a record of Leon's movements onto a map of the region, according to their memory. Within twenty minutes, they had drawn a radius around the limits they calculated.

Adrian was reassured by the concrete nature of the activity, but unsettled by the fact it was all based on assumption. Perhaps all detectives start this way. He got up to make coffee. The first pale ribbon of dawn floated on the horizon, offering all the clichés it always did. Hope, optimism, light, a new start and all the brightness of reality to chase away nightmares. As he waited for the pot to bubble, half listening to the conversation behind him, he gazed out over the valley as it came to life. The lake emerged from a velvety blackness to reflect the lightening sky, in which ripples of pink heralded the sun.

He poured the coffees and handed one to Will. Matthew had gone onto the terrace so Adrian took two more cups outside.

"Coffee?"

Matthew looked over his shoulder. "Yes, please. I think I may need more than one. Is there any warm milk at all?"

"Already in. I know how you take it. Quite a sight, a Portuguese sunrise, don't you think?"

They watched the mist lifting from the valley like lace curtains. The sky announced morning by flame-throwing its entire palette of fiery colours onto the underbelly of a shoal of cumulus clouds. On the lake, a fishing-boat puttered away from a pier, its motor chugging as a bass note to the dawn orchestra of a million birds.

"Quite a sight, as you say. I imagine how one experiences such a natural wonder depends on the state of mind." Matthew sipped at his milky coffee. "I might well be impressed by the delights of dawn, but my mind is wrestling with the stark horror of what I say to Tanya in a few hours' time. What would you advise? I'm not being sarcastic, I'd like some help. How do I tell my daughter her five-year-old son has disappeared from my care and we have no idea where to look for him?"

Adrian's eyes followed the small craft across the water as he tried to frame his apology, but he couldn't find a way of explaining without attaching blame to Matthew's other daughter. He simply didn't have the words. Far below, internal lights illuminated the little fishing-boat and Adrian involuntarily imagined the cramped, smelly interior. He'd experienced a particularly horrible journey across the Irish Sea in a similar vessel. Since then, he'd never quite felt the same about boats.

With a dizzying rush, random elements connected in Adrian's brain, like the tumblers of a lock mechanism falling into place. He grabbed Matthew's forearm, spilling his coffee.

"The boathouse! At the fish restaurant the other night. Remember? Luke disappeared and we all panicked. Will found him in the boathouse. He said he only wanted to have a look. The restaurant is closed for two weeks so the place is empty and private. It's a fifteen-minute drive from here and Leon knew no one would be there."

Matthew stared at him. "Good God. You might well be onto something."

Will's reaction after Adrian breathlessly announced his brain-wave was disappointing. Surely a detective should have leapt out of his seat and grabbed the car keys, shouting 'Let's go!'. But he didn't.

"Hmm. Could be a possibility." He returned to his screen, checking a map of the area.

Matthew had obviously held the same expectation. "I wonder if we ought not just get in the car? Creep up on the place while they're still asleep? Or do you think we should call the police first?"

Without lifting his gaze from the screen, Will said, "I am the police, Matthew. Which is why I want to do this properly. I'm going to inform Detective Machado of our suspicions and ask him to stand by with back-up. Adrian, on the off chance we do find Luke, can you get milk, biscuits and a towel or something comforting? I suggest we don't tell Marianne where we're going. If she's with us, her concern for Leon could override Luke's safety. Plus, someone should stay put in case we're wrong and Leon or Luke returns to the villa. Matthew, would you leave her a note saying we've gone out searching? Just don't mention where."

Matthew went off in search of pen and paper.

"Will, do we tell Beatrice what's going on?"

"Yes. But I don't want to wake her at this hour and leave her worrying about all of us. I'll drop her an email and hopefully we'll have Luke home before she gets up and sees it. I'll do that the minute I've called Machado."

While Will was on the phone, Adrian went upstairs to collect Luke's cuddly dolphin and a bath towel. He shoved them both into a carrier bag along with a bag of chocolate chip cookies and a carton of milk. As an afterthought, he added the First Aid kit from under the kitchen sink. Matthew returned and waited till Will had finished typing before offering his note for approval.

"Perfect. Right, I've spoken to the police and emailed Beatrice. Now I want you both to sit down and listen to me. We are potentially looking at a hostage situation and this is how we're going to play it. Follow these instructions to the letter, even if things go pear-shaped. Adrian, where's that shawl you were wearing?"

They sat, they listened, then they prepared themselves and trooped out to the car. Will drove, his mouth a hard line.

Chapter 29

Fifteen minutes later, the Peugeot passed through the village and into the forest. Two hundred yards from the turning to *Marisqueira do Miguel*, they stopped and parked between the trees. Through the copse, they could make out the restaurant and a little farther, the boathouse. The tension in the vehicle was heavy and the air not much lighter. As if reading Adrian's mind, Will turned the ignition and pressed the window button. Cool morning air flowed inwards, easing the pressure a notch.

Will twisted to look at them both and the smallest flicker of a smile crossed his face as he appraised Adrian.

"Right, one more time. What are we going to do?"

Adrian checked his costume in the rear-view mirror. Black T-shirt, black double sheet wound round his waist and fastened with a belt. Black shawl around his head like a caul, safety-pinned under his chin. Black trainers and the sleeves of one of Matthew's jumpers cut off and acting as woolly socks.

"I'm a fisherwoman heading down to my boat. I get out of the car, walk down to the turning as if I came from the village, go down the driveway and past the boathouse to the fishing boats at the end of the pier. I move slowly, like an old woman. I keep my head down, so my face is obscured by the shawl. I watch where I'm going and try not to trip over. When I get to the boats, I sit with my back to the boathouse and pretend to do something with nets. If I see the Fiat, I send you both a message.

The aim is to keep Leon's attention on me. I do not even look at the boathouse until I get your order to approach."

Will nodded once and looked at Matthew.

"I stay behind the tree line and watch. I must not fidget or attract attention. I stand still, watch and wait for your shout or message. If you say 'Retreat!', I go back to the car and call the police. If you say 'Approach', I come to your assistance. If I hear nothing within fifteen minutes of your entering the boathouse, I call the police regardless."

Seconds ticked past and the only sounds were those of the village waking; in the distance, the church bells struck seven, a cockerel crowed and a cacophony of barks responded to a moped's waspish rasp. Sunlight grew stronger, changing the colours of the foliage from dewy grey-green to a thousand brilliant hues.

Will pulled a black beanie down to his eyebrows to cover his blond hair and instantly transformed himself into someone terrifying.

"I'm moving left through the trees to approach the boathouse from behind the restaurant. If he's there and he's watching, his focus will be on the driveway and the old fishwife. I'll creep under the pier and enter the boathouse from beneath. If Leon's there, my priority is to disable him. Then I'll call for you two to get Luke out of there. He'll need to see a familiar face as soon as possible. Keep a cool head. If you panic, so will he. Mobiles on but switched to silent. We're now operating on stealth mode. Let's go and don't slam the doors."

Adrian had an urge to salute, not out of sarcasm but obedience. Instead, he crossed his fingers. They emerged from the vehicle and pressed the doors closed. Will seemed to melt into the foliage, while Matthew pressed himself against a tree trunk and peered through the branches. Adrian crossed the road and began the downhill slope to the lake while managing the uphill curve of learning to walk in a skirt.

After a minute's walk, he left the shade of the trees and found himself exposed, in full view of the boathouse. He kept his head down and concentrated on his character. *I do this every day. Down to my boat where I go fishing to feed my family. This is just a normal morning for me. Nothing to see here. This is just my normal gait, a bit of a limp and eyes on the track. No need for alarm. Just a fisherwoman off to work. Poor thing, widowed young and wearing mourning clothes. I have a family of five to support.*

He descended the dusty drive, passed the restaurant and the boathouse, then headed for the pier and its cluster of boats at the end. Apart from the riotous noises of nature, he heard not a sound. No voice calling his name or ordering him to approach. No one rushed out of the door and rumbled him. So far, so good.

Until he looked up. Four fishermen trudged along the lakeside from the opposite direction, heading for the same destination. Real fishermen, who very probably owned the boats. Dressing the part and faking the walk was one thing, but blending in with the locals? Adrian slowed, noting the curiosity on the approaching faces. He wished to God he'd shaved.

Chapter 30

The fishermen stopped in their tracks and gawped at Adrian with a mixture of surprise, suspicion and bewilderment.

With no other grasp on Portuguese than how to say hello and thank you, Adrian opted for mime. Performance, after all, was his forte. He pressed a finger to his lips and pointed back over his shoulder. He made sure his back was to the boathouse and his face to the fishermen. His impromptu audience watched intently, saying nothing, every brow a frown.

Adrian mimed rocking a baby and stroking its face. He indicated behind him again and then snatched the imaginary child from his own arm. He considered tracing his tears but judged that a touch too Marcel Marceau. Instead he pulled a face of pure panic. Two of the fishermen widened their eyes in an echo of his pantomime fear.

They were with him so far. He tapped his temple to signify thinking, followed by a Eureka! expression, backed up by a roll of the eyes to direct their attention to the boathouse. The men nodded and talked amongst themselves, articulating the narrative so far.

The youngest of the four made a beckoning gesture which Adrian translated as 'Do go on'.

So he did. He tapped his chest, waved a hand around his head, pulled his shawl tighter and spread a hand across his face. He could see from their faces they understood the reason for disguise. He jerked a thumb behind him and changed character. He pressed three fingers to his shoulder, having no idea how many stripes a Portuguese detective might wear, hardened his expression and pulled an imaginary gun. Then his fingers crept up his forearm, slowing towards the elbow until one 'foot' hovered in the air. The tension was unbearable. Eyes flicked from Adrian to the boathouse and the men discussed the situation in urgent whispers.

Adrian placed his finger to his lips once more. He pointed to his chest, pointed at the ground and glanced at his watch. He added a nibble of his nails and showed them his mobile phone. He received nods of understanding and sympathy.

The youngest asked a question. Faced with Adrian's incomprehension, he too mimed a babe in arms, then placed his hand palm-down by his knee, his thigh, his waist, with an enquiring look.

It clicked. Adrian splayed his hand. Five fingers. Luke was five years old.

One of the older men placed a hand at thigh-height and pointed first to Adrian's skirt and then at his own trousers.

Uncomprehending, Adrian looked from one to another for elucidation.

A second whiskery old bloke tutted and shook his head. He cupped his hands under imaginary breasts, then mimed waving his penis.

For the first time, Adrian spoke. "Oh I see! He's a little boy." He repeated the penis-waving mime, a gesture incongruous on its own, let alone dressed as a Portuguese fisherwoman.

The penis-waver's impressive eyebrows rose. "English?"

"Yes!" He dropped his voice. "Yes. You speak English?"

"A little bit. My name is Pedro Quintela. I come from Portugal. How do you do?" He held out his hand.

Adrian shook it. "My name is Adrian Harvey and I come from..."

At that moment his mobile vibrated and sent shockwaves through his system. He grabbed it and answered.

"Will? Are you OK? Will?"

The voice in his ear was a whisper. "They're here. I can see Leon watching you at the window and Luke is asleep in the corner. I'm going to tackle Leon but I need you to get Luke out of here. Retrace your steps as if you're going back to the village then as you pass the boathouse, rush through the door and look to your right. Luke is on a pile of tarpaulins. Grab him and get him out. I've alerted Matthew."

"OK," Adrian whispered. "The thing is, Will, there are some..."

A series of beeps indicated Will had ended the call.

Adrian looked at his new friends and made a decision. With a wave of his arm and a jerk of his head, he invited all four men to join him. Together, they walked back towards the boathouse. A movement to his left caught his eye and he spotted the Peugeot crunching down the drive. Matthew!

Right beside the entrance to the boathouse and out of view of its windows, Adrian tore off his 'skirt' and pointed at the door. He mimed again, this time for reasons of silence. He pointed at his chest, made a grabbing motion and rocked a baby. Then he counted with his fingers.

One, two, three.

He burst through the door and saw Will crouched on his haunches restraining a struggling, swearing Leon. The fishermen rushed past to help hold him down.

To his right, a small figure wrapped in a blanket sat up.

Adrian's heart thumped as he saw Luke's exhausted little face appear from beneath the folds. He reached out his arms.

"Luke! It's OK, we've got you."

Tears flooded the little boy's eyes and he scrambled up into Adrian's embrace, dragging his blanket with him. Adrian thought it best that Luke did not witness to the ugly scene behind him, and took him to the doorway.

"Come on, let's go. Grandpa's outside."

The Peugeot had just come to a halt. Matthew emerged, looking pale and gaunt, but determined. As Adrian walked out into the sunshine with Luke in his arms, Matthew's eyes creased with relief.

"Hello, Small Fry."

"Grandpa?" Luke got down and ran across the dusty car park, trailing his blanket. "Where have you been?"

His intonation, unconsciously mimicking his mother's, forced tears to Adrian's own eyes. He brushed them away and watched the pair embrace, Luke's small hand patting Matthew's back, as if he were the comforter. Which in a way, he was.

He went back inside to see what more he could do, but it was clear that Will had all the help he needed. Leon sat on an upturned rowing-boat, trussed like a pheasant between the two whiskery fishermen, who were watching him with belligerent expressions. Will shook hands with all of their unexpected helpers, with an *Obrigado* for each of them. He came towards Adrian, his face dirty but with the ghost of a grin.

"Don't know where or how you found these geezers but they're pretty handy with knots. He's not going anywhere until the police get here."

Under the circumstances, Adrian chose not to fling his arms around his hero.

"Considering I'm the first bearded fishwife they've encountered, they took it pretty well. Luke's outside with Matthew. What should we do now?"

"First priority is getting Luke home. He needs to get away from here and rest. I'll stay here to meet Machado, who should be here in around twenty minutes. You go with Luke and Matthew. Give Luke something to eat and drink then put him to bed. Don't give him a bath or a shower. We may still need to take physical samples." He gripped Adrian's shoulders and fixed him with an intense stare. "Listen to me. We don't know what he's been through. Take no risks. Resist the urge to cuddle or hug him unless he wants. Let him dictate terms, don't ask questions but listen to everything he has to say."

Adrian, too horrified to even consider the worst, gave Will a nod.

Will addressed the fishermen. "If you guys will stay with me for half an hour, we can keep the site secure."

"No problem," Pedro replied.

Adrian clasped his hands together to say a heartfelt thank you to all four men who had simply taken him at his not-quite-words. They all gave the universal thumbs-up and genuine smiles.

Outside, grandfather and grandson were still clutched in an embrace. On Adrian's approach, Matthew lowered the boy to the ground.

"Where's Mum?" asked Luke.

Matthew's eyes were still damp so Adrian jumped in.

"She's coming back today. We're going to fetch her later on. But we really should have breakfast before we go, don't you think? Talking of food, there's milk and biscuits in the car if you're hungry."

Luke rubbed his grubby face. Matthew took his hand and they started walking towards the Peugeot when Luke stumbled, dragging Matthew sideways.

Adrian stepped forward. "Did someone call for the Piggyback Taxi?" He hunkered down, allowing Luke to clamber onto his back and felt two little arms wrap round his neck. Matthew got into the driver's seat to chauffeur them home.

"Not awfully certain of the route, so all navigational advice is welcome," said Matthew, crunching the gears.

"Blind leading the blind," said Adrian, looking down at the small blond head beside him. He managed to swap the cuddly dolphin for the filthy blanket, which he dropped on the ground outside.

After two chocolate-chip cookies and several slurps of milk, Luke sat back and leaned against Adrian. Mindful of Will's advice, Adrian put his arm around the boy with great caution. Luke nestled closer and shut his eyes. Next time Adrian looked, he was fast asleep. Which was just as well, because Matthew's driving would have given anyone nightmares.

The jerky, hair-raising journey lasted twenty-five minutes after a couple of wrong turns, but finally they spotted the villa.

Adrian let out a huge sigh. "Has anyone called Beatrice?" he asked

"Not yet," said Matthew, his focus on the road. "I'll do so as soon as we get in. It is early, but I am sure she'd like to know he's safe. My other concern is ..."

"What to say to Marianne."

Matthew glanced across at the garden flat. "Precisely. Do you have any ideas? Other than 'your psychopathic boyfriend abducted your nephew and terrified your entire family', of course."

Adrian looked down at the small face resting against the seat. "Unless I get an hour's sleep, I'll never have another idea in my life. Why don't you go over and tell her we found him, at least. She must be worried. Leave the rest till Will gets back. I have faith in his judgement."

Matthew nodded. "So do I."

Luke barely stirred when Adrian lifted him out of the car, still clutching his dolphin. Matthew trudged across the lawn to inform Marianne of her nephew's return. Following Will's instructions, Adrian carried Luke upstairs, took off his little trainers and laid him in bed, still in his grubby shorts and Ice-Age t-shirt. He covered him with the duvet and watched for a few moments as the child slept soundly.

His own exhaustion dragged at him but he was reluctant to let Luke out of his sight. Footsteps on the staircase jolted him alert and he looked around to see Matthew coming through the door. He glanced at Luke with a sigh then turned to Adrian.

"She's gone," he whispered.

"Marianne? Why?"

Matthew shrugged. "No idea why or how. We had the only vehicle. But all her and Leon's things have disappeared."

"She must have called a cab. Where do you think she would go?"

"Home," said Matthew, rubbing his eyes. "Where else?"

Chapter 31

At seven o'clock, Beatrice bade Cher good luck, took one more chocolate croissant from the trolley and returned to her room. First priority now was checking on Luke. André and Xavier would be at the police station in Viana do Castelo already, Roman had left to seek out Fisher and Cher was waiting for the Buckinghamshire Assistant Commissioner to return their call.

Beatrice wished she could have spoken to the AC herself. She knew him in a nodding acquaintance sort of way. But as the man was unlikely to be in his office before eight, she had no choice but to put her trust in Cher.

While dialling Matthew, she looked out at the grounds, the pale morning sunshine casting a rosy light onto the white pagoda on the hill. The delicate beauty of the edifice and perfect natural illumination made Beatrice catch her breath. A summer wedding at sunrise would be a photographer's dream.

Matthew sounded far more relaxed than he had during his previous phone call an hour earlier. He assured her several times that Luke showed no obvious signs of physical or emotional damage and that he was still fast asleep. His voice was weary but cheerful, despite his concerns for his daughters. He was vague about what was happening with Leon.

. "Really couldn't say. That's Will's area of expertise. Talking of whom, he called twenty minutes ago to say they're filing the paperwork, whatever that means. Then he's going to the hospital to collect Tanya."

"I imagine he'll need her to make the decision about pressing charges against Leon. Poor Tanya, as if she doesn't have enough to cope with."

"Quite. I'm rather glad Will's handling this. He always knows what to do. As for Marianne, she's done a bunk. Cleared out the garden flat and gone. No note, nothing."

"Good grief! Are you all right? This must be immensely stressful for you," Beatrice asked.

"I'm fine now I've got my grandson back. I'll wait up till Will and Tanya come home, then I am going to bed for the rest of this holiday. You can join me if you like."

"I'll accept that offer. Will truly is a Superman. If Adrian does his usual trick of getting bored of his boyfriend after a few months, I will give him such a fourpenny one. William Quinn is perfect for him."

Matthew released a deep sigh. "I know. I can't even attempt to tell Will how grateful I am. I'm likely to break down and weep. Anyway, the most important thing is Luke is safe and asleep in his own bed. Likewise Adrian. What's the latest with you?"

Beatrice dissembled. "Everything is coming to a head. Should all be over very soon."

"Cryptic. Which is fine with me. I would rather avoid any drama for the next ten years. Plays havoc with my digestion."

"Oh you poor old devil, this must have been a wretched holiday for you. Well, we start anew tomorrow. Give the boys my love and ask Will to call me when he can. I have an interview this morning but plan to leave here at lunchtime, or just as soon as Ana can drive me. The more I think about it, the more retirement appeals. See you later and look after yourself."

"Will do and same to you, Old Thing."

Beatrice put down the phone and began making her third coffee of the morning. Her phone buzzed. A message from Cher.

Phone conf confirmed for 08.00 with AC of B.

Beatrice sent a thumbs-up icon in reply and returned to her deliberations over a ristretto or an espresso. After a sleepless night and with a dramatic day in prospect, she decided on both.

At seven forty-five on the dot, someone rapped on her door. Beatrice expected Roman with Fisher in tow, or possibly the local police detectives. Yet there stood Commander Gilchrist, dressed to impress, complete with smile.

"Good morning! The interview is taking place in my office. As I was on my way back from breakfast, I thought I'd escort you both. Are you ready?"

"Good morning to you, Commander. Unfortunately, Ana is still en route and unlikely to be here before ten. However, I'm ready to talk to the police and share everything I know."

Gilchrist's smile faltered. "Ah. That could be awkward."

"She sent her apologies and is prepared to drive to the station at their convenience."

"Let's deal with that later. Now we should get going, we don't want to keep them waiting. I take it you've eaten?"

"Indeed. Room service is a wonderful thing. Isn't it a glorious day?" She reached for her jacket.

"Glorious. Forecast is for 28 degrees, so I doubt you'll need a coat. Shall we?"

Beatrice picked up her bag and put on her jacket. She wasn't sure why, apart from her innate loathing of being told what to do. She followed Gilchrist out into the corridor, slipping her hand into her pocket to reassure herself the heavy little cockerel was still there. Somehow, he felt like good luck.

"Incidentally," he said as they walked along the hotel corridor towards his office, "I hear there was a touch of drama at your holiday home. The little lad is back safe and sound now?"

Beatrice narrowed her eyes. "Good gracious, news travels fast. Yes, thankfully Luke is home and none the worse for his ordeal."

"I'm in constant touch with local police, so naturally they

mentioned the situation. Very pleased to hear it all turned out well."

Her phone pinged. A message from Cher asking her to confirm where the interview would take place.

Beatrice replied in two words. *His office.* She looked up. Gilchrist had opened his door and was waiting for her. She stuffed her phone in her handbag and stepped inside.

Chapter 32

A private jet left Paris Orly at 04.20 with four passengers, two pilots and one not-quite-flight attendant.

If the four businessmen had been less focused on planning their negotiation strategy, they might have observed a certain clumsiness to the in-flight service, a worrying amateurism to the security announcement and an ill-fitting uniform on the young stewardess.

Yet the weather conditions were perfect, no coffee was spilt, the flight landed on time and a car was waiting to take the negotiating team to Matosinhos. Everyone was happy. Especially Ana Herrero.

She changed in the tiny toilet, yanked her bag from the rear cupboard and came down the aisle to hug the pilot.

"Antoine de Puits, you are the best. I know this was a mighty favour. Call me next time you're in Lisbon, OK?"

Antoine shook his head. "You are one crazy female. And I'm even crazier to take such risks for you. I will call you, don't think I'll forget. At the very least, you owe me a decent dinner."

"Deal! I have to run!" Ana clattered down the steps and raced across to the terminal. If she got out of Porto before rush hour, she could make Viana do Castelo by eight.

Sometimes, Fate is on your side. The car starts, the lights are green, the traffic is going in the other direction and music is your positive affirmation. Today, the stars are aligned. Christina tells me I'm beautiful, Annie says sisters are doing it for ourselves, George insists I gotta have faith and everything Bryan does, he does it for me.

Ana slugged her second shot of caffeinated fizz and switched off the radio. Awake, nervous and in no danger of napping, she needed to focus. The next few hours could be life-changing.

When she parked at the police station, it was a quarter to eight. She allowed herself a fist pump before announcing herself at the desk. Within minutes, she was shown to a waiting room containing Xavier, André and most importantly, a coffee machine.

"Ana!" Xavier leapt to his feet and kissed her on both cheeks. "Here so early?"

"I hitched a ride with an ex-boyfriend." She held out a hand. "Hi, you must be André."

André shook her hand. "Yes and I already know who you are. I watch you every evening on the news. It's a pleasure to meet you."

"Likewise." She yawned involuntarily. "Sorry, that wasn't meant for you. I need a shot of the black stuff to perk me up. What's the latest?"

André pulled some coins from his pocket for the machine while Xavier summarised the morning's events.

"Team meeting in the hotel at six, where we aligned our plan of attack. André and I arrived here at seven. It seems buying coffees, beers and sharing confidential chats with the local force paid off. They know me already. Although André is a new face, he commands respect through his own status, his father's reputation and of course, his Portuguese, which is so much better than mine. Detective de Sousa came in half an hour ago and listened to what we had to say."

André handed her a cup. "*Um cafezinho.* Then we had to repeat it all over again for his senior officer, Inspector Gaia. They have gone to make some calls but once protocol is satisfied, they'll order Gilchrist's arrest or apprehension."

"*Obrigada.*" Ana slugged the little coffee back in two gulps. "And what are the others doing now?

Xavier checked his phone. "Last thing I heard, Roman had filed a report with Interpol and was heading south to Porto to complete the formalities. Cher is going to speak to Gilchrist's superiors at eight. She'll have to do that alone as that's exactly the same time as the police will be questioning Beatrice, in the presence of Gilchrist himself."

"Where..." Ana was interrupted by the door opening. A crumpled-looking man in an open-necked shirt started to speak, spotted her and frowned.

André explained Ana's role in the investigation and introduced her to Detective de Sousa. He nodded, unsmiling, but shook her hand and asked them all to come to the interview room. Inspector Gaia awaited.

To Ana's surprise, Inspector Gaia was a tall, silver-haired woman with a firm handshake and impressive dark eyebrows. She welcomed Ana with good grace and invited them to sit. She spoke Portuguese in a slow, formal style, which may have been for the benefit of Xavier or all part of her dignified persona.

"We have contacted Interpol, Europol, the PGR or attorney general for Portugal, and informed the British Home Office. An arrest warrant is seen as unnecessary at this stage but all agencies agree the commander should be invited to answer some questions and that the investigation be reopened. In the light of this new information, the case will be handled by a senior detective from Lisbon, assisted by Detective de Sousa."

André cocked his head, rather like a puppy who heard the word 'walkies'.

Inspector Gaia gave a faint smile. "Your father would have been the ideal choice, Senhor Monteiro, but as I am sure you appreciate, personal involvement disqualifies him in these circumstances. Detective de Sousa will take two officers to Gêres and request the commander's assistance with our enquiries."

The crumpled-looking man gave a brief, weary nod and glanced at his watch.

Ana looked at the clock. Two minutes past eight. She caught Xavier's puzzled expression and she spoke without thinking. "Why not use the officers on site? It will take Detective de Sousa at least an hour to get there, but your officers are all in the same room as Gilchrist and DCI Stubbs as we speak."

Inspector Gaia frowned. "I'm sorry? De Sousa, you already have officers at the hotel?"

De Sousa shook his head, his frown more pronounced. "No. The case is closed. Why would I send men..."

"Officers," Gaia corrected.

"... officers when we filed the paperwork yesterday? All my officers have been reassigned new caseloads." He glared at Ana. "Who told you there were police at the scene?"

Ana stared at Xavier.

His face paled as his eyes grew large. "Commander Gilchrist asked DCI Beatrice Stubbs to be present for an interview with the local police at eight o'clock this morning. If there are no police at GCH, Gilchrist is acting alone."

Ana swallowed. "And he has Beatrice." She got to her feet.

"Hold on, you guys!" André called. "She's not alone. First off, the conference is full of police detectives. Second, Cher is on site. Someone can intercept him and get Beatrice out of there. Where is the interview taking place?"

All four faces focused on Ana.

"She didn't say. I'm not even sure she knew."

Inspector Gaia slapped a hand onto her desk. "De Sousa, call the hotel and see if the commander reserved a meeting venue for eight this morning. Authorise Housekeeping to open it, his office suite and even his own room if requested by nominated officers. They must also be given access to any security camera footage of relevant areas. Mr Racine, please alert your colleague and give her name to Detective de Sousa. I will arrange transport to GCH for all of you."

"I have a car!" Ana yelled. "Sorry." She dropped her voice. "I have a car right outside."

Inspector Gaia picked up the phone. "In that case, go ahead. Senhor Racine and Senhor Monteiro, go with her and take a police radio with you. De Sousa and his team will follow and I must insist you take no action without their permission. I will do all I can to ensure the safety of DCI Stubbs."

Ana jumped up so quickly that she bashed her knee on Gaia's table. She bit back a violent imprecation, rubbed her kneecap and limped to the door. She turned to say goodbye but de Sousa and his boss were already on their phones.

Rush hour, such as it was, drove Ana to the point of apoplexy. She swore and cursed and gesticulated at every single obstacle in their way, using the horn with abandon and wishing she had a flashing blue light. In contrast, Xavier and André spoke on their mobiles with a sense of calm urgency. Police training, Ana assumed, releasing a stream of expletives at a driver who halted traffic while he took three attempts to park.

André looked up, his hand over the mouthpiece. "Roman and Mr Fisher managed to get a meeting arranged with local government officials and senior police officers this morning in Porto. He asks if they should come back."

Ana watched Xavier in the rear view mirror.

"Can you hold one second, Cher?" He muted his call and replied to André. "How long will it take them to get back if they turn around now?"

André relayed the question and listened. "He's guessing an hour. They're on the outskirts of the city."

"In that case, they should continue and deliver the report in person. This must be done through official channels. We can get to the hotel sooner, so there's no point in them turning around."

Ana exhaled. "Xavier, we're a good thirty minutes from the hotel. Looks like we need Cher to step up." She scrunched her eyes in apology as she realised what she'd said, but opened them again to accuse the driver in front of bestiality.

Xavier returned to his conversation with Cher. His voice

carried a quiet authority. "Use the hotel security cameras. Ask for assistance from the staff but do not put them in danger. Find out where she is and..." He broke off and listened in silence. "Whose office?"

Ana flicked her eyes to the mirror and saw Xavier's brow crease. She overtook a bus, with her eyes on the road but her ears straining to hear one half of this crucial conversation.

"You're sure that's where they are?"

" ..."

"In that case, get your friend to show you the CCTV, just to be sure. And Cher, please wait for back-up. We'll get local police to..."

" ..."

"Half an hour, I think. Maybe less. We'll try to mobilise local forces to support you but you cannot go up there alone."

André's thumbs began twitching over his phone.

" ..."

"I understand that, but no officer should approach a hostage situation without back-up. You know that."

" ..."

"Cher, I agree, but as a colleague I am asking you, please, not to try this alone. You will put yourself and Beatrice at risk. Wait for us. We'll be there in...?"

Ana slammed on the brakes as a tractor pulled out of a field. "Twenty-five minutes if we're lucky, and it's not looking good."

"Listen to me, Cher, this is no time for individual heroism. You must wait! We'll be there in half an hour."

" ..."

Ana watched Xavier in the mirror. He took the phone from his ear and shook his head. She waited till André had ended his call.

"Xavier?"

"She says half an hour is thirty minutes too long for Beatrice."

André twisted in his seat. "She won't try to tackle Gilchrist alone?"

The tractor indicated left and drove off down an overgrown track. Ana floored the accelerator and raced along the road, dangerously over the speed limit. She knew without a doubt Cher would tackle Gilchrist alone. Because that's exactly what she would have done.

Chapter 33

"Come in and take a seat, DCI Stubbs."

She perched on the end of the sofa where she'd sat the night before, her handbag on her lap.

Gilchrist leaned against his desk, watching her with an intrusive intensity. "We have a few minutes before we talk to the police, so how about a little chat? I believe you and I can come to an agreement which will benefit us both."

Beatrice stared straight into his dead-fish eyes and shook her head. "I think that highly unlikely, Commander."

The silence solidified. Beatrice dropped her gaze, looking down at her own clasped hands. Dry, wrinkled, bearing small scars and large veins, these scruffy old tools had served her well. Every action, whether peeling a grapefruit or handcuffing a suspect had been decided and directed by her brain. A rather unpredictable organ. But in these circumstances, it was all she had.

Gilchrist's voice continued, smooth and assured. "I am in a position to be very supportive of your career, Acting DCI Stubbs. A word in the right ear and we could easily drop the 'Acting'. Or perhaps you'd prefer an advisory role, comfortable and well-remunerated."

"Commander..."

"As for your friend the journalist, there's every chance of aiding her career too. She seems like a smart young woman. I'm sure she'd recognise the value of a series of exclusives."

"Your offer is conditional, I presume. You would like us to lose interest in the murder of Samuel Silva."

Gilchrist flashed those showy teeth. "That case is closed. The perpetrator has been identified, but sadly not brought to justice. Local police are satisfied and it would be arrogant and patronising to assume our opinions are in any way superior. I think the best thing to do is respect the conclusions of the Portuguese force and move on. Both you and your friend should go back to your respective employments, at which you're both doing so well, and concentrate on the task in hand. Raking over the coals would be disadvantageous."

Anger surged through Beatrice's veins like molten lava. She clenched her fists as if holding the reins on her temper. Her imagination helpfully provided a slideshow of the photographs Samuel Silva had shown her. Marcia in the hospital, Marcia with her new parents, Marcia on the balcony with views of Lisbon's castle beyond, Marcia sleeping, her tiny fists beside her head.

"All my life, Commander, I've been raking over the coals. It's what I, what we, were trained to do. I turn stones, despite dreading what I might find under there. Some of the things I've found have had a permanent effect on my mental health. As I am quite sure you know, I have struggled with depression for many years. The first time I met my counsellor, he advised me to resign. In his words, I would have far less need of his services or medication if I took up a different profession. But that was not possible. I'm a detective and I do my job to the best of my ability. I've brought bad people to justice and set good ones free, if not as many of either as I would have liked. As for my career, it's over. I'm retiring at the end of this year. Further rungs on the ladder don't interest me as I'm not right for them. There are far better people for the job."

Gilchrist studied her. "I'm aware of your condition, yes. After your most serious episode, many of my management colleagues thought it might be time for your retirement. Hamilton stood in the way of that. So here you are. Personally, I'd like to see you leave us as a success story."

Donkey refuses carrot. Here comes stick.

"So would I, sir. But perhaps in a different way to Samuel Silva." She held his gaze.

"Let's make this simple. I expect no further muddying of waters in a case already closed by the investigating officers. This conference has already suffered from the consequences of an unexpected death. I would like you either to refocus or retreat to enjoy the rest of your holiday. The latter would be understandable under the circumstances."

Beatrice pretended to be in deep thought and considered her options. She could lie and accept his deal, then retract her promise when at a safe distance. She could refuse and deal with whatever consequences he planned. The one thing she could not do was forget it and move on. Gilchrist was no fool. He'd want some guarantee if she agreed. She played for time. The longer she kept talking, the greater chance there was that help would arrive.

"Commander Gilchrist, forgive me. I just don't understand. Samuel Silva was a friend of yours."

This time, Gilchrist laughed aloud. "And with searing ingenuity, the lady detective elicits a full and frank confession from the criminal mastermind, whilst fashioning a pair of home-made handcuffs out of crochet hooks. Don't be ridiculous, woman. I had nothing to do with Silva's death. If I can be accused of anything, it's putting the conference first and allowing the local jurisdiction to take control. Now can we step away from the conspiracy theories and work together to make this event the success it deserves? It's time to move on."

Beatrice checked her watch. "Yes, it is. The police are running late, aren't they? It's ten past eight already. "

When she looked up, she expected hostility. Which was exactly what she got.

Gilchrist levelled an Abadie revolver at her, while holding out his hand for her bag. His manner was as matter-of-fact as an airport security guard.

She gave it to him, clenching her fists to disguise the tremble in her hands.

"Walk ahead of me to the lift at the end of the corridor. Please do not attempt any theatrics or give me any reason to cause you unnecessary injury."

Adrenalin pumping through her, she could think of nothing else to do but obey. He stepped backwards, his eyes never leaving hers, and deposited her bag in a drawer.

Beatrice's mind scrambled to comprehend what he might have in mind. He couldn't be planning another execution. The man was a megalomaniac, undoubtedly, but even he must realise that the murder of another delegate would result in his eventual arrest. As an intelligent officer of the law, no matter how deluded he might be by his own potency, he had to know he was cornered. If he killed Beatrice, what of Ana? What of Xavier, Roman, André and Cher? No. He couldn't kill them all.

Gilchrist, still calm, still smiling, slipped the gun into his pocket and gestured for her to precede him through the door.

"Commander, I think it's time to..."

He shook his head. "Move, please. Walk to the lift at the end of the corridor. I should inform you that I have disabled the security camera on this wing."

Without a word, she did as she was told, frantically wondering how she could get a message to Cher. But even if she were able to make contact, she had no clue where this man intended to take her.

The lift doors opened and he pressed the button for the fifth floor. The top three buttons had a sign taped beside them.

DUE TO RENOVATION WORK, FLOORS 3, 4
AND THE ROOF TERRACE ON FLOOR 5 ARE
CURRENTLY CLOSED TO THE PUBLIC.
WE APOLOGISE FOR ANY INCONVENIENCE.

The roof. Somehow a sense of relief washed over Beatrice. Outside, in the open air, with birds singing and sun shining, the feeling that nothing bad could happen was irrepressible. She reprimanded herself for such stupidity.

The lift doors opened onto another corridor, one distinctly less manicured than the one they had just left. Underfoot plastic sheeting protected the carpet from dusty footprints and cables snaked their way towards a door at the end that led to the roof terrace.

The commander withdrew his gun and used it to point in that direction.

Beatrice picked her way among the builders' detritus; past rooms labelled Suite Douro, Suite Tagus, and Suite Dão and opened the heavy fire door into the fresh air. She rounded the corner to see the roof terrace stretching the length of the building, the size of an Olympic swimming pool. On the fifth floor, she realised, the two wings of the building were occupied by luxury suites leaving the long rectangular central section open for patrons to eat, drink and admire the view.

Tables and chairs were stacked against the back wall, next to metal shutters that probably concealed a cocktail bar. A stone balustrade ran along the front of the building, broken by a taped off section where the wall was missing. Beatrice eyed it, assessing how many tons of stone had fallen onto the ground floor terrace below. It must have been quite a storm.

"Take a seat, please." He motioned to the circular pond with a sculpture at its centre which formed the focal point of the empty expanse. Huge scallop shells decreased in size in three tiers, each bearing occupants. Dolphins arched out of the lowest, a female nude reclined in the second, her long hair covering her modesty and in the smallest and highest, seagulls perched around the edge, wings extended as if about to take to the air. At night, when the water flowed and the lights illuminated the arcs and curves, it would surely be a delightful sight.

At intervals around the water feature were benches made

of the same polished granite as the fountain itself. Beatrice sat on one, her back to the bar, facing out to the view. Gilchrist sat on the next bench and swivelled to face her, his gun no longer visible.

"Sorry to play rough, but I think it only fair to remind you there is a less pleasant way to do this." His voice had taken on an ugly harshness.

Far below, a blackbird sent its distinctive alarm call. The terrace remained cool despite the morning sunshine and Beatrice pulled her jacket tighter, the comforting weight of Matthew's souvenir against her leg.

"What do you say, Stubbs? Shall we let sleeping black dogs lie?" He laughed through his nose without a trace of amusement.

Her scalp prickled. Black dogs. What a low blow to use her depression as a weapon against her. The man was amoral. Even if she agreed to back down in return for some fictional promotion, she would never be anything more than a loose end. Sooner or later to be tied up. She had come too far and it was time to confront this inveterate liar, whatever the consequences.

If only she had a little more time. She looked straight at his face.

"I'm sorry, sir, I don't think we should lie any more. Least of all you."

His nostrils flared but he said nothing.

Beatrice continued, her voice calm. "The truth is that when Samuel Silva's book was published, it would have exposed you as the charlatan you are. His work would reveal yours to be plagiarised and self-aggrandising. Not a problem for an anonymous author, but I believe you planned to be 'outed'. A self-regarding personality such as yours could never remain in the shadows for long. You expected your 'creative non-fiction' to shake the world of law enforcement and eclipse previous insider works from such sources as MI5. You would never have been able to resist the glory.

"So you decided to publish first and call Silva out as the

plagiarist. However, he chose to release his findings as a blog, inviting discussion, offering proof, citing sources. Completely undermining your claims and exposing you as the cheat.

"I think you invited Silva to this conference with every intention of killing him. You switched rooms, staying one night in 1121 before requesting relocation. Of course your own fingerprints were all over the room, because it had been yours. And while it was, you got one of the gardeners to help you fix a stuck window. The gardener's name, which you took as you tipped him, was Marco Cordeiro.

"You put Silva in that room, next door to your office, from where you had access via the balcony. You knew he always returned to his room to call his wife at lunch because he told you so when refusing your Friday lunch invitation. You asked André Monteiro to come to that very room on Saturday lunchtime by faking a note. You recorded your own voice shouting into the phone and played it while Monteiro passed your door to provide you with an alibi. You shot Silva twice in the back of the head, framed Cordeiro and had him killed by local thugs.

"Samuel Silva was a husband, a new father, a great mind and altruistic educator. You killed him for purely selfish reasons, inflicting enormous suffering on his family and then covered your tracks by doing the same to Cordeiro. All this at a conference for police detectives. To think you could pull this off, you must have extraordinary levels of confidence. One might even say epic.

"Incidentally, my journalist friend Ana was included in our investigations at a later stage. Much of the legwork had been done and she merely filled in some gaps. As we speak, six high-profile international detectives are reporting our findings to your superiors, Interpol and the local force. We're not as stupid as you think, Commander. Neither are you as smart as you believe. I've come across some immense egos in my time, but you? You are off the scale."

The quiet following Beatrice's words seemed to echo back

at her. She'd lit the touch paper and now she waited for the explosion. In the next few seconds, he might very well decide to silence her permanently. He had the means. A shot to the head and he could attempt a getaway. Or he might try to push her from the roof and frame it as suicide. If he took her words at face value and realised he couldn't get away with Silva's murder, he had nothing to lose by killing her.

"Well, that is very disappointing."

Beatrice looked up and her heart began to race. His face was a mask of cold determination, his pupils shone dark and the only movement was the professional way he was putting on a pair of sterile gloves.

With a plummeting drop in her gut, she knew she had reached the end. Plenty of times she'd stared death in the face, but she'd never really believed it would happen. This time was different. She had finally run out of chances. No one was coming to help and she would face this alone. After all these years serving the force, she was going out at the hands of one of her own. Fear and self-pity pricked at her eyes and she hoped his choice of method would be a bullet. Falling from the roof or strangulation would be so much worse than a quick and sudden exit.

She tried to remember her last words to Matthew and experienced a profound sadness that they never would enjoy their long-anticipated retirement together.

Gilchrist stood up. "The tragedy due to unfold was for the mentally unstable detective to throw her journalist friend off of the roof and then shoot herself. I can still make that work. Come, Stubbs, on your feet."

Beatrice rose, her eyes fixed on his cold face. A movement behind him caught her attention as a wheelchair rounded the corner and a voice rang out.

"Here you are!"

Cher sat at the end of the terrace, phone held aloft. "Hello everyone, we're live on BluLite!"

Chapter 34

"Day Six of EPIC and we're onsite in Gerês! Today's BluLite reportage coming from Agent Cher Davenport of the FBI. Right now, we're on the terrace on the roof of the hotel. Beautiful spot, don't ya think?"

Cher rotated her phone around the scene and brought it back to focus on the couple in front of the fountain. "And did we just get lucky! Here's Commander Gilchrist, kingpin of the entire project. With him is Acting DCI Stubbs, of the London Met. Quite a coup to get these two guys in one place, if I say so myself. Let's share a few words with two of the most influential figures in British policing."

She steered her chair one-handed towards them, using the other to continue filming, but stopped at a distance of around fifteen feet. Well out of reach. Her smile was bright enough for daytime television.

"Good morning to you both!"

Beatrice returned the smile with a nod, watching Gilchrist in her peripheral vision. "Good morning, Agent Davenport, it's a pleasure to see you again."

Gilchrist switched on his beam. "It certainly is a surprise. You caught Acting DCI Stubbs and I having a quiet chat." He laughed heartily. "We assumed everyone was at breakfast so we sneaked off for a policy discussion. We should have known nowhere is private at a conference for detectives!"

Cher beamed right back. "Too right! Say, lemme ask you how you think the conference is going."

Gilchrist glanced at his watch. "In a word, fast! We hardly have time to cover all the topics and conversations we want to discuss with our European colleagues. Every moment counts. My next session begins at nine, in fact. I should be heading back."

"Just one last question, to both of you. How has the death of Samuel Silva affected morale? Of course the press are making the most of it but how did this event impact the conference itself? Is it business as usual?"

Beatrice turned her face to Gilchrist, in an ostensible gesture of politeness; in full knowledge the Commander saw it as a challenge.

"The death of a colleague is always a tragedy. Not one single delegate is unaffected, but we are professionals. We are here to do a job. The best way to honour our comrade is to carry on. The case is closed and my only regret is the perpetrator was not brought to justice. Thanks for the chat, but unfortunately, I need to get to my next appointment." Cher ignored him and kept the camera on them both.

Cher turned her attention to Beatrice. "DCI Stubbs?"

Beatrice took a deep breath. Their colleagues now knew where they were, so all she had to do was sit tight and wait for the cavalry to arrive. She had to filibuster.

"Commander Gilchrist has done an EPIC job at this year's European Police Intercommunications Conference. His achievement has been to bring international detectives together, encouraging collaboration in all kinds of unexpected ways. I am sure, in time, all his actions will be deservedly recognised.

"If I may, I'd like to pay a personal tribute to Samuel Silva. The loss of such a pioneer of intelligence is a blow to the entire law enforcement community. His research benefitted us all, in Europe and beyond. He knew this, yet he sought to take no profit. Instead he planned to share his work as a public resource.

I still hope his colleagues can make that happen. He was also a husband and father, mentor and godfather. He was a wise, decent man who will be greatly missed."

Gilchrist applauded. "Well said! Marvellous speech. Thank you. However, Acting DCI Stubbs, Agent Davenport, I have to get to..."

"So I would like to ask you all," intoned Beatrice, addressing the camera, "wherever you are in the world, to bow your heads for one minute and give thanks for a truly exceptional fellow officer. Ladies and gentlemen, Samuel Silva."

Sixty seconds. Gilchrist stood beside Beatrice, his head bowed and hands clasped behind his back. He couldn't go anywhere for the next minute without appearing a crass oaf. Then what? Beatrice bowed her head and squinted at her watch. 08.46. Come on! Roman? Xavier? Someone? Out of the corner of her eye, she saw Gilchrist slip a hand into his pocket.

The sound of a gunshot behind them both gave Beatrice such a shock that she stumbled sideways, the heavy ornament in her jacket pocket thumping against her hip. Gilchrist's head snapped up and he stared past Cher, at a wide open space.

"What are you doing? Get away from her!" Gilchrist launched himself forwards, as if at some invisible assailant. Cher attempted to spin round but couldn't turn quickly enough before Gilchrist ran behind her, snatched her phone and threw it over the edge of the balustrade.

The oldest trick in the book. *Look behind you!*

Before Beatrice could move, he trained his gun on Cher. "So Plan A it is, with a minor adjustment. Sorry ladies, no time for niceties. Let's make this quick."

He shoved Cher's chair in the direction of the red and white tape flapping in the breeze, his gun pointing at the back of her head. Time seemed to slow down as the chair rolled noiselessly towards the gap in the low wall. Cher released a howl of protest and yanked on the brakes. Gilchrist swore, shoved his gun in its holster then tipped the chair back and physically dragged it to the edge.

Beatrice's hand slipped into her pocket and took hold of the metal cockerel. Her fingers fitted around the sharp curves of its tail and comb as if it had been designed for her palm. Gilchrist lugged the chair closer to the crumbling stone, his face red and ugly.

Two could play at old tricks.

"Commander, *look out!*" she shrieked and hurled the cockerel with all the strength she had, aiming directly at his head. His face snapped up a second before the spiky souvenir hit him full in the mouth. He released the chair and recoiled, his hands covering his face. Cher reacted instantly, using both arms to wheel herself away and snatch the chance to escape.

So only Beatrice watched Gilchrist stagger backwards through the plastic tape and lose his footing. Only she saw his arms flail outwards and his mouth open to scream through broken, bloodied teeth as he fell. Only she covered her ears and counted the seconds until he hit the ground.

Chapter 35

Pancakes for ten, fruit salad, yoghurt, bread, poached eggs, bacon, cheese and ham for the continentals, all accompanied by plenty of coffee. Adrian whisked and chopped and arranged and brewed for over an hour until Matthew wandered into the kitchen, dressed in wrinkled linen.

"Something smells rather wonderful."

"Apart from me? Might be the strawberries. Can I pour you some freshly squeezed orange juice?"

"Yes please. Beatrice is in the shower, so you may as well pour her one too. Can I do anything to help? We've a few more mouths to feed."

Adrian smiled. "All in hand. Will drove me to the shop first thing and now he's tending Tanya. She wants to come downstairs today."

"Only because she hates being left out. Missing all these new faces, it must be more painful than her burns." Matthew cleared his throat, as if about to make a formal speech. "Adrian, while it's just the two of us, I have something to say."

"I see." Adrian poured two glasses of juice and sat down. Time to clear the air.

Matthew gave him a frank and direct look. "I blamed you for losing Luke. That was wrong and unfair. I realise now you could not possibly have overruled Marianne and I respect you even more for not assigning negligence where it was due. I am sorry, and I want you to know that I trust you and Will as family members with my grandson. Probably a lot more than some family members. Please accept my apologies."

Adrian reached over to shake his hand. "No need to apologise. I felt wretched about what happened, but only about a thousandth of what you must have been feeling. Thank you, anyway. I hoped you would feel that way, but it does my heart good to hear it."

Matthew's forehead smoothed. "I heard from her this morning."

"Marianne? Where is she?"

"Back in the UK. She's trying to get legal representation for Leon." He shook his head in a gesture of disbelief.

Adrian debated whether to speak his mind and decided against. "Shall we make a start on the pancakes?"

Several minutes later, Will helped Tanya into the room and eased her with great care on the chaise longue he'd dragged in from the living room. He laid a cotton sheet over her and poured her some juice.

"Adrian, are you very attached to Will?" she asked. "Because if not, I would be happy to take him off your hands."

Will laughed and kissed Adrian's cheek. "Sorry, Tanya. I'm a one-man kind of guy. I'm guessing you don't want any coffee?"

"Oh well, it was worth a punt. Actually, yes I do want coffee. Just add lots of milk and serve it in a sippy-cup."

Ana wandered in, phone glued to her ear, laptop under her arm. She gave everyone a thumbs-up, took some coffee onto the balcony and continued chatting and tapping away. Her story had the whole of RTP in a state of huge excitement.

Voices came from the hallway and a peal of laughter announced Luke and Beatrice.

Matthew's eyebrows rose. "Up before ten, Luke? I never thought I'd see the day!"

"Grandad, Beatrice taught me a rude song!"

"I don't doubt it. Go and enquire after your mother's health."

Luke planted a cursory kiss on Tanya's cheek. "Morning, Mum. Are you better yet?"

"Hello Trouble," she replied and stroked his hair. "It's getting better. But no swimming or sunbathing for me today. I'll have to stay inside and watch Poldark videos."

Adrian grinned. "What an awful ordeal. I might have to join you."

Luke returned to the table to help himself to pancakes. "Beatrice?" he asked, in a whisper.

"No, not in front of your mother," Beatrice replied, her hair a strange explosion of peaks and tufts. "Pass that maple stuff."

He giggled and handed her the syrup. "I wasn't going to ask you to sing it again!" He glanced at the garden flat and whispered. "Is that man really a Viking?"

Beatrice had a mouthful of pancake.

Adrian spoke for her. "Maybe we should go and ask him. Xavier went over there an hour ago to start work, so they must be hungry by now. Luke, wanna come with me to get Xavier, Roman and Shoop-Shoop..."

"Cher," offered Matthew.

"I know. I was just giving it the right build-up," said Adrian. At least Tanya and Will found it funny.

Luke dropped his fork and scrambled down from the table. He ran ahead across the lawn but hesitated as he got to the door. The three were clearly visible through the French windows, all bent over laptops on the dining-room table. No one had noticed their approach. Luke reached up for Adrian's hand.

Their polite knock turned all three heads.

"Just wondered if you're hungry? There's bread and coffee and other things I've forgotten. What did we make, Luke?"

"Pancakes! Bacon! Eggs! Juice! Maple syrup!"

Cher stretched. "That sounds exactly what the doctor ordered. C'mon, you guys, I need to break my fast. Luke, lead the way."

Breakfast was a success. Cher parked her chair beside Tanya and helped her by passing pancakes or juice as required. Will, Xavier, Beatrice and Roman ate with gusto, while Matthew and Adrian brewed coffee, poured juice and poached eggs to order. Luke spread honey on a piece of toast and cast covert glances at Roman as the adults discussed developments.

"Politically it's complex," said Xavier. "The case will be a collaboration between Inspector Gaia's team, Interpol, LIU and the British Home Office. Assuming Gilchrist survives his injuries, it will be at least a year before he can stand trial."

"He'll survive," Cher snickered. "So what if he got lucky with an awning instead of concrete? He's still due a sucker punch from the long arm of the law."

Will applauded. "Calamity Jane is alive and well and hiding in Gerês!"

When the laughter died down, Roman spoke. "Gilchrist will get what he deserves. Once the paperwork is filed here, he's the UK's problem. Interpol will actually enjoy dumping this on the Brits, according to Fisher."

Beatrice wrinkled her nose and Xavier spotted her reaction. "What is it, B? Not a fan of Interpol?"

She shook her head. "I have a great deal of respect for Interpol. But bloody Fisher rubs me up the wrong way. He's so... smooth. Like an oil slick."

Roman laughed, throwing his blond head back. Luke gazed up at him in awe.

"Well put. Not my kind of person either. Although I must say he was pretty effective when I tackled him yesterday morning. Listened, checked, acted and knew the right people to call. No hesitation in suspending the conference either. I respect him for that."

Will addressed the new arrivals. "It leaves a bad taste regarding EPIC as a concept, doesn't it? Rumours are getting more and more dramatic. Even if you have managed to keep it out of the press so far." He threw a curious look at Ana.

Dark rings shadowed her eyes but her expression remained animated and alert. "The way things look from the press side, I get an exclusive. Plus budget not only for reportage, but a full documentary. So I can spin this however I like. My gut is to tell the truth and praise EPIC for the good it achieved. Shame it was derailed by one power-crazed egomaniac who tried to get away with murder and shot himself in the foot."

"He didn't shoot himself in the foot," said Roman. "Beatrice knocked him off the roof with a cockerel."

His black humour hit the mark and no one could resist laughing.

Luke gawped at Beatrice. "You knocked somebody off a roof?"

"Only because I had to. It was a last resort."

Matthew coughed politely. "Luke, what about you and I going on lizard patrol? They'll be out sunning themselves on the rocks now."

"In a bit, Grandad."

Beatrice dabbed her mouth with a napkin. "I think now would be a good time, Luke. We need to have a police conversation and we'll need to borrow Ana and Will. Perhaps we should retire to the garden flat, out of the way? Adrian, thanks for a lovely breakfast. If you don't mind clearing up, I'll promise to take charge of dinner."

Luke released a disappointed sigh, but slipped off his stool and took Matthew's hand. "I'll take photos for you."

"You better had," replied Beatrice and led the team out through the garden door.

Chapter 36

Dear All

Hope you're all managing to chill after the stress of this past week. Sorry I couldn't join you today but I'm more useful here.

Just a few lines to let you know what's happening in Lisbon. Communication is constant between ourselves and Inspector Gaia's team. The case against Gilchrist is clear and it is simply a question of the jurisdiction in which to charge him. Due to his senior position and the international nature of EPIC, it is likely to be the UK. (TBH, we fought to keep it here, in honour of Samuel, but this is a political hot potato our domestic affairs department could do without.)

My father and I are arranging a widow's pension for Elisabete and we both intend to be very present and responsible in her and Marcia's lives. We debated trying to monetise Samuel's blog, but Elisabete agreed with his ethics and insists on making it free. I will test the blog in Beta version next month, with Xavier and Cher's help. If anyone else is interested, let me know and I'll put you on the list. Ana, that goes for you too. This is not exclusive to police.

I guess we'll all meet up at the trial, wherever and whenever it is, so right now I'm just going to wish you a relaxing weekend. On a personal note, I'm really glad I got to know you and earned your trust. You people made this happen and on behalf of Samuel's friends and family, I thank you.

Kind regards & beijinhos
André

Chapter 37

The sun-baked tiles around the pool radiated warmth, the sky was melting towards another spectacular sunset and the scent of grilling meat wafted across the pool. Cher, Roman and Will supervised the barbecue, while in the kitchen, Xavier instructed Matthew and Adrian on how to cook the bean stew. Ana and Tanya mixed *caipirinhas* behind the bar and did a fair amount of sampling, judging by the bursts of raucous laughter. Luke and Beatrice set the table, placing *citronella* mosquito candles at strategic points.

The vestiges of a mild headache induced by dealing with emails, a lengthy discussion with Ranga and endless repetition of yesterday's events ebbed away as Beatrice looked forward to the evening. Despite her promise to Adrian, she'd actually contributed very little to dinner.

Xavier's suggestion of a traditional Brazilian *feijoada* earlier that afternoon had met with general enthusiasm. Will and Adrian took him shopping for ingredients. Cher, Ana and Tanya prepared the salads and by the poolside, Roman taught Luke some kind of martial arts.

This gave Beatrice and Matthew an hour or so for a nap. They lay on the bed with their eyes closed but neither slept.

"Are you really OK?" she asked him, for the fourth time that day.

"Yes, I am. I do have a whole bagful of concerns regarding

my daughters, in the light of recent events. If Marianne does side with her nephew's kidnapper, I really can see no future relationship between herself and Tanya. I struggle to comprehend her myself."

"If it comes to that, which I doubt. Leon's relationships rarely last long. Marianne will wake up to him sooner or later. Keep the doors open."

"The doors will always be open. She's family. By the way, I apologised to Adrian," said Matthew. "I should have known it wasn't his fault."

"Good. It's obvious Adrian and Will both adore Luke."

"Yes, and they're both good role models in the absence of a father figure." He sighed and reached for her hand. "For some reason, perhaps because I almost lost two people closest to my heart, loved ones seem awfully precious today. Your rooftop drama will give me nightmares for months. Isn't the DCI post supposed to keep you safely in a carpeted office?"

They lay side by side, hand in hand.

Beatrice decided to put it into words and thereby make it real. "The DCI post will keep me in a carpeted office for one more month exactly. I called Ranga for a debrief and asked to resign from the post of Acting DCI. My time is up and I know it. He promised to replace me within a month and then I can officially retire."

He released her hand to put his arm around her and she curled into his shoulder, watching a tear leak from his closed lids. The time, she sensed, was finally right.

She closed her eyes, drawing peace and restoration from his presence. For five minutes. Then she sat up.

"Don't know about yourself, but I'm hungry."

"Ah-ha. Normal status restored."

Beatrice took another paper napkin from Luke and rolled it into a hanky shape to poke in a wine glass. Pure elegance.

"Beatrice?" asked Luke.

"No! Never. Pinch me, tweak my ears or take away my bean stew, if you must. But I shall never sing in public."

Luke creased up with laughter. "I know! That song is just for us. Guess what I learned from Roman today?"

"Karate chops and kick-boxing?"

"No. He says feet and fists are your weakest weapons."

Beatrice stopped and raised her eyebrows. "Give me another napkin."

He handed her one, his face eager.

Beatrice rolled and stuffed. "So what is my strongest weapon? No, don't tell me, I want to guess. Is it my bottom?"

"No!" he giggled and handed her another napkin. "Guess again!"

"For your information, my bottom can be pretty lethal, depending on what I've eaten." This time Luke laughed out loud. "All depends on the individual, I suppose. It must be something superior to your opponent. Hmm." She placed a knife, fork and spoon around a place setting. "Whoever I'm up against might have bigger fists, bigger muscles, bigger guns or in extremely rare cases, a bigger bottom. How can you deal with all of those?"

Luke placed the pack of napkins on the table and pressed an index finger to each of his temples, his eyes wide. "Your mind."

"Oh really? So where does the karate come in? You two were pulling some judo moves this afternoon, I saw you."

"Not judo or karate, it was Tai Chi. Roman says it's a very different kind of discipline."

Beatrice moved on to position cutlery, but her eyes had filled with tears. Luke was an open book, influenced by everyone he met, easily convinced and enthused. She made a decision to offer as much support as she could to Tanya and to her sort-of-grandson. She had to fill his life with good people and the Viking was an ideal example.

"Maybe in the morning, you can teach me how to do it?" she said, beckoning for the napkins.

"OK. It's very slow and easy so I reckon you could handle it.

Why are there only nine places? We're ten, including me."

Beatrice laughed at his accurate assessment of her level of fitness. "Mum can't sit at the table so she's on the sun bed. You will have to act as waiter for her."

"Oh yeah. Course. Beatrice?"

"What?"

"I don't want to go home tomorrow. I like this place."

"Good. So do I. Anyway, we're not going home tomorrow but on Sunday. That's the day after tomorrow. So you have one and a half more days to swim and play and watch the lizards and learn Tai Chi. Feeling sad on Friday about leaving on Sunday is a waste of time, so we'll have no more of it. Right, the table's done. Go put a napkin in your mum's wine glass and let's get this show on the road."

By sundown, the table stood testament to a feast enjoyed by all. Empty plates, a few wilted lettuce leaves, bones, bits of bread and an almost-empty pot of black bean stew sat among wine bottles and shot glasses of *aguardiente* muddied with bean juice. The night air rang with laughter and a giddy sense of release. Beatrice started to clear the table, assisted by Xavier and Adrian, both pink of cheek and magnanimous. The *cachaça* had worked its magic.

Will joined them as they took the citrus sorbets from the freezer. He produced three bottles of champagne. Beatrice beamed at him.

"That's a thoughtful gesture. Such a nice way to celebrate the rescue of Luke and Gilchrist's downfall."

Adrian and Will stared at her in disbelief.

"I can't believe you just said that!" said Will. "Sometimes I think you do it on purpose."

"Of course she does it on purpose." Adrian placed a tray of sorbets on the hostess trolley and pushed it at Will. "Put the bubbles on the bottom shelf. I'll load the dishwasher and be with you in a sec."

Beatrice stood in the doorway for a moment, inhaling the night, listening to the cicadas, anticipating the sorbet and champagne, watching the pool lights ripple and flicker across the party.

Adrian appeared behind her, his hands on her shoulders. "Come on, you of all people must be present for this."

"For what?"

"Ssh. Listen."

Will was on his feet, tapping a spoon against a glass, while Xavier and Roman distributed glasses of champagne. With a gentle shake, Matthew woke a dozing Luke who blinked at Beatrice as she sat down.

"It's been quite a week!" Will announced. His voice rang down the table as far as Tanya's sun bed, where she sat with Ana.

"This has been a holiday to remember. There's been fun, sadness, drama and more than the usual amount of stress. Some were lost, some were wounded, and we also gained new friends. Welcome to Xavier, Cher, Roman and Ana, again."

Laughter and smiles bounced around the table. Luke applauded.

"All these are things we should celebrate. But there's one more cherry on the cake I want to share with you all. Yesterday, I asked Adrian Harvey to marry me. I still quite can't believe it myself, but he said yes!"

Beatrice leapt to her feet with everyone else, except Tanya and Cher, who applauded with hoots, cheers and whistles. Will and Adrian accepted all the hugs and congratulations with tears and delight. Matthew proposed the toast and they raised their glasses to 'Will and Adrian!' at least three times.

"When is the wedding?" asked Tanya. "Can you at least give me a couple of months to get better? Assuming I'm invited, of course."

Will took Adrian's hand. "Everyone's invited! We want a massive party, but we've not discussed a date yet. Probably next year. Plenty of time for you to heal."

Conversation turned to possible locations and the optimum season for nuptials, with opinions ranging from springtime in Venice to Brampford Speke in early autumn.

Xavier fetched more champagne from the fridge and set off another round of toasts. The clock struck twelve and Luke began rubbing his eyes. Beatrice beckoned Roman.

"Luke is ready for bed. Tanya isn't but if you could help her upstairs and Ana takes a bottle of fizz, the girls can party on while the little chap gets his rest. None of us wants to leave him unattended."

"Sure. I'd be happy to. You ready?" Roman raised his eyebrows at Tanya, who pretended to fan herself.

Cher wheeled herself up to Beatrice. They watched Tanya lean on Roman and limp indoors. Ana scooped up two glasses, a bottle of champagne and held out her other hand for Luke.

"Coming, little fella?"

He nodded and took her hand. "Tomorrow is Saturday, you know. Not Sunday."

"Thanks be to God! Otherwise I'd have to go to Mass."

"So we have another holiday day here. All of us together."

"Isn't that grand?"

"Yes, it *is* grand," he agreed.

The small group went inside and closed the curtains. Beatrice sat down on the stone bench and faced Cher.

"Love is in the air..." she sang, quietly.

Cher laughed, a throaty contagious sound. "Love is all around us..."

Beatrice snorted. "Feels like it, I must say. What about you and the Viking? Is there a future?"

"Who knows? We've had such a great time together. He's like no one else I ever met. But long-distance relationships are not really my thing."

"Bugger. We could have had a double wedding."

"Nah. If you're going for the full house of political correctness, you need gay, disabled *and* black. That tall handsome blond ruins the whole damn thing." Cher threw back her head and gave a gurgling infectious laugh.

Adrian joined them, his eyes shining. "Is this the rowdy ladies' corner? If so, may I have guest privileges?"

"Sure you can! Hey, congratulations again. He is one helluva catch," Cher said.

"I think so." Adrian chinked glasses with them both. "Mind you, yours is rather easy on the eye. Love his hair."

Roman sauntered across the terrace, making for the group at the bar, with all the grace of an inhabitant of Asgard.

"Is there a place you can go where they teach you to move like that?" Beatrice asked. "Catwalk school, or something?"

Cher sighed. "With some people it's genetic. Look at Ana. She comes into a room and jaws drop. Roman's got damn good genes. And while I still got the chance, I'm going to get into them thar jeans." She gurgled again, setting Adrian and Beatrice off into laughter, and wheeled herself away towards the Viking.

Beatrice nudged Adrian. "You're getting married."

"I know. Beat you to it by a country mile."

"Seeing as I've been running in the other direction for twenty-five years, that's no surprise. But honestly, I could not be happier for you two. Will is a lovely, kind, smart man and he adores you. No surprise there either." Her throat constricted. "I feel like an emotional auntie with her favourite nephew. I'm going to miss you so much."

He pulled her into a sideways hug. "I'm getting married, not joining a monastery. We'll still be neighbours, at least till the end of the year."

With a sniff, Beatrice patted his leg. "End of next month, actually. I asked Ranga to release me early. I can retire at the end of September and move to Devon."

Adrian twisted his body to face her. "Oh my God, you're actually going to do it, aren't you?"

"Yes, I am. You can visit us, we can visit you, we'll go on trips, and on top of that, I have to come back every month to see my counsellor. I could use a friendly place to stay. If you like, I'll even help plan the wedding. Adrian, we want you and Will to be a part of our lives. And Luke's life. We're family now."

Adrian dropped his head onto her shoulder. "Yes, we are."

A gale of laughter drifted from the bar and a head poked out of an upstairs window.

"Oi!" yelled Ana.

"Sorry," called Xavier. "We'll keep it down."

"No, don't worry, Luke's next door and he's out for the count. The thing is, has anyone got a cigar?"

Will reached behind the bar and threw a small flat tin up to Ana, who caught it one handed in the dark. She blew them all a kiss and retreated within.

Adrian's voice was low and discreet. "Beatrice?"

"You sound like Luke. Are you going to ask me to sing smutty songs?"

"No." Adrian faced her, his expression serious. "I'm just a bit worried. You've always been so preoccupied by your job. How will you deal with retirement? What are you going to do with yourself?"

Beatrice drained her glass and gazed up at the night sky. Stars twinkled back at her, reassuring in their permanence. She met Adrian's eyes with a mischievous smile.

"As a matter of fact, I'm thinking of writing a book."

Acknowledgements

As always, sincere thanks to Gillian Hamer, Jane Dixon Smith, Catriona Troth and Liza Perrat, aka Triskele Books. Gratitude for intelligent insights from Julie Lewis and Florian Bielmann, refinements from Perry Iles and cover design by JD Smith.

Also by JJ Marsh

Behind Closed Doors

"Beatrice Stubbs is a fascinating character, and a welcome addition to crime literature, in a literary and thought-provoking novel. I heartily recommend this as an exciting and intelligent read for fans of crime fiction." – Sarah Richardson, of Judging Covers

"Behind Closed Doors crackles with human interest, intrigue and atmosphere. Beatrice and her team go all out to see justice is done. And author JJ Marsh does more than justice to the intelligent heroine who leads this exciting and absorbing chase." – Libris Reviews

"Hooked from the start and couldn't put this down. Superb, accomplished and intelligent writing. Ingenious plotting paying as much attention to detail as the killer must. Beatrice and her team are well-drawn, all individuals, involving and credible." – Book Reviews Plus

Raw Material

"*I loved JJ Marsh's debut novel Behind Closed Doors, but her second, Raw Material, is even better. While Beatrice is fully occupied with the London crime, Matthew, and Beatrice's neighbour, Adrian, decide to investigate in Wales and what starts out as a light-hearted caper turns into something horribly grim. The truth is more terrible than Matthew, Adrian, or even Beatrice, could ever have imagined and the final chapters are heart-stoppingly moving and exciting.*" Chris Curran, Amazon reviewer.

"*Some rather realistic – if not particularly laudable – human exchanges reveal honest personal struggles concerning life's bigger questions; the abstruse clues resonate with the covert detective in me; and the suspense is enough to cause me to miss my stop.*" – Vince Rockston, author

Tread Softly

"*The novel oozes atmosphere and JJ Marsh captures the sights, sounds and richness of Spain in all its glory. I literally salivated as I read the descriptions of food and wine.*

JJ Marsh is an extremely talented author and this is a wonderful novel." – Sheila Bugler, author of *Hunting Shadows*

"*There are moments of farce and irony, there are scenes of friendship, tenderness and total exasperation - and underlying it all a story of corruption, brutality, manipulation and oppression with all the elements you'd expect to find in a good thriller, including a truly chilling villain. Highly recommended*". – Lorna Fergusson, *FictionFire*

Cold Pressed

Editor's Choice – *The Bookseller*
This is J J Marsh's fourth, snappily written crime mystery featuring the feisty but vulnerable Stubbs, a most appealing character. It's all highly diverting, and an ideal read for those who like their crime with a lighter, less gruesome touch. – Caroline Sanderson, The Bookseller

Marsh is an excellent story-weaver. The plot twists and turns, the suspense is compelling. The intertwining of the details of the case and Beatrice's personal demons is clever and credible and gives the plot a multi-layered feel. All the characters, major and minor, are well drawn and believable. As a reader, you're drawn in and made to care about them as you feel the terror and panic that sweeps the ship.

Marsh's economical, highly visual prose make this book a deceptively easy read, but at the same time a most satisfying one. – Angelica Reads

Human Rites

The opening leads the reader straight into the atmosphere and the story and Stubbs aficionados (of whom I am one) will sink into it as into a comfortable armchair. All the usual Stubbsie goodies are here – a carefully worked out and clever plot; a sense of location that enables us to see clearly places we have never been to; human vulnerability; real emotions and genuine affection; and a threat that is only warded off by the cleverness and dedication to which we have become accustomed. – The Bagster, Amazon reviewer

An accomplished and original crime novel that's a serious pleasure to read, "Human Rites" infuses JJ Marsh's subtle sharpness into its

menace, its urbanity and its humour. Spare, spectral, classy and down-to-earth, all at once, it manages to pack resonant detail into its natural coolness of exposition, with intriguing dives into international art theft, European police procedures and Expressionist art history, among other worlds of endeavour, along with sparky glimpses of contemporary urban romance and a suitably unhealthy dusting of religious lunacy. – Rohan Quine, author of The Imagination Thief

Thank you for reading a Triskele Book

If you loved this book and you'd like to help other readers find Triskele Books, please write a short review on the website where you bought the book. Your help in spreading the word is much appreciated and reviews make a huge difference to helping new readers find good books.

Why not try books by other Triskele authors?
Choose a complimentary ebook when you sign up
to our free newsletter at

www.triskelebooks.co.uk/signup

If you are a writer and would like more information on writing and publishing, visit http://www.triskelebooks.blogspot.com and http://www.wordswithjam.co.uk, which are packed with author and industry professional interviews, links to articles on writing, reading, libraries, the publishing industry and indie-publishing.

Connect with us:
Email admin@triskelebooks.co.uk
Twitter @triskelebooks
Facebook www.facebook.com/triskelebooks

CPSIA information can be obtained
at www.ICGtesting.com
Printed in the USA
FSOW01n2040071117
40907FS